THE FORTRESS IN ORION

Also by Mike Resnick:

Starship: Mutiny
Starship: Pirate
Starship: Mercenary
Starship: Rebel
Starship: Flagship

The Buntline Special—A Weird West Tale
The Doctor and the Kid—A Weird West Tale
The Doctor and the Rough Rider—A Weird West Tale
The Doctor and the Dinosaurs—A Weird West Tale

Ivory: A Legend of Past and Future

New Dreams for Old

Stalking the Unicorn
Stalking the Vampire
Stalking the Dragon

THE FORTRESS IN ORION

DEAD ENDERS BOOK ONE

MIKE RESNICK

an imprint of Prometheus Books
Amherst, NY

Published 2014 by Pyr®, an imprint of Prometheus Books

Cover illustration by Dave Seeley
Cover design by Nicole Sommer-Lecht

Inquiries should be addressed to
Pyr
59 John Glenn Drive
Amherst, New York 14228
VOICE: 716–691–0133
FAX: 716–691–0137
WWW.PYRSF.COM

18 17 16 15 14 5 4 3 2 1

Library of Congress Cataloging-in-Publication Data

Resnick, Michael D.
The Fortress in Orion / Mike Resnick.
pages cm. — (Dead Enders ; Book One)
ISBN 978-1-61614-990-1 (paperback) — ISBN 978-1-61614-991-8 (ebook)
1. Imaginary wars and battles—Fiction. 2. Human-alien encounters—Fiction. 3. Space warfare—Fiction. 4. Science fiction. 5. War stories. I. Title.

PS3568.E698F67 2014
813'.54—dc23

2014023891

Printed in the United States of America

PROLOGUE

Everything hurt.

Pretorius lay on his back, trying to focus his eyes on the door some ten feet away from the foot of his bed. It took him almost two minutes of intense concentration for it to stop swiveling like a belly dancer.

He gingerly tried flexing his left hand and felt the fingers move. He tried the same thing with his right hand and felt nothing.

He ran his left hand over his torso, winced as it came in contact with medical dressings, and lay perfectly still until the pain subsided.

Finally he turned his head to the left and saw half a dozen tubes leading from his body. Some went to what he recognized as the standard life-support machines, but two of them were connected to translucent vats. There was *something* in each of them—a pair of dissimilar somethings, actually—but he couldn't make out what they were.

A white-clad figure—he couldn't focus enough to determine its gender—approached him and began manipulating something on his left side.

"Damn, that smarts!" he muttered.

"Ah, you're awake," said the figure in a feminine voice.

"I'd prefer to think that I'm having a nightmare," he replied.

"You have a visitor, Colonel Pretorius, one who is very anxious to see you."

Colonel Pretorius. Right, that's me. I'd forgotten. Then: *I wonder what my first name is?*

"Tell whoever it is to go away," rasped Pretorius. "We are not entertaining visitors."

The woman—he could focus enough now to see that it was a female doctor—laughed. "Same old Colonel Pretorius!"

He frowned. "I've been here before?"

"It'll come back to you."

"In this lifetime?" he asked.

She chuckled again. "I'll let your visitor explain."

She walked to the door; it opened. She gestured to someone on the far side of it and stepped aside as a burly man with a shock of white hair and a matching mustache entered the room.

"Thanks," he said. "I'll take it from here." She nodded and walked out the doorway, which snapped shut behind her. "Welcome back, Nathan."

Son of a bitch! Nathan is me!

"I've been gone?"

"In every possible way."

Pretorius managed to focus even better and saw that his visitor wore a general's uniform.

"How many possible ways would that be?"

The general smiled. "You went out on a mission—I'll give you all the details later, if you have trouble remembering them—and you accomplished it, as you always do."

"I don't remember a damned thing," said Pretorius.

"That's because you've only been awake a few minutes."

"So where am I back from?"

The general smiled. "You're back from Benedaris IV in the

Albion Cluster." He paused. "You're also back from whatever the hell is on the Other Side."

Pretorius frowned. "The other side of *what*?"

"Life. You died for a few minutes during surgery."

Pretorius tried to shake his head and winced. "I don't remember a damned thing."

"Too bad. There's plenty that would pay through the nose to know what it's like there."

"On Benedaris IV?"

The general looked amused. "You have one more guess."

Pretorius grimaced. "I don't want it."

The general threw back his head and laughed. "That's my Nathan!"

Pretorius stared at him. "I seem to remember you. Kind of."

"You ought to. We've been working together for a dozen years. I'm Wilber Cooper. Name ring a bell?"

Pretorius concentrated, then frowned. "You're the bastard who keeps sending me out on these missions."

"See?" said Cooper with a grin. "You *do* remember."

"What happened to me?"

"We're hoping you'll tell us when you're strong enough to be debriefed. But it was messy. See these two cases?" Cooper tapped the two translucent vats. "One of them is cloning you a spleen, and the other a pancreas. They should be ready for you, or you for them, in a week." He paused. "Looks like we're also going to give you a prosthetic foot, to replace the artificial one you ruined. There's not a whole lot of the original Nathan Pretorius left."

"How long have I been here?" asked Pretorius.

"A few weeks."

Pretorius frowned. "*Weeks?*"

Cooper nodded. "You've been in a medically induced coma. They just let you wake up about an hour ago."

"And I fulfilled my mission?"

"You always do."

"What was it?"

"You led a team into a buried facility on Benedaris where the Bolio kept the weaponry they planned to use to disrupt the upcoming Spiral Arm Games. It was pretty sophisticated stuff. There's not a scanning station in the Democracy that can spot it. Ten of those bastards could have wiped out, oh, eighty or ninety thousand spectators before we killed them."

"And I disabled the weapons?" asked Pretorius.

Cooper smiled. "That's one way of putting it. You blew up a third of the goddamned planet." He paused. "They killed your men while you were escaping and came damned close to killing you. You were quite a mess when we found you."

"I thought you said I *did* die."

"In surgery, not in the field," responded Cooper. "Though I suppose it comes to the same thing in the end."

"So since I'm clearly damaged goods, I suppose I should ask about my pension and the best retirement communities."

Cooper emitted a heartfelt belly laugh. "Forget it, Nathan! We're in the middle of a war!"

"*You're* in a war," said Pretorius. "Me, I'm in a hospital."

"For the fourth time," said Cooper. "Or is it the fifth?"

"How the hell should I know?" demanded Pretorius. "I didn't even know my name ten minutes ago."

"It'll come back to you. It always does."

"I get shot up a lot, do I?"

"It's a dangerous business," replied Cooper. "But you're the best covert agent we've got, and there's no way you're walking away from this." The general paused, then added: "And once your brain and body are working again, you won't want to."

Pretorius stared at him and had the uneasy feeling that he was right.

1

Pretorius was sitting in his room, staring out the window at the gardens just beyond, when the door opened and a tall orderly, not quite human but clearly humanoid, entered the room.

"Excuse me, sir," said the orderly in a harsh, rasping voice. "You have a visitor."

"I'll excuse you if it's anyone but that Cooper."

"That's *General* Cooper, sir," said the orderly.

Pretorius grimaced. "How did I know?"

"May I show him in, sir?"

"Absolutely not," said Pretorius. "He's the last man I want to see."

"This is a military rehab center," said a familiar voice from beyond the room. "You let me in and make yourself scarce or I'll have you court-martialed."

"He's lying," said Pretorius. "He does that a lot."

"Sir," said the orderly, "may I present General Cooper."

Cooper strode into the room and turned to the alien orderly. "Scram, son," he said.

"Good-natured as ever," noted Pretorius.

"Nathan, my boy!" said Cooper expansively. "How are you?"

"I was fine until thirty seconds ago, and I haven't been a boy in twenty years."

"Do I detect some veiled hostility here?" said Cooper with an amused smile.

"Absolutely, except for the veil," replied Pretorius. "Leave me alone."

"The medics tell me you're being released tomorrow," continued Cooper. "It's time to talk business."

"It's time to talk recuperation," said Pretorius. "Leave me alone."

"Can't do that, Nathan my boy! There's still a war on."

"I'm not your boy, and there'll still be a war on whether I listen to you or not." He glared at Cooper. "I'd prefer not."

"That's exactly what you said the last two times," noted Cooper cheerfully.

"You mean the last two times I was almost killed carrying out your hair-brained schemes?"

"Need I remind you they were *your* schemes?"

"They were *your* fucking impossible targets."

"Nonsense," said Cooper. "You accomplished your missions, didn't you?"

Pretorius glared at him. "Go away."

"Do we have to go through this every time?" said Cooper with a heavy sigh.

"No," answered Pretorius. "You could just leave me the hell alone instead."

Cooper frowned. "What's gotten into you, Nathan?" he asked with mock concern.

"You want a list of every alien piece of crap they dug out of my body?"

Cooper laughed heartily. "You always had a fine sense of humor, my boy!"

"I'm thrilled that you appreciate it," said Pretorius. "Now go away. Visiting time's over."

"Oh, I'm going," responded Cooper. "Just as soon as you get

your clothes on. I'd wait outside, but first, we're old friends, and second, you'd lock and barricade the door the second I walked through it."

"I'm not going anywhere."

"Yes, you are. We've come up with something really unique, a plan that'll excite even you." He paused. "*Especially* you."

"The only thing that excites me right now is the thought of solitude."

"I'm not kidding, Nathan. This is something we've been working on for three years. When you see it, it'll just blow you away."

"I've *been* blown away," said Pretorius. "It hasn't got a lot to recommend it."

Cooper leaned forward, unable to keep the excitement from his face. "This is the Big One, Nathan—the one that could change the entire course of the war."

"It seems to me I've heard that before."

"Those missions you've gone on were major, there's no question about it." Cooper paused. "But this one's a game changer, Nathan. It's *the* game changer."

Pretorius sighed deeply. "All right, tell me about it."

Cooper shook his head. "I'm going to show you. Start getting dressed."

"Whatever happened to 'Just listen'?" asked Pretorius.

"I can explain it," replied Cooper, "but it'll make much more sense if you see it for yourself." A pause. "You're going to love it, Nathan!"

"If it's so great, why did you bother sending me out on the last couple of missions?"

"This one wasn't ready until now." Cooper's face brightened. "Wait 'til you see it, Nathan! It may change the course of the whole damned war."

"I've heard that before," said Pretorius.

"Not from me. Trust me on this, Nathan."

"It seems to me that I'm learning how to walk and breathe and eat again because I trusted you the last few times."

"This is war, goddamnit!" snapped Cooper, pounding the wall with a fist that made a metal clanging sound. "You think you're the only soldier who was ever injured?"

"All right," said Pretorius with a defeated sigh. "Tell me what this is all about."

Cooper shook his head. "I've got to show you. It'll make more of an impression."

"Are you trying to impress me or prepare me?"

"Both."

"All right," said Pretorius, getting to his feet. "Where are we going?"

"Not far," said Cooper. "Climb into your clothes and follow me." A moment later Cooper was leading him out the door, down a corridor, and over to an airlift. They floated up to a docking station, emerged a few feet from Cooper's personal flier, and were aloft a few seconds later.

Before Pretorius could ask how far they were going, Cooper gave some coded orders to the autopilot and the flyer banked right, slowed down, hovered over the roof of a building Pretorius had never seen before, and descended slowly, landing with barely a tremor.

"This way," said Cooper, climbing out of the flyer and heading off for an airlift. When he got there he waited for Pretorius, who was still getting used to his new leg and still recovering from his organ transplants, to catch up with him.

"How're you holding up, son?" asked Cooper.

"I'm managing, and I'm not your son" was the reply.

"Follow me," said Cooper, entering the airlift.

"Is this thing working?" asked Pretorius as they passed the ground floor and kept descending.

"Perfectly," Cooper assured him.

They descended five more levels and finally came to a stop. When they emerged, Pretorius found himself flanked by heavily armed officers, who fell into step with him behind the general.

They walked down a corridor, entered a large room, crossed it, and came to a halt at a heavy door that reminded Pretorius of a bank's safe, complete with what seemed to be a pair of state-of-the-art locks.

Cooper uttered a coded command so softly that none of the men could hear him. The instant he did so a narrow beam shot out, examined the insignia on his uniform, matched it against his face and skeletal structure, and the door slid open.

"You men wait here," ordered Cooper. "Nathan, come with me."

The two of them walked into a large chamber, and the door snapped shut behind them.

"Alone at last," said Pretorius sardonically.

"Not quite alone, Nathan," replied Cooper. "Come this way."

He led Pretorius off to the left, where there was a single table, some ten feet long. On it rested a translucent container, almost eight feet long, three feet high, and four feet in width, topped by a shimmering energy field. As they approached it, Pretorius was able to make out the form of an alien. It was some six feet tall, with a prehensile nose, more like that of a proboscis monkey than an elephant's trunk. It had two very wide-set eyes, both of them shut; earholes but no ears; and a sharply pointed chin. Its arms were the length of a gorilla's and just as heavily muscled. Its feet were almost circular. Its head and body were devoid of hair, and its color, top to bottom, was a dull red. A number of small wires were attached to its head. And it was breathing.

"Okay," said Pretorius, "so you've got a Kabori. Get four hundred million more, and that's one less threat we'll have to face in this war."

"Is that all?"

"Other than the fact that he's breathing?"

Cooper grinned. "Take a closer look."

Pretorius frowned, stepped closer to the alien, studied it, and suddenly looked up.

"Jesus H. Christ!" he exclaimed. "You've actually captured Michkag!"

Cooper's grin grew wider. "Well, we've finally managed to impress you."

"You're damned right you have."

"A clever ruse," said Cooper.

"Are you trying to say that *isn't* Michkag?" demanded Pretorius.

"In a way."

"All right," said Pretorius, stepping back and staring at Cooper. "What are you talking about?"

"Well," said Cooper, "that's Michkag *genetically*."

"Explain!" demanded Pretorius.

"The Democracy, at the cost of quite a few lives, has managed to steal a sample of General Michkag's DNA from his own medics, and we've managed to clone him. That's what you're looking at—the clone. He's in a state of stasis right now, with language and history being fed into his brain—but he's been awake most of the time since we created him two years ago." He paused and gave the unconscious clone a loving pat on the shoulder. "There is a Kabori psychologist named Djibmet who has ample reason to hate Michkag and the coalition he leads, and for the past two years, even since we created the clone, Djibmet has been teaching him everything else he needs to know—schooling him in Michkag's gestures, verbal inflections, everything he can teach him to help him pass as the real Michkag."

"*Will* he pass?" asked Pretorius.

"We think so," said Cooper. "Even as he lies there, he's being fed tapes. Still, there's only one way to find out." He flashed Pretorius another grin. "That's where you come in."

Pretorius stared at him but said nothing.

"Your job will be to lead a team that will kidnap the real Michkag if you can, secretly assassinate him if you can't, but in any event put *our* clone in his place, where he'll misdirect the enemy's forces and find some way to funnel vital information to the Democracy.

Pretorius shook his head. "This is crazy. We won't get within five light-years of Michkag's headquarters. He's better protected than our own leaders are."

"But he won't *be* in his headquarters two months from now," replied Cooper. "We've intercepted a coded message to the effect that he'll be meeting with members of a federation of human rebels, trying to convince them to join his side. The meeting will take place at a fortress in Orion in two months. You have that long to prepare your team. You can select it from any officers or enlisted men in my command."

"Not a chance," replied Pretorius. Cooper opened his mouth to object, but Pretorius held a hand up to silence hm. "I used your people the last three times, and there are parts of me scattered all the hell across the galaxy. If I go, I'll pick my own team—and they probably won't be members of the armed forces."

"That's absolutely out of the question!"

"Fine. Get yourself another boy. I'm going back to the rehab center." Pretorius began walking to the airlift.

"Damn it, Nathan, it's got to be a military operation!"

"Round up your own military team and good luck to you."

"I could court-martial you for refusing a direct order in wartime!"

"Go ahead. I'll be safer in jail than trying to kidnap or kill the most important general the enemy has."

Cooper stared at him for a long minute. "You really mean that, don't you?"

"I really do."

There was a long silence.

"All right," said Cooper at last.

"All right, I can choose my team, or all right, you're court-martialing me?" replied Pretorius.

"Choose your fucking team!" growled Cooper, walking past him and heading to the airlift. "Don't just stand there! You've only got two months to turn the tide of this goddamned war. Time to get to work!"

2

Pretorius sat on his couch, with his favorite symphony playing in the background. It was some four hours after he'd spoken to Cooper, his first night out of rehab.

He sat perfectly still for half an hour, letting the music wash over him, trying to get used to the feel of his new body parts. Then he pressed his right forefinger against the chip that had been embedded in his left wrist, and an instant later the entire wall of the room became a computer screen.

"Orion," he said, and the Orion constellation appeared.

"Please tell me it's not in the Rigel or Betelgeuse systems," he muttered.

"It's not in the Rigel or Betelgeuse system, Nathan," replied the computer obediently.

"Thanks a heap," growled Pretorius. "And call me Colonel.

You want to show me where the damned thing is?"

"What damned thing would that be?" asked the computer.

"The goddamned fortress!" snapped Pretorius. "Cooper said it was programmed into you while I was in the hospital."

A bleak, barren, dust-covered brown world appeared.

"That's it?" asked Pretorius, frowning.

"Yes."

"So where's the fortress?"

"Beneath the ground," said the computer. "No member of the armed forces has seen it, so I cannot image it for you."

"Can you pinpoint its location?"

"I just did. It is on the fourth planet of the star known to the military as Petrus."

"Can you pinpoint it any more accurately?"

"Not without further data," replied the computer.

"I assume it's not an oxygen world?"

"You are correct."

"Wonderful," muttered Pretorius.

"I am glad you are pleased."

"You go to hell."

"I have been instructed by your superior to ignore that command," replied the machine.

Pretorius glared at the screen for a long moment, then got up, poured himself a glass of Alphard brandy, and began pacing restlessly around the room.

"I don't suppose anyone has told you what kind of armaments and defenses the damned planet or even the fortress has?" he said at last.

"No."

"Or how big the fortress is?"

"No."

He leaned back, closed his eyes, and considered his options. Finally he sat up again.

"All right," he said. "If we don't know what's awaiting us there, and we're going to have to approach it world by world, some hostile, some neutral, hardly any of them friendly, I'm going to have to put together a very eclectic team. And a *small* team. I approach with a ship than can hold too many, they'll blow us apart while we're still approaching the damned planet, before I can even start lying about why we're there." Suddenly he shrugged. "What the hell.

If he thought he could approach it with a large military ship, he wouldn't have tossed the damned job into *my* lap."

He drained his glass, then uttered a curse.

"Is something wrong?" asked the computer.

"I'm supposed to sip that stuff," answered Pretorius. "I got caught up in the problem and drained it, and it burned all the way down."

The computer offered no comment.

"All right," said Pretorius. "I'm going to rattle off a series of names, people I've either used before or at least seen in action. I want you to show me a holograph of each and a readout telling me how old they are, where they are now, if they've received any disabling wounds since I programmed their bios into you, if they've recovered from any such wounds—and wipe any who are deceased. Got it?"

"Yes, Nathan."

"That's 'Yes, Colonel,' damn it."

"Yes, Colonel Damn It."

Pretorius glared at his wrist and wondered how soon they could give him a new wrist and hand if he cut this one off just above the embedded chip. Finally he rattled off forty names, studying each as the computer produced a holograph and a readout for each.

When it was done, he leaned back again and shook his head. "Nine of them dead," he said. "That's hard to believe. These were the best."

"I can produce copies of the death certificates if necessary," offered the computer.

"Definitely not necessary," said Pretorius. He closed his eyes, lost in thought, for another long moment. "Okay," he said at last. "I'm off to bed. You've done your job. Tomorrow I'll start doing mine."

3A

Pretorius walked down the midway, past the barkers, the hucksters, the hints of sinful pleasures within the old-fashioned canvas tents. There were strippers of both human sexes and three other sexes that had very little in common with humanity. There were half a hundred games of skill and even more games of chance. There were trained animals from a dozen exotic worlds, their number of limbs differing wildly.

There were grifters, pickpockets, hookers, everything you'd expect to find in a carnival except a freak show. With over two hundred known sentient races in the galaxy and hundreds more presumed out there somewhere, one entity's freak was another's lifemate.

"Kill a Pizo!" cried a barker, holding up some wicked-looking spears. "Three throws for fifty credits!"

Pretorius grinned and continued walking. He'd seen Pizos in action. They looked reasonably normal: humanoid bipeds with two eyes, two ears, a purple tint to their skins, and totally without hair, down, feathers, or any other natural covering—and they could absorb just about anything from a dagger to a bullet to a laser blast with absolutely no ill effects.

"You sure you want to walk away, fella?" said the human barker, grabbing his arm. "For you, we'll make it four throws."

"Keep your spears," said Pretorius. "I'll pay you fifty credits if you'll let me feed him a candy bar."

"Get outta here!" snarled the barker.

Pretorius grinned. Not much killed Pizos, but contact with chocolate or sugar did it instantly.

He continued walking, looking at the various signs, and finally he saw the one he'd been searching for: *The Galaxy's Strongest Creature.*

And in smaller type, just beneath it: *Is he Man, Alien or Machine?*

Pretorius paid his admission and entered the tent. Only eight other spectators were there, two humans, four Robalians, and two whose races he couldn't identify.

Standing on a makeshift stage was a man, or rather, thought Pretorius, what was left of a man. He wore only a loincloth. His head was bald, and his eyes seemed to be entirely pupil and iris, with no white showing. He had gleaming metal prosthetic arms, heavy prosthetic legs made of a heavier metal, and his left ear was also artificial.

"Okay, Samson," said a voice over a speaker system, "show 'em what you can do."

The man walked up to a pair of metal weights, each emblazed with "500 pounds," inserted his artificial hands into grips at the top of each, and lifted them until both arms were extended straight out from his body. There was mild applause, and he lowered the weights to the ground.

"Now," continued the voice, "if any member of the audience can lift even one of those weights, the management will refund double your money to every member of the audience."

One of the Robalians climbed up onto the stage, tried to lift a weight, grunting ferociously, and gave up after about half a minute.

The mostly prosthetic strongman offered four more demonstrations of his prowess, and then the show was over, and the audience walked out.

All except Pretorius.

"Not bad, Felix," he said. "Not bad at all."

The strongman peered into the darkness. "I'm Sampson," he said.

"You're Felix Ortega, and you're wasting yourself here," said Pretorius.

The strongman peered more intently, then straightened up. "Nathan," he said. "What the hell are you doing here? Have you come to gloat?"

"I've come to offer you work," replied Pretorius. "*Real* work, not this bullshit stuff."

"I *got* this way from what you call real work," replied Ortega. "And then," he added bitterly, "when it was over, the military wouldn't take me back. They gave me a bunch of money and medals and basically told me to go away. I think it made them uncomfortable to look at me."

"Nonsense," said Pretorius. "You're as good as new. Better, even. Could the old Felix Ortega lift a thousand pounds? And what do those eyes see? Infrared, telescopic?"

"Both, plus microscopic, and I can also see well into the ultraviolet spectrum."

"Then what's the problem?"

"The problem is that I'm not a man anymore," said Ortega. "I'm a goddamned machine."

Pretorius shook his head. "You're an *enhanced* man, and the military was crazy to let you go. What's in your head and in your heart is still Felix Ortega. The rest is just improvements."

"Easy for you to say," replied Ortega.

"You want a list of every body part I've had replaced?"

Ortega stared at him for a moment. "No."

"So do you want to hear my deal?"

"I don't know," said Ortega. "Why me?"

"Because with your enhancements, that's four or five normal men and women I don't have to take."

"Normal men," repeated Ortega bitterly.

"That's right," said Pretorius. "And thanks to science, you're a superior man. Maybe even a superman."

"I'd rather not be."

"I'd rather be happily married, working at a desk, going home every night, and looking forward to being a grandfather," replied Pretorius. "But there's a war on, and if we do our job, maybe some other poor bastard can enjoy those simple pleasures a few years from now."

"How long will this take?" asked Ortega.

Pretorius grinned. "The sales pitch or the assignment?"

"The assignment."

"Three months at the outside. If we haven't accomplished it by then, we're dead."

Ortega was silent for a long moment, then finally nodded his head. "I'll do it."

"Good!" said Pretorius. "I'm glad to have you aboard."

"You didn't ask my price."

Pretorius stared at him. "Well?" he said at last.

"When it's over, if we're still alive, I want a body and a pair of eyes that'll pass for normal."

38

Pretorius walked down the long line of cells. Finally the officer who was leading him came to a halt.

"I'm sorry, sir," she said, "but I'll have to frisk you first."

"I turned over my weapon at the front desk."

"Even so, sir," she said apologetically. "You have no idea how dangerous this prisoner is."

Yes, I do, thought Pretorius, as he extended his arms out and stood for the frisk.

"You're sure you wouldn't rather communicate with her via holographic video?"

"I'm sure."

The officer gave him a *Well, you've been warned* shrug, proceeded another fifteen feet, and faced the prisoner in the cell.

"Stand back," she said harshly and waited until her order had been obeyed. Then she drew her burner, held it on the prisoner, and ordered the cell door to slide open. Pretorius stepped through, and the door immediately closed behind him.

"Hello, Snake," he said.

The inmate, a slender woman barely five feet tall, with her hair clipped as short as his, walked over and gave him a hug.

"Hi, Nathan!" she said. "It's good to see you again. Did you make my bail?"

He shook his head. "There's no bail, Snake. You were convicted, remember?"

She frowned. "If you're not here to spring me, use my real name."

He smiled. "Snake *is* your real name. Sally Kowalski is just the name the government knows you by." He looked around the small cell. "You're the best—or at least you were. There was almost no space you couldn't slither through, no locked room you couldn't break into or out of. How the hell did you ever wind up here?"

"I trusted a man."

He shook his head. "You should have known what scumbags they can be."

"All except you, Nathan."

"How come you haven't broken out of here?"

"See the sink and the toilet?" she said, gesturing toward a corner. "No metal. Same with the bars, front and back. I don't even have a hairpin." She grimaced. "And the cell's electrified, Damned hard to short it out with no metal." She pointed to a camera that was mounted in the ceiling just outside her barred door. "Watch." She walked across the call. The camera swiveled and followed her every move.

"So they've finally build a Snake-proof jail," said Pretorius.

"Oh, I'll find a way out," she said. "It's just taking a little time."

He shrugged. "Well, if that's the way you want to get out . . ."

"You got a better way?" she asked, suddenly alert.

"It's a possibility," he said. He looked around the small cell. "I don't know how you keep in shape in a place like this."

"Watch," she said, twisting her body in ways he would have sworn no human could bend. "Satisfied?"

"You're still the best contortionist I ever saw," he said.

"Don't need a whole lot of room to stay limber," she replied. "Though I probably can't run a four-minute mile these days."

"Could you ever?"

She grinned. "It depended on who was after me."

Pretorius laughed aloud. "Damn, I've missed you, Snake!"

"Enough to spring me from durance vile?"

"That's what I'm here to talk about." He paused and pulled a small metallic cube out of his pocket. "Activate." The cube suddenly glowed with power. "Okay, no one can monitor us now."

"You mean spy on us."

"Comes to the same damned thing in these surroundings."

"Okay." She smiled at him. "Who do you want killed?"

"Maybe no one."

"Robbed?"

"Try not to get ahead of me," said Pretorius.

"Okay," she said. "But every minute you drag this out is another minute I'm stuck in this goddamned cell."

"You ever hear of General Michkag?"

"Who hasn't?"

"What would you say if I told you I was putting together a team to kill or kidnap him and put a double in his place?"

"You know better than that, Nathan," she said. "They'll spot him in ten seconds."

He shook his head. "Not this one, Snake. He's a clone."

"How the hell did they pull that off?"

"I'll tell you all about it if we can come to an agreement," said Pretorius. "I ran all the factors through the computer. It says it's a suicide mission. It gives us a six percent chance of surviving." He paused. "But it gives us a ten percent chance of pulling off the replacement *before* we're killed. How do you feel about ten-to-one odds against?"

"Sounds generous," she said.

"Probably is," agreed Pretorius.

"You think there's a better-guarded person in the whole damned galaxy?"

Pretorius shook his head. "I doubt it."

"I hope they're paying you a lot for this," said Snake. "Because right off the bat, you need to buy a computer that can dope out the odds better."

He laughed. "So . . . you want in?"

"I want *out*," she replied. "Of here."

"Okay."

"Does this job pay anything?" she asked. "I mean, besides the cost of my funeral?"

"Not much," said Pretorius. "But before the mission starts I can get your entire record expunged."

She laughed. "Fat lot of good having a clean record'll do when they bury us in . . . ?"

"Somewhere in Orion."

"Right," she said. "You found anyone else with a death wish besides you and me?"

"Felix Ortega."

"Never heard of him."

"You'll meet him soon enough."

"May I make a suggestion?" she asked.

"I'm listening."

"Get Toni Levi to join us."

"I'm way ahead of you," said Pretorius. "I'm having dinner with her tonight."

3C

Toni Levi, who hated her nose, her eye color, and the name Antoinette, sat across the table from Pretorius. She'd had two cosmetic surgeries, had spent countless hours in a local gym, and was on her third hair color—and was still disappointed with her appearance, and the fact that most people didn't find her ugly but indeed quite ordinary did nothing to alter her opinion.

"That was an excellent dinner, Nate," she said as a robotic waiter took the empty plates from the table. "I've always loved Belargian shellfish, and this is a great wine."

"I'm glad you liked it."

"Are you going to tell me why we're here, or would you rather wait for dessert?"

"I may have a big job for you," said Pretorius.

She laughed aloud. "Of course you do, Nate," she said. "When's the last time either of us worked on a *little* job?"

"Point taken," said Pretorius, pulling out the security cube and activating it. "It won't pay that well, it'll take three months out of your life, and the odds are that you won't survive it."

"You really know how to charm a girl," she said with a smile.

"If it'll make you feel any better, the Snake's coming along."

"Sally Kowalski? I like her." She paused. "I hate the nickname you've given her, though."

"She gets into places even a snake can't penetrate."

"It's even worse than what you call me."

"Pandora?" said Pretorius. "But it fits. There isn't a computer or lockbox or anything else that you can't open."

She laughed. "So far," she replied. "But I don't like it anyway."

"It fits," he said, holding up the cube. "Remember this?"

"Remember it?" she replied. "Hell, I created it."

"All the more reason for calling you Pandora. I can't give you a name in some code that only you and three computers in the whole galaxy can speak."

"Even so."

"Settle for it. It's better than Sexpot."

"And those are the only two nicknames you know?"

He smiled. "The only two that are left and that fit you."

"I'm almost flattered," she replied. "Okay, what's this mission that you thought was worth the most expensive dinner in town?"

"Even been to Orion?"

"Not many people have—and even less have returned to tell about it."

"Aren't you even a little curious about it?"

"Of course I am," she answered, "but I think General Michkag might have a little something to say about it."

"Oh, I doubt it," said Pretorius with a smile.

She studied his face for a moment. "Okay, what do you know that I don't know?"

"Not a hell of a lot, according to your resume."

"Cut the bullshit, Nate," she said irritably. "What do you know about Michkag that I don't know?"

"He's going to be traveling with us."

She stared at him. "You don't *look* crazy, but that's as crazy a thing as I've ever heard you say."

"We've got a clone—not a look-alike, not an android, but a living, breathing clone of Michkag."

"Great," she said. "So now there are *two* genocidal geniuses with the same DNA."

Pretorius shook his head. "We grew this one up from his DNA, and we've got a turncoat Kabori who used to work for Michkag and is teaching the clone his mannerisms, his choice of words and phrases, the way he carries himself, everything." He paused. "I've seen him, Pandora. He really exists."

"Okay, he really exists," she said. "Now, I suppose you could put him on video and have him surrender. That might fool some of his troops. Or you might shoot him in cold blood—always assuming these Kabori bastards *have* any blood—and ruin the morale of his troops and countrymen, or country*things*, or whatever the hell they are. But no, that's not half dangerous enough for Nate Pretorius." She looked him full in the eye. "You're putting together a suicide mission to replace the real Michkag with the clone."

"Well, it's a mission, anyway," acknowledged Pretorius. "And with the right team, it might not be a suicide mission."

"Hold on," she said, reaching for one of the seven miniaturized computers she wore attached to her belt and tapping in a code with her forefinger. A moment later a response flashed briefly on the screen. "I just put the proposition to the Master Computer on Deluros VIII," she continued. "You know what it says the odds of any member of your team living through it are?"

"Six percent."

"Close," replied Pandora. "Seven percent."

Pretorius smiled. "Damn! I'm doing something right!"

"What the hell are you talking about?"

"It was six percent before you and Snake joined the team."

"I haven't joined anything, Nate."

"But you will," he said.

"Why?"

"Because no one's ever broken into Michkag's personal computer, and no one's ever deciphered their secret codes—and you can't resist that kind of challenge."

"You think not?" she said pugnaciously.

He shot her a confident smile. "I think not."

"You're a fool," she said. "You never asked why I retired from the service two years ago."

He shrugged. "I figured you had your reasons."

"I did," she said, nodding her head. "I *do.* Close to a billion reasons as of last month." She lowered her voice. "Since I quit, I've robbed seven of the enemy's biggest banks, and now you want me to actually go to Orion and kidnap or kill their most powerful and best-protected general?"

"Yes."

"You know the odds against it?"

He smiled. "You just told me."

"Well, you're crazy."

"I've been called worse."

She stared at him. "Do I look crazy to you?"

"No."

"Well, there you have it."

"Okay," said Pretorius. "If you're still talking to me, I'll order dessert."

She nodded her assent; he signaled to the robotic waiter, ordered two soufflés, and turned back to her.

"By the way," she said, "if no one's broken their code, how do you know what planet to go to and when?"

He smiled. "We've broken their partners' code."

"Ah," she said. "Of course."

"So who do you recommend? Tomas Sanchez?"

She shook her head. "Not good enough, not for something like this."

"Benny Scaparelli?

"No."

"Well, when you think of someone, let me know."

"It may take some time," replied Pandora.

"You know how to reach me."

They finished their desserts, Pretorius signed for them, and they got up to leave.

"I'll take you home," he offered as they stepped outside.

"Not necessary."

"Well, I'm sorry we couldn't work together one more time," he said, "but at least it was nice to see you again."

He began walking away when she called out: "Nate!" He waited until his smile had vanished before he turned to face her.

"Yes?" he said.

"What day are we leaving and where do we all meet?"

30

Deluros VIII, the capital world of the race of Man, was the home to basically a single city that had spread over every inch of dry land and burrowed under most of the oceans as well. It was said that it housed some eight billion bureaucrats who were charged with administrating the Democracy's thousand-plus worlds and pursuing the ongoing war against the Transkei Coalition.

Pretorius parked his ship in an orbiting hangar and took a shuttle to the surface. Even though Deluros VIII was considered a fascinating city-world, he always felt claustrophobic. The Customs hall was large and crowded, but his military uniform and rank got him into a special line, his passport was okayed, his retina read, his fingerprint and DNA matched against his profile in the Master Computer, and he was passed through in only twenty minutes.

He went to a transport station, fed the address he sought into a computer, and was instantly given three different routes to his destination: the fastest, the least expensive, and the most scenically beautiful.

What the hell is scenically beautiful about a goddamned tunnel? he wondered, and he decided to find out.

He bought passage on an airsled, took an airlift down some twelve levels, found a sled with his name in glowing letters, sat down, waited for the harness to embrace him and the door to shut and lock, and then he leaned back and smiled. The airsled took off so smoothly he was sure he wouldn't have known it if his eyes had been closed, and it began skimming above the floor of the broad tunnel.

Suddenly it began slowing down, and then tunnel became brighter up ahead—and suddenly the metal walls were replaced by glass, the lighting got even brighter, and he was slowly passing huge fish, larger and far more colorful than whales, on both sides. He stared at them in rapt fascination and was annoyed when the reversion from glass to metal indicated the end of his ride.

"You may exit now, Colonel Pretorius," said a mechanical voice.

"There's no station," he said.

"Just exit, please. You are expected."

His harness disappeared, the door vanished, and he stepped out of the airsled. He thought he'd be standing on the tunnel floor, but instead he found himself on a narrow beltway that carried him to an airshaft, where he quickly rose to ground level and walked out of what appeared to be a small kiosk, identical in every way to dozens of other kiosks that were scattered around the street and the slidewalks.

He had wondered how he'd know where to change slidewalks, but the airsled had let him off within fifty yards of the address he sought, and that section of the slidewalk on which he was standing came to a halt opposite the entrance. He got off, walked into the building, looked for a directory, couldn't find one, and at the nearest airlift simply uttered the name of the person he was there to see.

He was gently lifted some forty stories on a cushion of air and stepped off at the door to a large office.

"Who are you here to see?" asked a disembodied voice.

"Circe," he replied.

"Have you an appointment?"

"No."

"I'm sorry, sir, but—"

"Send him in," said a feminine voice.

The door irised and Pretorius stepped through. A narrow beltway transported him past a dozen offices until he came to a large glass-enclosed office that theoretically overlooked the city but actually just looked at other skyscrapers.

A beautiful, exotic blonde woman—so beautiful and so exotic he doubted that she was quite human—sat at a desk.

"Have a seat, Colonel," she said, and a chair instantly moved across the room to him. He sat down, and it promptly carried him forward until he was positioned across her desk, staring into her pale blue eyes. "The retina scanner has already identified you, or you would not have been allowed access to this floor, but I would nonetheless like to know your name."

"Nathan Pretorius," he replied.

"And you are here for . . . ?" She let the question linger in the air.

"Why don't you tell me?" he said.

She stared at him and frowned. "Just what do you think I am, Colonel Pretorius?"

"I really don't know," he answered truthfully. "I suspect you're not entirely human." He paused. "But I've been told what you can *do.*"

"You have doubtless been misinformed," said Circe. "I am an investment counselor."

"I'm sure you're that, too," said Pretorius. "But I ran a thorough check on you before I made the trip here to see you. I know you have gone under the names of Cybele, Vacuna, and Epona before you started calling yourself Circe; a friend named Felix Ortega worked at the same carnival as you when you were calling yourself Saunders; I know you copped a plea on Sarazan II, where you promised to leave the system and never return in exchange for no jail time; and I know that you're no more a financial advisor than I am. My guess is that you're vetting the customers to see which ones actually have cash to invest and which are just looking for market tips."

"You're thorough, Colonel," she said. "I'll give you that."

"Call me Nathan."

"Let's keep it formal until I know what you want of me."

"Don't you know already?"

"I'm not a mind reader, Colonel," said Circe. "I read emotions—but if you spoke to Ortega, you know that."

"And what do my emotions tell you?" he asked.

"That you're very tense, that you want me to agree to something, and that you're not thrilled with your surroundings, though I can't tell if that is just this building or extends to the whole planet."

"The planet."

"And of course, since you're in the military, you want me for something." Suddenly she smiled. "And the second I said that, your emotions intensified."

He withdrew the small security cube from a pocket and activated it. "I'm putting together a very special team. I think you'd be a valuable addition." He returned her smile. "You might even live through it."

"Now you're lying."

"Well, I *hope* we both live through it."

"What does it concern?"

"Assassinating five highly placed traitors in the Democracy's government."

"That's a lie," she said promptly.

He smiled again. "Yes, it is."

"Why are you wasting my time telling me lies?"

"Because I wanted to make sure you could spot them."

Suddenly she looked interested. "Proceed, Colonel."

"We've developed a clone of General Michkag," said Pretorius. "Not a surgically altered being, not an android, not a turncoat Kabori who looks like him, but an actual clone."

"Interesting," she said, leaning forward.

"The team I'm putting together has been charged with the task of kidnapping or secretly killing the real Michkag and substituting the clone in his place. And before we leave the poor bastard behind, I need to be sure that no one suspects that he's not the real Michkag. That's where you come in."

"You're going to need me for a lot more than that," she replied. "Just where is the switch to be made? Certainly not his home planet."

Pretorius shook his head. "In Orion."

"Where in Orion?"

"On Petrus IV."

"We'll be lucky to get halfway there," said Circe.

"We?"

She grinned an almost human grin. "This is the craziest idea I've ever heard. There's no way we'll live through it or even come close to accomplishing anything."

"That's too bad," said Pretorius, "I'd have loved to have you on the team."

"Oh, I'm coming," she said. "The Kabori killed the only three people I have ever loved." Suddenly she smiled. "Besides what audacity! I'd rather die doing that than expire of boredom here at my desk."

"Good!" said Pretorius. "The rest of my team is a few light-years from here. How soon can you be ready to leave?"

"Give me five minutes to clean off my desk and cancel all my appointments."

"Five minutes?" he said, surprised.

"What the hell," she said with a not-quite-human shrug. "Make it four, Nathan."

4

Pretorius gathered his team at a small government facility on Torvill IV, at the edge of the Democracy's territory. From the outside it looked like a small, rundown boardinghouse and even had a "No Vacancy" sign posted, but the interior was something completely different: half a dozen security systems, armed robotic guards, luxurious private rooms, an excellent kitchen/dining area, and a large meeting room equipped with every imaginable video and sound system.

Ortega and Circe knew each other, as did Snake and Pandora, and it took them only a few minutes to all feel comfortable with each other. The same could not be said for the Michkag clone and his instructor.

Djibmet.

"Goddamnit, Nathan!" said Snake, backing away from the two Kaboris. "He looks exactly like every holo I've ever seen of Michkag."

"He *is* Michkag," answered Pretorius. "Or a version of him."

"Give us a little time to get used to him," added Pandora.

"We haven't got much time," said Pretorius.

"It's like putting a prisoner in a room with Genghis Khan or Hitler or Conrad Bland and saying 'He's actually a friend,'" said Snake. "How soon do you think *they'd* have adjusted?"

"I assure you that I sympathize with your reactions," said the clone in heavily accented Terran. "But I have been created and trained for the sole purpose of replacing the original Michkag and bringing this war to a peaceful conclusion."

"He even *sounds* like Michkag!" complained Snake.

"He has to," interjected Djibmet. "He will be under constant guard as well as constant scrutiny. He has been taught to think of himself only as Michkag, to speak Kabori with Michkag's inflections and other languages with Michkag's accents. His gestures mirror Michkag's."

Pretorius nodded his agreement. "The thing to remember is that we're not substituting an actor or a double, at least in the usual sense. This is really and truly Michkag, just a sane and rational version who wants to make a peaceful accommodation with the Democracy."

"I know, I know," muttered Snake. "But it's going to take some getting used to."

"Circe?" said Pretorius. "Do you detect any hidden hostility in Michkag, any indication at all that he's not telling the entire truth?"

"None," she answered.

Pretorius shrugged. "There you have it."

"So you got us all here," said Ortega, "we're all fed, we've met the reason for our mission, so how do we get from here to there?"

"A direct approach is out of the question," answered Pretorius. "We couldn't get ten light-years into the Coalition's territory without being challenged, any more than they could get anywhere near Deluros, and I'm not prepared to fight off half the Kabori fleet."

"Then what's our plan?"

"Cube," commanded Pretorius, and instantly a holographic cube, some four feet on a side, popped into existence in the middle of the room. "Show the Democracy in blue, the Coalition in yellow." The cube responded instantly with a three-dimensional holograph. "There's some neutral space over here," he continued, pointing to the left side of the cube. "I'll call it a No Man's Land, or No Man's Space, if you prefer. Maybe two hundred systems, sixty-two of them inhabited or at least colonized. I don't think more than a dozen have sentient native populations."

He paused while Ortega's artificial eyes extended on stalks, microscopically examining the worlds in the neutral area.

"Anyway, we have friends on five of these worlds, and on at least one of them we should be able to swap our ship for a Kabori vessel."

"Swap?" said Circe, arching an elegant eyebrow.

Pretorius smiled. "A euphemism for 'appropriate.'"

"Which in turn is a euphemism for 'steal,'" she said, returning his smile.

"In essence," he agreed. "Except that it'll be more than a simple theft."

"Oh?" said Pandora.

He nodded. "We'll have to kill every member of the crew, any witnesses, anyone who might be able to signal to the Coalition that we're approaching them in a stolen ship." He paused. "The trick is to decide whether to steal a military ship, if one's available, or a private ship. There are advantages and disadvantage to both."

"I can see the advantage of a military ship," said Ortega. "We probably won't be stopped and boarded or that carefully scrutinized. But what's the disadvantage?"

"Simple," answered Pretorius. "Wherever we land—and if we're in a military ship, it almost has to be a military base—they're going to instantly recognize our Kabori passenger. And since it won't have been announced that he's in that ship or that sector of the Coalition, it'll take them about ten seconds to see if the real—or let's call him the *original*—Michkag is where he's supposed to be, and it'll probably take them another ten seconds to kill or incarcerate the lot of us."

"Okay," said Snake. "Then we eliminate the crew of a private ship and appropriate it. It sounds less dangerous start to finish."

"Well, it's certainly less dangerous at the start," agreed Pretorius. "Not much less at the finish. Just about any member of the Coalition, in or out of the military, is going to know that Michkag doesn't fly in a private ship with no bodyguards, no subordinate officers, just a bunch of the enemy."

"You don't like easy assignments, do you?" said Snake.

"If it was easy, I wouldn't need all of you," replied Pretorius.

"So what the hell *is* our plan?"

"We've got two months to get our Michkag safely and secretly to Petrus IV. We plan to leave this world in another day, head through No Man's Land, stop at a few friendly, or at least nonhostile worlds, land on Petrus IV, kill or kidnap their Michkag and replace him with *our* Michkag, and escape unseen and safely." He paused. "Everything else will be improvised on the fly, and you represent the best talents I can assemble for any eventuality."

"I'm flattered," said Pandora, "but I also think I just heard you pronounce my death sentence. Surely you have thought this through more thoroughly than that. After all, you're Nathan Pretorius, the man the military goes to when everyone says it can't be done."

Pretorius nodded. "Yeah, I've got a number of ideas, but probably half of them, maybe more, will have to be scrapped along the way."

"Let's hear them anyway," persisted Pandora. "Maybe we can scrap some right now and replace them with better ones."

Pretorius shrugged. "Why not?" He paused, ordering his thoughts. "If we're spotted after we change ships, especially if we're spotted as we approach the Petrus system, one ruse that *might* work is for a Kabori to claim to have captured us. We'd have to hide Michkag, of course; they'd know he's an imposter. It might get us on the ground and even into Michkag's presence, especially if we claim to have information to sell him, but . . ."

"But?" said Ortega.

"But Djibmet is undersized, probably too old, and would never pass for a military officer or even the kind of private citizen who could have captured all of us."

"This is true," put in Djibmet. "They would see through such a ruse in seconds."

"Then why even mention it?" asked Pandora.

"Because we may need to try it."

"But—"

"Does anyone know a shape-changer?"

There was a general shaking of heads and murmuring of negatives. Pandora pulled one of her tiny computers off her belt and spoke softly into it, then looked at its answer.

"There are only three shape-changing races in the galaxy," she replied, "and none of them are politically aligned."

"To which I repeat: does anyone know one?"

No one did.

"All right," said Pretorius. "Hopefully we won't need one, but we'll see if we can find one on one of the No Man's Land worlds."

"What else?" asked Snake.

"We'll see if any races we can impersonate have aligned themselves with the Kabori."

"The answer is no," said Pandora.

"The answer is no as far as Deluros VIII and the military know," replied Pretorius. "But every alliance is in a constant state of flux. I mean, hell, it's not as if the Democracy and the Transkei Coalition are the only major players. As we get closer, we'll see if that option is open to us."

"You're not giving me a lot of confidence," said Snake. "What else?"

"The closer we get, the more likely we'll run into some Kabori. And the more Kabori we run into, the more likely we are to be able to appropriate their ship or computer and let Pandora get to work finding the fortress and maybe even the essential rooms of the fortress. She may be able to totally mislead the planetary defense, have them all looking the wrong way as we approach and sneak in."

He turned to Ortega. "We've got the strongest being in the galaxy, short of those dinosaurs on that little world out on the Rim—Skyblue, I think it's called. If we need to disassemble anything from a ship to a small building to an enemy, he's the guy to do it. And if we're incarcerated or something vital to our mission is well beyond everyone's reach, or behind an impenetrable lock, that's why we have Snake."

"And why do we have *her?*" asked Snake, indicating Circe.

"To tell us who's lying and who isn't, who's about to take some kind of action and who isn't, who trusts us and who doesn't," answered Pretorius. "As I said, you were chosen to improvise in any situation, but thanks to Circe, we'll know up front if the situation *requires* a change in our plans." He paused. "Now, before we're done here, I'll have our initial itinerary—the trip through No Man's Land—available to each of you. If you have any contacts among the inhabited or colonized worlds there, I'd like to know about it.

If any true telepaths have joined the Coalition, we definitely need to know about that. I've checked you all out pretty thoroughly, but if any of you have any restrictions—gravity, abnormal oxygen content, endurance, anything that I might not be aware of, this is the time to tell me so we can make adjustments in our plans or eliminate you from the team." He turned to Djibmet. "I know the Kabori are oxygen-breathers, but if you'll have any difficulty with our oxygen-nitrogen ratio, let me know."

"We're fine," responded Djibmet. "But your gravity is about ten percent lighter than that of Rigel XV or Petrus IV, so—"

"It is?" interrupted Pretorius.

"Yes," answered Djibmet. "So we'll have no difficulty at all on the ship."

Pretorius shook his head. "You're not trying to fool anyone on the ship. I want our Michkag to take strength exercises twice a day, for an hour each time. We can't have him staggering from the gravity on Petrus after all of his subordinates have seen him walking and reacting comfortably."

"Yes, sir," said Djibmet.

"All right," said Pretorius. "This meeting is over. You can go to your quarters. Make sure you study the itinerary, and at dinner tonight we'll discuss any further suggestions or observations. But as I said at the outset, I expect this to require more improvisation than planning."

"I don't think of myself as an improviser," remarked Ortega.

"Haven't you figured it out yet?" asked Circe with an amused smile.

"Figured *what* out? asked Ortega.

"*He's* the improviser," she replied. "*We're* the tools."

5

They took off the next evening and left the Democracy two days later. As much time as he'd spent in space, Pretorius never ceased to be awed by its vastness. Once Man had thought that finding ways around Einstein's equations and reaching, then exceeding, light speeds would turn the rest of the galaxy into his backyard. But a galaxy that was one hundred thousand light-years across still took one hundred millennia to cross, even at light speeds. Wormholes, which seemed to exist outside of normal space, certainly helped, allowing ships to travel parsecs in mere minutes, but one took one's wormholes where one found them, and no one entered one until it had been charted, because it was just as likely to dump you halfway across the galaxy as in that system six light-years away.

Literally thousands of technicians had been charting wormholes for centuries, but the job was nowhere near completion. For one thing, about a quarter of the technicians—Pretorius preferred to think of them as galactic explorers—never came back, and it was impossible to know the reason. Did they emerge in hostile territory? Were some wormholes only one-way? Did some damage or destroy ships? Until a second, or a third, or a tenth exploration of the wormhole produced tangible results, commercial and even military traffic avoided it.

The ship emerged from the Boise wormhole, so-named for the birthplace of its explorer's great-great-great grandmother), and since Bortai III, the first planet on its itinerary, was only one day away through normal space, Pretorius didn't even have the ship's navigational computer search for wormholes.

The crew kept busy, each in their own way. The most obvious was Snake, who underwent a rigorous exercise regime every few hours, twisting and contouring her body in ways that no human body had never been designed for.

Ortega sat and watched her. Finally she turned to him and said, "Are you just gonna sit there all day? There's room for both of us to work up a sweat."

"No, thanks," he said. "I don't exercise."

"Ever?" she asked, surprised.

"Ever," he replied. "When I get up, from sleeping or even from just sitting down to eat—or to watch you, for that matter—if my arms and legs are working, they're working. They never tire, they don't get any stronger with exercise, they're powered by tiny batteries embedded just below my right ear in one of the few original parts of me, so stamina never enters into it. Once a day I test my various visions—telescopic, microscopic, infrared, ultraviolet—but that only takes maybe a minute."

"I envy you," said Snake.

"Don't," he said unhappily. "There's not a lot of the original me left to envy."

Pandora sat in a corner with her computers, oblivious to the others, and kept picking up distant signals, translating or deciphering them, very occasionally replying to them, saying nothing, letting the cup of coffee in the flat arm of her chair grow cold.

Michkag, having completed his physical therapy, was in his quarters, where Djibmet would spent the rest of the day, like all the previous ones, schooling him in his country's recent history;

in military protocols; in the original Michkag's personal likes and dislikes in literature, entertainment, food, and associates; as well as working on his speech inflections.

Circe sat by herself, plugged in to an ancient classic, living the life of Elizabeth Bennet as she first met Mr. Darcy, oblivious to all else.

And Pretorius continued to go over the checklist of possibilities and eventualities in his mind, wondering how many he was missing, wondering if he had recruited the right team. They were better than any crew Cooper would have provided, but that didn't mean they could break into the enemy's stronghold, kill or kidnap its best-guarded leader, replace him with a clone who as of this moment had only encountered a single member of his own race, and somehow escape intact. He almost wished there was a bookmaker aboard; he'd have loved to bet against being able to pull it off.

After a few hours, Pandora began composing messages in Kabori and having Djibmet make any necessary corrections so that if she had to send a phony one within the Orion constellation its construction wouldn't give it away. The evening was pretty much a repeat of the morning, and Pretorius decided the only reason he hadn't gone mad from boredom preparing for so many missions was that, having experienced them, he'd have traded the excitement and especially the danger for some nice peaceful boredom every time.

When they were within three hours of the Bortai system, Pretorius got his crew's attention.

"Okay," he announced. "Bortai's got about ninety-four percent of Standard gravity and an oxygen-nitrogen ratio within two percent of Deluros VIII. It was colonized by a race that calls itself the Bort—I have no idea if they took their name from the planet or vice versa.

They have their own language, but most of them speak and understand Terran." He turned to Djibmet. "They understand Kabori, too, though I gather their mouths have some difficulty forming the words correctly. You're welcome to come with us or stay on the ship." He jerked a thumb in Michkag's direction. "He stays."

"We can disguise him so that he doesn't look like General Michkag," said Djibmet. "And surely Pandora can create a passport for him under any name we choose."

"There's no doubt that she can," agreed Pretorius. "But he stays anyway."

"But why?" asked Djibmet.

"I don't want him answering to any other name, speaking in any other dialect or tone of voice, or carrying himself in any other way. There's an old scam, dating back thousands of years, though it applied to livestock, not sentient beings. The term was 'ringer,' and it was a different, usually less valuable, look-alike animal that was substituted for a more valuable one. Well, we're trying to pull off the biggest ringer scam in history, and the odds are already too stacked against us." He turned to Michkag. "I'm sorry, but you are Michkag and no one and nothing else, not even for an hour in a non-Kabori town three thousand light-years from Orion. I hope you understand, but whether you do or not, you're staying on the ship until the impersonation begins."

Michkag inclined his head slightly. "I understand."

"Now, at some point you've got to meet some Kabori," continued Pretorius, "and convince them you're Michkag. We need a trial run, but we'll have to dope out the proper scenario. It'll almost have to involve them coming aboard whatever vessel we're on, where, if you do make a mistake, it won't be fatal to the mission."

"When will that be?" asked Djibmet.

"I'll work it out and let you know," replied Pretorius. He looked around. "Any other questions or comments?"

There was no initial reply, but just as he was about to get up and return to his cabin Pandora spoke up.

"Got a problem here," she announced, looking at one of her tiny computers.

"Oh?" said Pretorius.

"Yeah," she said. "We'd better not land on Bortai."

"Why not?"

"If these codes weren't so hard to break I could have warned you yesterday," continued Pandora. "The Coalition has entered into a secret agreement with the Voche Empire, which consists of twenty-three systems, including Bortai. It's been in effect for five Standard days, which means when you ask for landing coordinates they'll direct us to a military base and intern us."

"Okay, it'll cost us a few extra days, but let's give this new arm of the Coalition a wide berth." He checked his navigational computer and had it lay in a course for Belladonna.

"Belladonna," said Circe. "That certainly doesn't sound like an alien world."

"Just means it was named by a human and programmed into our maps that way. The Kabori and other races probably call it something else. Anyway, it's got much the same atmosphere and gravity as Bortai III. Only difference is that this one has a native population, and Bortai was a colony world."

"It'll cost us a few more days, then?" asked Ortega.

"Not a problem," replied Pretorius. "No sense getting there before Michkag does."

"I wonder . . ." said Pandora.

"About what?"

"*Is* there some advantage to be gained in getting there first?"

Pretorius considered it for a long moment, then shrugged "There are pluses and minuses either way. If we get there first, we'll have time to acquaint ourselves with the fortress, to determine the best place to make the switch, to learn the routines of their security forces. But on the other hand, the longer we're there, the more chance we'll be discovered." He paused. "And if *he* gets there first, at least our target will be there on the ground, but so will all his massive security. Six of one, half a dozen of the other."

"Oh, well," said Pandora with a shrug. "It was an idea."

"Keep coming up with them," said Pretorius. "You never know which improvisation will work, just that the best-laid plans usually fall apart when dealing with alien races and worlds."

And though he didn't know it then, twenty-two hours later they would have a chance to test the truth of that statement.

6

"Incoming message," announced the computer.

"From a planet?" asked Pretorius.

"From an approaching ship."

"Is it military?"

"No."

"Okay, let me hear the message."

There was some brief static, and then a voice in heavily accented Terran said: "Ahoy the ship!"

"Ahoy?" repeated Pretorius, frowning. "No one's said 'Ahoy' in centuries."

"SOS! SOS!" continued the voice. "We have three severely wounded females aboard, and our fuel supplies have become corrupted. May we approach and transfer our sick and wounded to you?"

Pretorius turned to Circe. "Bullshit?" he asked.

"They're way too far away for me to tell," she replied.

"I don't like it," added Snake. "Females, not women?"

"The speaker's clearly not human," said Ortega. "He's learned the language the way they teach it in textbooks, not the way we speak it."

Pretorius waited to see if anyone else had any comments, and when they remained silent he replied to the signal. "You may approach us. Please state your race, so we can determine the nearest medical facility that can accommodate you."

"The females are human."

"But you're not," noted Pretorius.

"No, I am a Beldorian."

"All right. Disable your weapons and continue approaching."

"Thank you."

The communication was cut off, and Pretorius waited until the ship got to within ten miles.

"Are they sending to anyone else?" he asked Pandora.

She checked her various machines and shook her head.

He ordered the computer to put the approaching ship on visual.

"Okay," he said. "Is that Beldorian?"

"No," answered Pandora. "But Beldor is a long way away from here. It's probably just some local transit service."

Pretorius was silent for a moment, then he shrugged. "Okay, direct him to us and make sure any weapons are disabled."

"So are we going to take the women back to base?" asked Ortega.

"There aren't any women," replied Pretorius.

"But he said . . ." began Ortega, and then his voice trailed off.

Pretorius glanced over at Circe. *Can he really be this naive?*

She stared back at him with a knowing grimace.

"They're almost here," announced Pandora.

Pretorius nodded. "Let's have a look."

A holograph of an approaching ship, a little larger than their own, came to life.

"Not heavily armed," reported Ortega.

"Makes sense," commented Pretorius. "We're in No Man's Land or so close to it as makes no difference, so every ship needs *some* weaponry—but you don't want so much that bigger ships, and there are a lot of them, start to covet them." He studied the ship again. "Still, they've got enough to cause trouble."

"I take it you don't believe them," said Pandora.

"I get paid for not believing them."

"More to the point, he survives by not believing anyone," added Snake with an amused smile.

Pretorius turned to Circe. "I think you'd better go to your cabin."

"Why?" she said. "If they're not legitimate, I'll be able to tell you instantly."

"If they're not legitimate they might enter the ship shooting," answered Pretorius. "If you sense that they *are* legit, come on out and join us." He stared at her. *Don't make me explain in front of the others that you're the only who can't take care of yourself in an attack.*

She couldn't read his mind, but she could read his emotions and his concern, and left for her cabin without another word.

"You, too," said Pretorius to the clone. "I don't want anyone to report that Michkag was seen on a ship in the company of Men."

The clone nodded and went to his quarters, while Pretorius turned to Pandora and pointed to the half-dozen miniaturized computers hanging from her belt. "I assume at least one of those is a weapon?"

She nodded and patted one that rested on her left hip.

"Have it ready," he said.

"You're sure these guys are enemies?" asked Ortega.

"I'm not *sure*," answered Pretorius. "But my experience tells me that a small nonmilitary ship like ours is definitely at risk anywhere outside the Democracy, and my brain tells me the odds of a ship with three injured human women chancing upon us before contacting anyone else are pretty damned long. So be ready."

Ortega shrugged his prosthetic shoulders. "You're the boss."

"Let's all remember that," replied Pretorius.

The approaching ship reached them in another five minutes, docked alongside, and extended an enclosed walkway between the two ships' airlocks. They requested permission to come aboard.

Ortega, who was closest to the airlock, turned to Pretorius. "Do I let them in, or should we insist on a visual inspection first?"

"If they haven't got three wounded women, they'll find a way to substitute a holo of them, and we won't know the difference until we see them," answered Pretorius. "Let 'em in and keep alert." He turned to Snake. "Make yourself scarce."

She nodded and curled herself up in a near-impossible fashion beneath her seat.

The airlock door slid into the ship, and suddenly four burly Beldorians, heavily boned and heavily muscled, mildly humanoid in form, entered the ship, weapons in hands.

"If you want to survive," said the one who seemed to be their leader, "do exactly as you're told!"

Pretorius checked their weapons, saw that they were all computer-operated, and quickly glanced at Pandora, who seemed to be fidgeting nervously but was actually manipulating two of the microcomputers she had on her belt.

"Disarm yourselves, slowly and carefully," said the leader.

Pretorius looked at Pandora, who smiled and nodded her head almost imperceptibly.

"I don't think so," he said.

The leader turned, aimed his weapon at Pretorius, and pressed the firing mechanism.

"It tickles," said Pretorius.

The other three Beldorians tried firing their weapons, also to no effect.

"Felix, I think our visitors would like a little exercise," said Pretorius.

Ortega grinned and knocked the nearest one senseless with his prosthetic left arm. Then he turned and pointed at the leader—and as he did so, his arm instantly extended almost the length of the bridge, sending the leader flying into a wall where he collapsed with a resounding *thud!*

One of the two remaining intruders turned to face Ortega and tried to advance toward him but instead fell on his face, with Snake wrapped like a boneless grapevine around his legs.

The final Beldorian dropped to one knee. "I surrender," he said in Terran.

"And you think we're going to let you live, do you, Pirate?" asked Ortega.

The Beldorian turned to Pretorius. "You are the leader," he said. "Let me live and I will join you, serve you, fight, and even die for you."

"We're not in the pirate business," replied Pretorius. "We could save a lot of time and trouble by killing you right now."

The pirate stared at him for a long moment. "I have offered my fealty once. I will not do so again."

"Snake, see if either of the first two is alive," said Pretorius.

She checked them out. "They're breathing," she said. "I can't speak for their condition, what might be broken, which innards are still working."

"We're going to kill enough sentient beings before we're done," said Pretorius after a moment's silence. "I don't see any reason to kill these too."

"They'll report what they've seen," said Ortega.

Pretorius shook his head. "What have they seen?" he replied. "Pandora, go over to their ship and make sure the controls are responsive to us, or at least that you can make them responsive. Ditto the weaponry. Ortega, go first, just in case they left someone behind."

He nodded and walked to the airlock, then crossed over to the other ship, followed by Pandora.

The Beldorian that Snake had tripped began groaning and tried to sit up.

"Whack him on the head with the butt of his weapon," ordered Pretorius. "We're no match for him physically. If he gets up I'll have to kill him."

She took the weapon from the floor where it lay next to him and cracked him across the front of his skull as he was getting to his feet. He dropped back down without a sound.

Ortega returned a few minutes later. "Pandora says there's no problem with the ship or the weaponry. And since she suspects you're planning on moving us there, she also says that the galley is capable of creating food we can metabolize."

"Sounds tasty," said Pretorius, making a face. "Okay, drag the three unconscious ones into three cabins, pack up any of our effects, and lock them in. Then escort this last one to another cabin and do the same. Have Snake lend a hand."

Ortega lifted an unconscious pirate as if he were a baby, slung him over his shoulder, and deposited him in a cabin, then repeated the process twice more. The fourth Beldorian walked to his indicated cabin on his own power.

"Okay," said Pretorius. "Felix, move the luggage and whatever else you pulled out of the cabins to the other ship. Snake, get Circe,

Djibmet, and the clone, and have them gather their gear and go to the pirate ship."

"What about you?" asked Snake.

"I'll be along in a few minutes."

Pretorius went to the control panel, where he jettisoned most of the fuel. Then he set the locks on the cabin doors for forty-eight hours. Finally he permanently limited the radio range to three light-years.

Then, satisfied that his prisoners could survive but couldn't cause him any trouble, he entered his new ship, cast his former one adrift, and began planning his next move.

7

"Nice ship," said Pretorius, looking around the interior. "Certainly roomier, more modern galley, better weaponry. And what looks to be a big cargo hold—big enough for our stuff and their booty, with room left over—at least, judging from the outside." He turned to Pandora. "How's the navigational computer?"

"Seems to be fine," she replied. "Even the chairs are more comfortable."

"This thing is Beldorian registry, right?" asked Pretorius.

"That's correct," answered Pandora.

"How hard will it be to change it?"

"I can do it," she replied. "But why bother? We'll reach Petrus before anyone finds our ship. Well, our *former* ship."

"I'm not worried about them," he said. "They're pirates, and the likelihood is that they'll lie their heads off if anyone in authority comes across them."

"Well, then?"

"The fact that they were still free until a few minutes ago implies they were *successful* pirates," answered Pretorius. "That implies that someone—or more likely, a bunch of someones, has a grudge against them and is looking for this ship."

"Ah!" she said with a smile. "Okay, what registry do you want?"

"Something neutral," suggested Snake.

Pretorius shook his head. "Not *too* neutral. We don't know which neutral planets they've pacified in the past month or two. See who's not in the Coalition but has a most-favored planet trading status with them."

Pandora fed the data into her one of her computers. "Moreno II," she said. "It seems perfect. A former human colony world, broke away centuries ago when we were still the Republic, hasn't had any contact with the Democracy since it was formed, and exchanged ambassadors with the Coalition." She smiled. "It gives us an excuse for looking like Men."

"Sounds good," said Pretorius. "Okay, give us a Moreno II registry."

"What name would you like?"

"Something unexceptional and unmemorable."

"How about *Goodwill?*" suggested Ortega.

Pretorius made a face. "My God, that's awful."

"But it is unexceptional," noted Circe.

"And unthreatening," added Snake.

Pretorius sighed deeply. "Goodwill it is." He turned to Djibmet and Michkag. "Have you inspected the galley? Does it meet your needs?"

"It'll be fine," said Djibmet.

"Good. I'd hate to have to go out and steal another ship."

"The navigational computer would like your input," announced Pandora. "Where do you wish to go?"

"Let's finish inspecting this ship first," replied Pretorius. "Maybe it'll tell us."

"I don't follow you," said Circe, frowning.

"It's a pirate ship. They have to have *some* booty locked away somewhere. Let's make sure it's not perishable or set to explode if we don't hit it with the right code every hour or day or whatever."

"There are only two secured areas," announced Snake. "One of the cabins and the panel leading to the cargo hold."

"I can batter the door down," offered Ortega.

"I don't doubt it," replied Pretorius. "But let's proceed on the assumption that they knew whoever took over the ship could batter it down, and took precautions against that eventuality. Pandora, check it out."

"I already did. It's not a computer lock."

"All right," said Pretorius. "Snake, do your thing."

"I'll have to improvise," she said heading off to the galley. "The fucking government confiscated my tool kit."

She spent a few minutes examining various eating and cutting implements, walked to the cabin in question with a few of them in her hand, began cursing under her breath when her first few efforts were unsuccessful, and then uttered a victory bellow that seemed like it couldn't have come from such a small body when the door finally slid into the wall.

"Okay," said Pretorius, walking over. "Let's have a look."

The treasure, such as it was, was sorted into jewelry, currency not recognized by the Coalition, art, weaponry, and a few miscellaneous items.

"Not the most successful pirates I ever saw," muttered Ortega.

"Who knows?" said Circe. "Maybe they cashed in a month ago, and this is all from the last few weeks."

"All right," said Pretorius, standing in the doorway, hands on hips. "I hate to do this to the artwork, but we're going to have to jettison it, as well as any weapons that might be registered and any jewelry that is so unique that it can be identified. Keep the cash until Pandora finds some worlds where we can use it, keep any unregistered weapons that seem to be in working order, and keep any jewelry that's not unique and is small enough to be carried in a pocket or pouch until we need to use it as a bribe."

"I'll take care of it," said Snake.

"Felix, help her with the heavy stuff," said Pretorius. He gave Circe a look that said *And you let me know if anyone pockets anything*, and returned to the bridge.

Within two hours they'd jettisoned anything that could identify them as a pirate ship, found that the galley could make edible but not very appetizing food, and began discussing their options.

"We have to kill a few weeks," said Pretorius. "We might as well not approach the Petrus system before we have to."

"Why not?" asked Ortega as they sat in the galley, trying not to think of their favorite dishes.

"Because if anyone stops and inspects us, they're going to find our Michkag, and even if we convinced them he's the real thing, that'd only last until the true Michkag shows up. Remember, we're not here just to insert our Michkag, but to kill or kidnap the best-protected being in the Coalition."

"Besides," added Pandora, "we're Men, and we're at war with the Coalition. Even if they didn't know about our Michkag, they'd have no reason not to blow us out of the ether."

"Then how *do* we expect to approach Petrus, let alone land on it and make the switch?" asked Djibmet.

"I'm working on it," said Pretorius.

"Is that the only answer we're to be given?" demanded Djibmet.

"I could tell you the thirty-four approaches I'm considering and let you pick holes in each of them," answered Pretorius, "but I'd rather wait until I had one that was foolproof."

"He's the best," added Snake, "or they'd never trust him with this mission. Once it works, the damned war'll be over in a year, our Michkag will make peace, and the combination of the Democracy and the Coalition will be all but invulnerable."

At least I'm traveling with an optimist, thought Pretorius wryly.

Circe couldn't read his thought, but she had no problem reading his reaction and smiled.

He sighed. *Yeah, I know. The only thing worse is for* nobody *to believe in this thousand-to-one scheme.*

"So do we just cool our heels here in No Man's Land for a month?" asked Pandora.

"We'll keep busy," replied Pretorius. "It'll give our Michkag another month to prepare for his impersonation. It'll give you time to monitor more of their messages. It'll give all of us time to probe for weaknesses. Also, in a few days I'll adjust the ship's gravity and atmosphere to match that of Petrus IV."

"There's a couple of pretty powerful pulse weapons that we didn't jettison," said Ortega. "We might start practicing with them, and maybe even hunt up some more on some of these worlds out here."

"Waste of time," said Pretorius.

"Oh?"

"We're going to be five Men and an imposter on a planet that, for the duration we're there, will be the most heavily guarded world in the Coalition. If there are less than half a million uniformed Kabori there I'd be surprised. Short of slipping a Q-bomb into a molar and blowing the whole world to smithereens—and nine out of ten Q bombs never detonate—just how much difference do you think heavy artillery will make?"

Ortega's prosthetic face contorted into a hideous grimace.

"I just hate it when you lay it out like that," he growled. "I like to think we have a chance of succeeding in this damned enterprise."

"We do," replied Pretorius. "But not by outshooting the bad guys." He saw Djibmet offer the Kabori equivalent of a frown. "Excuse me," he continued. "I misspoke. We won't do it by outshooting the temporary enemy."

The Kabori inclined his head slightly in acknowledgment.

"So we just float here for a month and hope no one will spot or question us?" said Snake.

"Not exactly," answered Pretorius. "As we learn more about their defenses, we'll gradually get closer to them. We'll stop on the occasional planet where we might pick up something useful."

"Useful?" asked Circe.

"Information, for the most part."

"For the most part?" persisted Snake. "What else?"

Pretorius shrugged. "You never know."

"I know you are good at your trade," began Djibmet.

"The best," said Snake.

"The best," said Djibmet. "Therefore, I cannot believe that you have as little planned as you say. Are you—what is the expression?—are you holding out on us for some reason?"

Pretorius smiled. "As a matter of fact I am."

"Do you distrust us?"

"No. At various times my life will be in each of your hands. If I distrusted any of you, I wouldn't have accepted the assignment or solicited the aid of those assembled here."

"Then why are you unwilling to confide in us?"

"Because our next port of call is not going to meet with universal approval aboard this ship," answered Pretorius.

"Oh?" said Snake.

"Where are we headed?" asked Pandora.

"I'd like to know too," said Circe.

Pretorius took a deep breath and exhaled it slowly. "We're going to McPherson's World."

"There's only one thing on McPherson's World," said Pandora.

"A Tradertown?" suggested Ortega.

"A Tradertown with the most notorious whorehouse on this side of the galaxy!" snapped Pandora.

Circe closed her eyes and concentrated. "He's not kidding," she said, frowning.

"A whorehouse!" repeated Snake angrily. "The most important mission in the history of the Democracy, and he's stopping off at a whorehouse!"

Pretorius stared at Djibmet. "You had to ask," he said at last.

8

The Tradertown was named for McPherson, as was the world, though no one quite remembered who he was or why he'd stopped there long enough to give the world his name. It was rumored that he'd found gold or fissionable materials there, but a couple of survey teams, three centuries apart, concluded that there was nothing worthwhile on the planet. It had some underground water (which had to be purified) and some sunny days (and one had to protect against the strong ultraviolet rays of its yellow-orange sun). There was enough vegetation to keep a few thousand herbivores alive, and enough predators to keep their herds from increasing, but most species stayed far away from the Tradertown.

McPherson—the town, not the planet—consisted of a landing field, a boardinghouse, a message-forwarding station, a spare parts shop for the more popular types of smaller spaceships, a general store that sold everything from dry goods to medicine to antique weaponry, and then there was Madam Methuselah's, which had a fame far out of proportion to both its size and clientele.

From the outside it looked like a run-of-the-mill boardinghouse, with absolutely nothing special about it. The interior gave lie to that. The walls were covered with exotic and erotic art from half a hundred worlds; there was a huge, elegant bar, a trio of smaller drug dens—each accommodating a number of different races—and perhaps fifty elegant rooms, most of them hidden unobtrusively below ground level.

It was a brothel, with females of more than a dozen races, and a few males as well. It had been patronized by dictators, kings, and celebrities from all fields of endeavor. It was even said that the legendary Santiago himself had once stopped in, though no one really believed it.

There was one person who could have confirmed it, or definitively denied it, and that was Madam Methuselah, who was the most exotic thing about the brothel, for she had been its madam since the day it had opened some eight centuries earlier. She looked like a woman in her early twenties, though some said her eyes, which had seen so much, appeared ancient. But the madam wore no makeup, never dyed her hair or wore a wig, had not undergone cosmetic surgery or spent a day away from the brothel in half a millennium, and yet she possessed not a wrinkle nor a single gray hair, and she moved with the grace of a woman not long out of her teens.

Which is not to say that she didn't rule her domain with an iron fist. There were other brothels around the galaxy, some on nearby worlds, but Madam Methuselah's was unique for two of the services it offered: privacy and confidentiality. Not necessarily between bedmates, although that was private and confidential as well. But when people, often of different races, required absolute privacy in which to consummate their business, be it economic, military, or political, they knew that the madam would provide them a soundproof, windowless room that had no hidden microphones or holo cameras, and that there would be no record anywhere of their having been there.

Her rules were strict, and her word was the only law in the only town on this world. Her assistants—she disliked the words "bouncers" and "enforcers"—were unobtrusive until a weapon was drawn or a prostitute was abused, and then their response was swift and deadly. A running total of recently deceased rule-breakers was kept on the wall over the magnificent polished bar as a reminder that civilized behavior was not only requested but insisted upon.

Madam Methuselah herself was not beyond conducting some private business of her own—not sexual business, for it had been hundreds of years since anyone had seen her take a client to bed, but business of a different sort. Many a man or woman came to the brothel, sat down for a private conversation with the madam, and left a few minutes later with the information they had come for. She never sold such information but rather traded it, so that she always had new information to trade and hence new reasons for people to make the trip to McPherson's World and perhaps spend a day or a night sampling the brothel's more usual services while they were there.

She was waiting for Pretorius when he entered.

"Hello, Nathan. They told me your ship had landed." She smiled at him. "It's been awhile. Are you here to fertilize any of my frail flowers?"

"Have I ever?"

"One can always hope. Let's have a drink in the bar, and then we'll go to my quarters for a chat."

"Let's skip the bar," said Pretorius.

"That's not like you, Nathan."

"I've got three furious women on my ship who only half-believe I'm here to talk. The sooner I get back there, the better."

"Three?" she said, arching an eyebrow. "I think your eyes are bigger than your—"

"Don't say it," he interrupted, and she laughed.

"All right," she said. "Follow me."

She led him through the bar to the elegant entrance of an airlift. A moment later they had ascended to the expansive and beautifully furnished fourth floor, which constituted her living quarters and was filled with eight centuries of memorabilia.

"Computer," she said, "secure this level." She turned to Pretorius. "Have a seat, Nathan."

"Thanks," he said, sitting in a chair that immediately changed its shape to conform to his body.

"I heard you had some difficulty on your last assignment," she said, lighting up a thin Altairian cigar.

"There are bits of me all the hell over the galaxy," he acknowledged. "The last one was no different."

"And you're on another one now?"

He nodded.

"Care to tell me about it?" she asked.

"This one you'll have to keep to yourself."

She grimaced. "For how long?"

"You'll know when."

She considered it for a moment, then nodded her consent.

"I need two things," he continued "First, I need to know exactly when Michkag is due to land on Petrus IV."

If the mention of Michkag's name surprised her she didn't show it.

"Thirty-four Standard days from now."

"He's moved it up?" said Pretorius.

"I don't know what your information was," she replied. "I just know when he's due there."

"Okay, thanks."

She smiled at him. "Come on, Nathan. I'm sure you needed that, but you could have gotten it other places. What's the second thing you need?"

He stared at her for a long moment. "I need a shape-changer, and I need it soon."

A broad smile spread across her face. "You're going to try to replace Michkag!" She took a deep breath, exhaled it slowly, and shook her head. "You'll never get away with it, Nathan. When's the last time you touched a doorknob or a computer or damned near anything else that didn't read your DNA?"

Pretorius saw no reason to tell her about the clone, so he merely shrugged. "I don't create the plans," he responded. "I just carry them out."

"Oh, come on, Nathan, everyone at your level improvises. At least tell me that I'm wrong, that this isn't what you want a shape-changer for."

"You're wrong," said Pretorius. "This isn't want I want a shape-changer for."

She stared at him intently. "I can't tell if you're lying or not."

He grinned at her. "Good. I'm getting better at this. Maybe I'll join the Diplomatic Corps."

"If you live through this foolishness," she said.

He nodded seriously. "If I live through it."

"You know there are only three shape-changing races in the galaxy," she said, "none of them especially friendly to the Democracy, none of them especially inimical to the Coalition—and unless some of the major wormholes have moved, none of them within twenty days of the Orion constellation."

"If it was easy, I wouldn't be spending time talking to you while three women aboard my ship are planning a humiliating death for me for coming here," he said with a smile.

"All right," she said. "You'll have to stretch the definition, but I can help you."

"Stretch the definition?" he repeated, frowning.

"If he—or *it*, I'm really not sure which—functions as a shape-changer, do you really care what he is?"

"He can change into any shape the situation calls for?" persisted Pretorius.

"Any *living* shape," she replied. "I very much doubt that he could pass for a hospital or a spaceship."

"That's no problem. Even the Domarians can't do that, and they're supposed to be the most accomplished shape-changers in the galaxy."

"Good," said Madam Methuselah. "Then I'll be able to help my old friend"—she suddenly stared hard into his eyes—"*who will not forget that he owes me one—a* big *one.*"

"I won't forget."

"You had better succeed in this cockamamie scheme, whatever it is. Dead men never pay their debts."

"I assure you it is my earnest intention to live through it," he said with a smile.

"Good. Then I think I shall help you." She got up, walked to a nearby bar, opened a bottle of Alphard brandy, and filled two exquisite crystal glasses, carrying one over to Pretorius and sitting down with the other.

"Thanks," he said, taking a sip. "Good as ever."

"We don't water the liquor or misrepresent the frail flowers," she replied. "All right, Nathan. The creature you want—there's no sense pretending he's a Man—is Gzychurlyx."

"Say that name again?"

She did so.

He sighed. "I'll die of old age before I pronounce it right." He finished his brandy. "Is he here?"

"In the house?" she asked, surprised.

"On the planet."

She shook her head. "No. I heard he was on Belore V last week. I imagine he's still there."

"You're sure?"

"Unless a countryman has made his bail, and he's the only one of his kind I've ever seen or even heard of."

"How many jails has Belore got?"

"Just one," she replied. "It's not much more heavily populated than this world."

"Okay," he said, getting to his feet. "I'd better get back to the ship and convince them that I actually did come away with information," he said with a wry smile.

"Good luck," she said, rising and walking him to the door. "I'll be watching. So to speak."

"Thanks," he said. "And I owe you one."

"Maybe only a half," she said as he stepped out into the hall.

He frowned. "A half?"

"He's got a shortcoming."

Pretorius was about to ask what she was referring to, but the door had already slid shut, and a burly assistant was escorting him to the airlift and then out the door.

9

Belore V was a dirtball of a planet. Not much grew on it, not many people chose to live on it. The air was a little thin, the gravity a little heavy, the sun a little hot . . . but its location was perfect for a huge gambling emporium that catered to all races. It was almost exactly equidistant between Deluros, Orion, Sett, and the headquarters of four minor alien empires. One had only to look at the spaceport to see the vast array of races that frequented the casino.

Pretorius set the *Goodwill* down in that section reserved for ships of its type, about three miles from the small town that encircled the huge building, then had the computer pinpoint the jail.

"You must be feeling a bit cramped in this ship," he announced to the others. "Unlike McPherson's World, there's actually something for you to do here, so if you want to take a few hours at the casino, grab an upscale meal, or just breathe a little of what passes for fresh air here, go ahead, since I don't know the next time you'll have an opportunity to do so." He turned to Circe. "All except you. I want you with me. And of course Michkag can't be seen, so you'll have to stay on the ship."

"I will remain with him," announced Djibmet.

"Okay," said Pandora. "I've activated the ship's security and tied it into the spaceport's security headquarters, so we'll be under a double watch while we're gone—our own and theirs. The password is 'football.'"

"What the hell is football?" asked Snake.

"A human sport from a few thousand years ago," answered Pandora. "Remember to say it when you touch any part of the ship after we leave it, or you're going to get one hell of a correction."

"Correction?" asked Ortega, frowning.

"Shock," she replied. "Not lethal, but it'll knock you on your ass for a few minutes."

"All right," said Pretorius as the airlock's door slid into the hull and a stairway lowered to the ground. "Try not to come back drunk or dead broke."

Pandora checked the security one more time, nodded her approval, and Snake and Ortega left the ship. She followed them a moment later, and a driverless vehicle pulled up within seconds, waited for them to enter, and raced off toward the casino.

"You ready?" asked Pretorius.

"Let's go," replied Circe, walking to the airlock.

They climbed down, and when the ship sensed that they were on the ground the stairway retracted and the airlock was instantly sealed.

A vehicle appeared almost instantly and paused while they climbed aboard.

"Welcome to Belore V," it said. "Have you reservations at the hotel?"

"No," said Pretorius.

"Then I shall take you directly to the casino. Would you like a list of all the many games available?"

"No, and we don't want the casino."

"I am afraid the hotel is full or fully reserved," replied the vehicle.

"We don't want the hotel, either," said Pretorius.

The vehicle, which had been heading toward the casino, paused, awaiting instructions.

"Take us to the jail," continued Pretorius.

"Acknowledged," replied the vehicle, changing directions and heading to the southern edge of the town. It arrived in four minutes, then stopped, opened its doors, and waited for them to exit.

"Will you be wanting a ride back to your ship?" it asked.

"Yes, but I'm not sure how soon."

"I will wait here unless called away," replied the vehicle. "If I am not here when you emerge, just stand in front of the building, and another vehicle will be by in a maximum of two hundred Standard seconds, usually sooner."

"Thank you," said Pretorius.

"It was my pleasure to serve you, sir," said the vehicle, and suddenly Pretorius and Circe could sense that almost all of its systems had shut down.

"Well, let's go in," he said.

"I'm still not totally clear about this shape-changer that isn't really a shape-changer," replied Circe.

"Welcome to the club," said Pretorius. "Madam Methuselah was a little vague about a couple of things."

"Are you sure we really need it?" she asked. "I mean, we've got the Michkag clone."

"Pretty sure," he said. "At any rate, it can't hurt."

She smiled. "Of course it can. That's why you've brought me along."

"To protect me?" he said, returning her smile.

"Oh, not physically," she replied. "But to protect you against believing him if he's lying."

"True enough," he said, approaching the door. "Shall we go to work?"

"Let's."

They entered the jail and were confronted by a robot custodian.

"May I help you?" it said.

"Yes," answered Pretorius. "I'm here to visit a prisoner."

"And which prisoner is that, sir?"

"I'm going to mispronounce his name, I'm sure," said Pretorius. "But it's something like Grizcharly."

"Are you referring to Gzychurlyx?"

Pretorius nodded. "That's the one. What's he in for?"

"Cheating at the casino, striking an officer, impersonating an officer, and impersonating an attorney."

"That's him, all right," said Pretorius. "What's his bail?"

"You are of the race of Man, are you not?" asked the robot.

"Yes."

"His bail, in your currency, is one hundred thousand Democracy credits."

"Okay," said Pretorius. "Let us see him."

"Follow me," said the robot, as another robot took its place by the door. It took them past two security stations, down two levels below the ground, and along the length of a short corridor to the very last cell.

"We have arrived," it announced.

Pretorius looked through the shimmering force field than encircled the cell.

"You must be mistaken," he said.

"This is the cell of the prisoner you named."

"But there's nothing there but a lump of . . . I don't know . . . fur, it looks like."

"That is Gzychurlyx."

"But—"

Circe touched his arm, and he looked at her.

"It's sentient," she said.

"*That?*"

She nodded her head. "That."

He turned back to the robot. "Does it understand Terran?"

"Is that what we are speaking?"

"Yes."

"Then yes, it does."

"Okay," said Pretorius, "you can leave us. We can find our way back to where we met you."

"I cannot leave you alone with the prisoner," replied the robot.

"Okay. Move as far from us as you can and don't listen to what we say."

The robot moved to the far end of the short corridor.

Pretorius turned back to the blob of fur. "Hey, can you hear me?"

"I have heard every word you have said since you arrived at my cell," said a very human voice in near-perfect Terran.

"You know Madam Methuselah?"

"I know *of* her" was the answer.

"She says you're a shape-changer."

"She is mistaken."

"Damn," said Pretorius. "Then we're wasting our time here."

"Possibly not," said the inmate, and suddenly Pretorius was staring at a gray-haired blue-eyed man, an inch or two under six feet, dressed in an expensive suit, perhaps twenty pounds overweight.

"This is *you?*" said Pretorius, staring at him.

"Yes."

"Then you *are* a shape-changer."

"I told you I am not."

Pretorius turned to Circe, who nodded her head that the alien was telling the truth.

"Then what the hell are you?" insisted Pretorius. "Why do you look exactly like a Man?"

"I cannot change my shape," answered Gzychurlyx. "But what I *can* do is change your perception of my shape."

"Explain, please."

"Any security machine will know my true appearance. So will cameras. But I can project an image of myself that will fool any living being of any race, no matter how close or far away they are."

"I see," said Pretorius, frowning. "That makes it more difficult, but I think we can still use you."

"Who is this 'we,' and how do you propose to use me?"

"Let me answer that with a question," said Pretorius. "We're in neutral territory between the Democracy and the Coalition. Which side do you favor?"

The Man who was not a male grinned. "I favor any side that will get me out of this dungeon."

Pretorius turned to Circe for confirmation, and she nodded again.

"All right," he said. "If I pay your bail, will you come to work for me? I warn you, it will be dangerous."

"It can't be any worse than being bored to death in this cell," replied Gzychurlyx.

"Okay. It'll take me perhaps an hour to raise the funds for your bail."

"I am not going anywhere."

"One more thing," said Pretorius.

"Yes?"

"I can't begin to pronounce your name, and neither can anyone else on my team. Have you got a nickname or an alias?"

"No."

Pretorius lowered his head in thought for a moment, then looked up. "All right. From this moment forward, your name is Proto."

"Proto?" repeated the alien.

"For protoplasm, and the way you sling it around."

"But I don't."

Pretorius smiled. "We'll let that be our little secret for the time being." He turned to the robot. "Okay, we're ready to leave now."

The robot escorted them to the ground level and out the front door. Their vehicle was gone, but another pulled up in less than a minute, and shortly thereafter they were aboard the ship.

"You look troubled," noted Circe.

"I was hoping he and maybe Djibmet could masquerade as members of Michkag's military and march us into the fortress as prisoners, but we'll never pull that off, not if he can't fool a security system."

"Then why are we getting him out of jail?"

"He's got a talent. We'll find *some* use for it. Besides, I don't think Wilbur will let us keep the pirates' loot, so we might as well spend it."

"Wilbur?"

"General Cooper," he answered. "Okay, let's get some of that stuff we appropriated from this vessel's former owners. As many losers as a casino this size has, there's got to be a lot of jewelers and pawnbrokers circling it like carnivores to the kill."

Djibmet, Michkag, and Circe helped him sort through the booty, and a few minutes later he and Circe returned to town, where they quickly sold enough of it to make up Proto's bail.

Then it was back to the jail, where Proto still appeared as a gray-haired man.

"You made my bail?"

"Yeah," said Pretorius. "And you remember our deal?"

"Yes."

Pretorius turned and signaled to the robot, and a moment later the force field vanished.

"All right," he said, "let's get this show on the road."

10

The other three humans were still at the casino, and the two Kabori were in their quarters when Pretorius and Circe returned to the ship with Proto.

"Let's see just how good you are at what you do," said Pretorius after showing his newest recruit where his quarters were.

"You've already seen it," answered Proto.

"You appeared to be a middle-aged man that neither Circe nor I had ever seen before," answered Pretorius. "How long does it take you to create an image or whatever it is that you do?"

"Instantly."

"Okay. Take a good hard look at Circe, study her voice when she speaks, study her gestures and mannerisms. Then, when I tell you to, *become* her and see if you can fool her crewmates." He turned to Circe. "When we see them pull up to the ship, go to your cabin for a few minutes."

She smiled. "At least we'll find out right away how good he is."

Proto kept the shape of the middle-aged man and spent a few minutes acquainting himself with the ship, then went to the galley and ordered it to mix him a foul-smelling drink.

"Heads up," said Circe a moment later. "They're on their way."

"Okay," said Pretorius. "Off you go." She got up and walked directly to her cabin. "Proto, do your thing and sit over there where she was."

And suddenly, as the words left his mouth, he wasn't talking to a gray-haired man anymore, but to Circe, who moved gracefully across the bridge to her chair.

"Amazing!" said Djibmet. Michkag merely blinked his eyes rapidly and then smiled.

A moment later Snake, Pandora, and Ortega entered the ship.

"So did you find what you were looking for?" asked Snake.

Pretorius shrugged and gestured to Proto. "Ask her."

"So did you?" continued Snake, facing Proto.

"I hope so," answered Proto, mimicking Circe's voice and inflections.

"Don't you know?"

"I think that's for you to decide," said Proto.

"Me?"

"The three of you."

"Well, you sure as hell had better luck than we did," said Pandora. "I really should stick to my machines." She smiled. "At least no one tried to pick us up. That's one advantage of going there with Felix."

"How much did you lose?" asked Proto.

"Not much," answered Ortega. "But then, we didn't start with much."

Pretorius let them chat for a few more minutes, then turned to Djibmet. "Tell our friend to come out of the cabin now."

Djibmet went to Circe's cabin and returned with her a moment later.

"Well, I'll be damned!" exclaimed Ortega, looking from Proto to Circe and back again.

"Our Michkag can't look like the real one any more than whichever of these isn't that Circe looks like the real one," added Snake.

Pandora turned to Proto. "I commend you. That is one hell of an impersonation."

“What makes you think she’s not the real Circe?” asked Pretorius.

“She made a mistake. A little one, but a mistake.”

“Oh?”

“Our Circe always wears red nail polish. This one doesn’t.”

“Damn! You’re right!” said Ortega.

“Yes, you are,” said Pretorius. He turned to Proto. “I’m not sure exactly how we’re going to use you, but you can’t mess up any details, no matter how minor.”

Proto nodded his head. “I’ll work on it.”

“What do you really look like?” asked Snake.

“Like this,” answered Proto, the image gone, appearing in his true form again.

“I’ve never seen anything like you,” said Pandora. “Where’s your home planet?”

“I don’t know.”

“What do you mean, you don’t know?”

“I gather I was not a very good citizen,” he answered. “I know I have been banished from my planet, but I do not know why. My entire life there, including its location, has been expunged from my memory.”

Snake frowned. “Now I’m going to be up all night wondering what a shape-changer can do to get himself exiled from a world of shape-changers.”

Proto then launched into an explanation about how he was not really a shape-changer at all, which led to more questions, including how a being who could appear to be the arresting officer or the judge could land in jail on Belore V, leading Pretorius to conclude that the newest team member was simply a very ordinary being possessed of extraordinary skills.

"All right," he said at last. "There's nothing more to be accomplished here. We might as well take off."

"And go where?" asked Pandora.

"The team's complete," he replied. "Time to start moving closer to Petrus. I think Tiroga II is one of the last planets as we approach Coalition territory that's reasonably friendly to Men."

"Not a bad idea, at that," said Pandora. "There were four pirates. There are eight of us. It wouldn't hurt to lay in some more supplies, especially if our newest member doesn't eat human or Kabori food."

"Well, yes, I suppose we *could* do that," said Pretorius.

"You had something else in mind?"

"Yeah," he replied. "I thought we might steal a Coalition ship. Not a military one—we don't know the codes—but a civilian one, something that will arouse a little less suspicion when approaching Petrus than this one."

Ortega nodded his head. "Makes sense."

"It may even be easier than I thought a couple of days ago," continued Pretorius. "Proto?"

"Is that her name?" asked Snake.

"*His* name," said Pretorius. "And trust me, you couldn't pronounce his real name. Proto, you've seen Kaboris before. Let's see you appear as one—and not as either of the two in this ship."

Instantly Proto projected the image of a Kabori.

"Damn, that's impressive!" said Ortega.

"You'll need a military uniform," said Pretorius.

Proto became a general.

"Not too high ranking," continued Pretorius.

Proto's rank was reduced to the Kabori equivalent of a lieutenant.

"Yeah, that'll do. We'll find some way to make use of that."

Proto appeared as his true self instantly.

"Why aren't you king of the universe?" asked Snake.

"Don't tempt him," said Pretorius. "For all you know, that's what he had in mind when they exiled him."

"I hope not," said Proto, whose natural voice was a hoarse and guttural-sounding.

"I have a request," said Snake.

"What is it?" asked Pretorius.

"Of Proto."

"Yes?" said Proto.

"Could you please appear as a Man while you're on the ship?" she said. "I'm afraid I'll trip over you, and I find your true voice disconcerting."

"That won't be a problem," said Proto, immediately appearing as the middle-aged man that seemed to be his favorite projection.

"Thanks," said Snake. "No offense meant."

"None taken."

"All right," said Pretorius. "As long as we're all being thoughtful, we can stop on an uninhabited planet for a day if our Kabori friends are going stir-crazy in here."

Djibmet looked at the clone, who responded with the Kabori equivalent of a negative head shaking.

"We are fine," said Djibmet.

"Okay," said Pretorius. "But understand: our Michkag is almost certainly going to be confined to whatever ship we're on until we actually reach Petrus. So if he thinks he'll need some exercise or fresh air, now's the time to let me know."

"I will be fine," said Michkag in badly accented Terran, and it occurred to Pretorius that those were the first words he'd heard him speak in any language.

"How's your education coming along?" he asked.

"He will be ready," Djibmet said with certainty.

"I sure as hell hope so, for all our sakes."

"I suppose in a pinch we could always use Proto," suggested Pandora.

The gray-haired man shook his head. "I do not speak Kabori."

"At all?" asked Pretorius.

"Very little," answered Proto. "Certainly not enough to pass as its most famous leader."

"Just as well to find out on the front end," said Pretorius. "Djibmet, we've got another job for you. When you're not schooling Michkag, help Proto work on his Kabori language skills."

"We haven't much time," replied Djibmet.

"Just give him some everyday basic phrases, nothing special," said Pretorius. "Just enough so they won't spot him the second he opens his mouth."

The Kabori shrugged. "I will do what I can."

"And once I figure out exactly how we're going to use him, I'll give you some exact phrases that you can translate and have him work on."

They fell silent for a moment.

"Shall I tell the ship to take off?" asked Pandora.

"Yeah, might as well, unless some of you want to go lose more money at the casino."

"I'd like to get some back," said Ortega. Then: "Ah, what the hell. I'd probably just lose again. There's an alien game called *jabob* that I've been trying to beat for years. Haven't managed it yet, certainly wouldn't if I went back tonight."

Pretorius nodded to Pandora, who gave the order to the ship, and had the navigational computer lay in a course for Tiroga II, which would be the last neutral world on their itinerary.

11

There were no convenient wormholes, and the trip took four days at light speeds. Once in the Tiroga system they announced their presence, got landing clearance and coordinates, and set the ship down in a spaceport on the outskirts of the largest town, which fell somewhat short of being a full-fledged city.

"All right," said Pretorius, when they were set to disembark. "Pandora, see if you can monitor any messages to or from Petrus or Orion. Snake, hang around the spaceport here, see if you can spot a likely Coalition ship that we can appropriate and then wait for Pandora to make sure it hasn't got some state-of-the-art security system. Circe, it's a mundane job, but someone's got to lay in supplies. See if you can pick up any political gossip along the way."

"What about me?" asked Ortega.

Pretorius stared at him, frowning. "Of all of us, Felix, you're the one people are most likely to remember. We sure as hell can't have you doing anything covert here. Let me think." He lowered his head for a moment. "Okay, *you* hunt up a ship for us. Snake, we used up most of the booty, and we can't keep hoping to find unsuspicious pawnbrokers. We need some currency that's good within the borders of the Coalition. Steal some."

Snake smiled happily. "Good! I was going to be bored to tears looking at ships all day."

"Just try not to get bored to tears in some Tiroga jail cell," responded Pretorius. "Pandora's made up passports and IDs for all of us. They'll get you through customs, but we don't know how they'll hold up under a close examination, even out here in No Man's Land, so try not to get into any trouble."

Pandora spent the next few minutes passing out the passport and ID chips, after which the three women left the ship.

Pretorius turned to Djibmet and Michkag. "Same as last time. You"—he indicated Djibmet—"can go into town if you want. But you"—he nodded to the clone—"can't be seen. In fact, once we decide which ship to steal, we'll still have to wait until dark, just to make sure no one walking to or from their ships can spot you."

"I understand," said the clone.

"I think this time I will go into town for an hour or two," said Djibmet.

"Up to you." He handed the Kabori his false ID. "Be back before dark."

Djibmet left the ship, and Proto approached Pretorius. "You seem to have forgotten about me. Surely I can be of some use to you."

"I haven't forgotten," answered Pretorius. "You'll be coming with me."

"In this guise?" he asked, indicating his human features.

"For the moment."

"Might I ask what our mission is?"

"Passports and IDs."

"But Pandora made them already," said Proto.

"Pandora made up a bunch of phony passports that list us as citizens of various neutral worlds, and which probably can't stand a close inspection. You and I are going to steal some valid IDs from members of the Coalition. They change them every few months, and we've no idea what kind of coding the current ones possess. But this is the last non-Coalition world we figure to touch down on, and the closer we get to Petrus, the more rigorously they're going to inspect IDs."

"Won't the people we steal them from just report them missing?"

"Of course," answered Pretorius. "But we're not duplicating them. Pandora just needs to know what the current codes look like so she can copy them. We may kill some Kabori along the way—in fact, we almost certainly will have to—and we may very well appropriate their passports and IDs, but we don't want to kill anyone, especially a Kabori, on a neutral world."

Proto nodded his head. "Makes sense."

"I'm glad you approve," said Pretorius, but his sarcasm was lost on his companion. "Let's get started."

As with the last world, a vehicle soon pulled up alongside the ship, waited for them to enter, and offered them a choice of half a dozen locations.

"Center of town," said Pretorius.

"The geographic center, the population center, or—?" began the vehicle.

"Middle of the biggest business district," Pretorius interrupted it.

"This will take approximately six minutes," announced the vehicle. "Would you like me to point out the sights of interest as we proceed?"

"No."

"Would either of you like something to drink?" it continued. "I can supply libations for the following races . . ."

"Not necessary," said Pretorius.

He almost felt the vehicle was sulking the rest of the trip, but it finally let them off at mid-block in the major business section of the town.

"Thank you," he said.

The vehicle sped off without an acknowledgment.

"What now?" asked Proto.

"Now we wander around a bit, go into a couple of stores and bars, maybe a drug den or two, and get a feel of the place and the clientele."

"I thought we were just looking for Kabori."

Pretorius shook his head. "Outside of Djibmet and the clone, only you can pass as Kabori, and that ends the second you open your mouth. No, we're looking for any citizens of the Coalition."

"There are no Men," noted Proto.

"But there are a number of humanoids. We don't need to look like them, we almost certainly won't be presenting IDs in person, but we'll travel more freely within Coalition space if we can identify ourselves as some minor humanoid race rather than as Kabori. It'll explain the non-Kabori ship, any accent if we make verbal contact, and any minor variation in IDs."

"Variation?" asked Proto, frowning.

"Ideally we'd like to present ourselves as being from a very minor planet, one that's part of the Coalition but so remote that if they're changing IDs every week or two, we could be a few days behind."

Proto looked dubious. "I don't know . . ."

"Neither do I," admitted Pretorius. "But if a team of eight is going to overthrow a government that controls eight thousand worlds, the first thing to do is proceed with confidence."

Proto smiled.

"What's so funny?"

"You're making that prison cell look mighty comfortable."

Pretorius chuckled. "We could return you."

Proto paused and considered it. "Let's see how today goes first," he finally replied.

Pretorius couldn't tell if he was joking or not, decided not to bother figuring it out, and entered a clothing store with Proto just a step behind him. He went directly to the section for humanoids and decided that what he and the women were wearing wouldn't necessarily identify them as members of the Democracy—there were quite a few million Men on the thousands of neutral planets, and many of them had occasional business inside the Coalition. He studied a number of humanoid customers but was simply unable to tell which ones might be from within the Coalition.

He went back outside, looked around, and spotted what he wanted.

"I think," he said softly, "that if we can't find a fight, we're going to have to start one."

"I don't understand," replied Proto.

"I can't tell by looking at them who's in the Coalition and who isn't. I mean, the Coalition isn't all Kabori, just as the Democracy isn't all Men. There are a number of races that have spread their seed; some are from neutral worlds, some from Coalition worlds. There's simply no way to tell by looking at them."

"What does this have to do with fighting?"

"We're going to go into that bar there," he said, pointing across the street, "and I'm going to get drunk and start cursing the Kabori and Michkag and the Coalition, and you're going to defend them, and we're going to get into a fight, and I'm going to be winning, and when someone comes to your defense, we'll have a pretty good idea that he's from the Coalition."

"It won't work," said Proto.

"Oh?"

"You're forgetting. I *look* like a Man, and I can look like any other race, but I am just projecting an image. If you aim a punch at my jaw, it will go clear through the image, perhaps three feet above the top of my head."

"Shit!" muttered Pretorius. "You look so real, I keep forgetting." He paused. "There's no sense getting into a fight with one of these bozos for real. I could get myself killed, or he could have enough friends that win, lose, or draw we can't get him alone long enough to remove his ID. We'll need a totally different plan. I've *got* to remember what you can and can't do."

He lowered his head in thought for a moment, looked up, blinked twice, and suddenly a huge grin spread across his face.

"I'm an idiot," he said.

"You have an idea?"

"Yeah. I just said it myself. We have to concentrate on what you *can* do."

"I don't follow you."

"We go to the bar. Wait until half a dozen humanoids are using their IDs to pay for their drinks. They'll be lying on the bar waiting for the bartender to pick them up and run them through his machine, or he'll have just returned them, and because they plan to order more they won't put them away." Pretorius smiled again. "Then you do your thing."

"My thing?"

"You stand twenty feet away, where everyone will be able to see you, and then you roar and project an image of some fire-breathing monster twenty feet high."

Suddenly Proto returned the smile. "Yes, I can do that."

"They'll be startled and probably scared shitless, and while they're staring at you I'll pick up a few IDs, passports, anything else that's lying on the bar. And the beauty of it is that it's just an image. If they shoot for your heart or where they think your heart is, they'll be ten or fifteen feet above you. And once you see me walk away from the bar, kill the image, and while they're looking for it, take this identity, or become whatever race seems to be most popular in the bar, and just walk out after me."

Proto considered it. "You know," he said at last, "I think it'll work."

"It will," agreed Pretorius. "And if a true shape-changer tried it, he'd be shot dead in two seconds."

They entered the bar. There were tables and chairs to accommodate a dozen races, and liquor for even more. It wasn't very crowded, and half the clientele were Kabori, so Pretorius nursed his drink while Proto pretended to nurse his, and within half an hour the place was crowded, and most of the clientele was human or humanoid.

"Now?" whispered Proto.

"Wait another minute," said Pretorius, studying the bar. When enough customers were in mid-transaction he nodded his head; Proto walked about twenty feet away, stood in front of a wall with holos of Michkag's and of the bartenders' home worlds—and suddenly, in place of the man who had wandered over, there was a twenty-five-foot monster that looked very similar to illustrations of mythical Chinese dragons Pretorius had seen on disks as a child.

There were shouts of surprise, some of terror, and three or four customers drew their burners and screechers and turned them on the dragon's image, which only made it roar in rage.

Pretorius moved quickly, picked up five sets of ID, and walked quickly out the door. A moment later Proto joined him, and they could still hear cries of "Where did it go?" and "What was it?" as they walked down the block and crossed the street at the corner.

"Did you get what we need?" asked Proto.

"I think so," said Pretorius, patting his vest pocket. "I *hope* so. Pandora will let me know. I don't think that stunt works too many times in the same place."

They went back to the ship, where Ortega and the two Kabori were waiting for them.

"I found a ship," announced Ortega. "Just about perfect. Let's just hope they don't come back for it before we're ready to leave."

"You're sure it's from a Coalition world?"

"It's got the Coalition's emblem emblazoned all the hell over it," replied Ortega. "Looks like it fits ten, maybe twelve."

"Any armaments?"

"Just the usual," came the answer. "It's not really equipped for battle."

"That'll do," replied Pretorius. "We don't want to get into a shooting match with Michkag's fleet."

Circe was the next to arrive, ordering her vehicle to use its extensions and deposit all the food and medicines she'd purchased into the ship's hold.

"Seems a waste, since we're just going to be moving it again," she said. "But the alternative was to order the vehicle to remain here, and that would attract too much attention."

Pandora arrived an hour later. When Snake didn't show up, they ate dinner without her. After another few hours, Pretorius got to his feet.

"She must have been caught," he said. "I'd better check the local jails and see if I can buy her out or if we'll have to break her out."

"Don't bother," said Circe.

He turned to her. "Why not?"

"She's on her way."

"You're sure?"

Circe nodded. "And she's furious as hell. I could read *that* emotion from miles away."

"But she's all right?"

"I don't detect any pain, just anger."

Pretorius opened the hatch, they waited another two minutes, and finally Snake climbed up the stairs, a bag over her shoulder.

"You okay?" asked Pretorius.

"There's a department store I want to blow up!" she snapped.

"What happened?"

"I figured they were taking in more than any other store in the area, so I stayed in the restroom until closing, then cracked the lock on their business office, jimmied the safe, and pulled out wads of cash—Coalition cash."

"So why are you so late and so mad?"

"I was just about to leave when four employees unlocked the door, pulled up chairs around the desk, and began playing cards. I knew if they saw me they'd report it, and there was no way I could make it back to the ship, so I hid. They couldn't have bet the equivalent of fifty credits between them, but they acted like guilty kids getting away with something because no one knew they were there. I was hiding in a fucking file drawer for five fucking hours until they left!"

"Damned good thing you're a contortionist," said Ortega.

"Well, I am one very pissed-off contortionist, let me tell you!"

"How much did you come away with?" asked Pandora.

"How the hell should I know? I had to hide before I could count it."

"Felix," said Pretorius, pointing to the sack, "do the honors."

Ortega knelt down and reached into it. "There's a *lot* here," he said. "Hope it's not all low denomination."

It wasn't. When they were through counting and recounting, Pretorius got to his feet.

"Okay, grab your gear and let's go steal a ship. We've got to be off the planet before that store opens up in the morning, because there's no way the authorities'll let anything take off once they find out that we robbed them of the equivalent of seven million credits."

"I should have swiped another million for my trouble," muttered Snake.

12

"So what's our name?" asked Snake as they took off in the new ship.

"It translates as *Victor*," replied Pandora, "which is an odd name for a ship with so few armaments."

"What race does it belong to?"

"Us, now," said Pretorius.

"I mean, who built it?" said Snake.

"A race that called itself the Dreen," said Pandora.

"Called itself?"

"They've been extinct for about twenty years, according to my computer," answered Pandora. "Evidently the Kabori pacified them a little too vigorously."

Djibmet looked upset but said nothing.

"So who was the most recent owner?"

"A Torqual," said Pretorius. He shook his head in wonderment. "Must have spent every voyage bent damned near in half." He tapped the hull above him. "It feels kind of cramped to me, and I never saw a Torqual less than maybe nine feet tall." He turned to Pandora. "Have you checked out the IDs and passports?"

She nodded. "Three are good. I destroyed the other two."

"How can they be good?" demanded Ortega. "They didn't belong to Men."

"Let me correct that," said Pandora. "They'll be good when I'm done with them—and they'll let me make three more, which will cover the five Men and Proto. Djibmet's got his own, which is still valid. And if our Michkag needs one, then we're on the wrong mission."

"Sounds good," said Pretorius. "How long will you need on them?"

"Creating them will take maybe an hour apiece. The trick is creating three more identities that won't set off any alarms. That'll be maybe a day if we're lucky, two or three if we're not."

He nodded. "Okay. Circe, you and Felix can start monitoring any news items within, say, a hundred light-years. We need to know if there's any change in the political situation. And we especially need to know if anyone thinks stealing the ship was anything more than a simple act of theft."

"We might even find out if they've stumbled on the pirates yet," said Ortega.

"Makes no difference," replied Pretorius. "They don't know anything about us, we took anything that could possibly be identified out of the ship, and we're well clear of No Man's Land."

"Okay, that's what they're doing," said Snake. "What do you want *me* to do?"

"I think our next port of call will be Brastos III," answered Pretorius. "It's a small mining world, oxygen atmosphere, seems well out of things. We'll stop there, ostensibly to refuel, but actually to see if the real Michkag has left for Petrus yet, and if we're real lucky to pick up a humanoid military uniform or two. Even if it doesn't bear any fruit, we still don't want to get to Petrus too soon. We might be able to hide there for a few days. I wouldn't want to try it for, say, two weeks."

"So what do *I* do?" persisted Snake.

"Open an account at the biggest bank on Brastos III and transfer about a third of your loot there."

She frowned. "Why? The only thing you're going to spend money on is fuel, if we even need any."

"Some of you will pick up information in the local bars or drug dens or"—he glanced at Ortega's head—"barber shops, always assuming they'll work on a Man. But I have a feeling a bank officer might be better wired into a government that's still a thousand light-years from here, and the easiest way to find out is to have a chat with him or her or it. And the easiest way to do that is to deposit a million credits or the equivalent now, and then visit the bank to see if we want to deposit any more."

Snake stared at him. "Damn! You're even more devious as I am!"

He smiled. "I have to be. I can't hide in a file drawer for five hours."

"All right," she said, heading off to another workstation. Suddenly she stopped and turned back. "How about half a million, just in case?"

"A million."

"But—"

"Snake, if we need more, we'll get it," said Pretorius. "Stealing money is easy. Winning wars is difficult."

She seemed about to argue, decided that it wouldn't do any good, shrugged, and went to the station.

"Is there anything I should be doing?" asked Proto.

"I was just coming to that," answered Pretorius. He turned to Djibmet. "We are going to need your expertise here."

"What do you want me to do?" asked the Kabori.

"Just watch." Pretorius turned back to Proto. "I want you to appear as a Kabori. Not Michkag and not Djibmet. If you've seen one in a military uniform, so much the better, but we can always bring up holos of that later."

"All right," said Proto. "When?"

"Now."

And as quickly as Pretorius uttered the word, Proto seemed to vanish, to be replaced by a Kabori soldier.

Pretorius turned to Djibmet. "Well?"

"The uniform was out of date even when I was still in the Coalition," answered the Kabori, "but physically he almost looks the part."

"Almost?"

"His eyes are brown. Ours are black."

No sooner had he voiced the observation than Proto's eyes became black.

"The right number of digits on his hands, and his feet are covered by boots," said Djibmet. "The ears are moving correctly. Walk toward me."

Proto approached him.

"Yes," said Djibmet. "Quite good."

"If you saw him right now for the first time, would you have any suspicion at all that he wasn't a Kabori?" asked Pretorius.

"No, none."

"All right. Your job for the next three days, when you're not working with Michkag, is to teach him a few simple sentences in your language, especially anything he might need at customs or if he's being questioned by the military."

"I'm not very good at languages," said Proto, who was once again in his familiar human guise.

"How are you at dying?" asked Pretorius.

"I beg your pardon?"

"This isn't a war game," said Pretorius. "It's the real thing. You'd better be good at one or the other, because I don't think you have a third choice."

The team kept busy for the next two days, and when Pandora announced that she'd finally created and certified ID chips and passports, Pretorius increased the ship's speed, and a few hours later they landed at a small spaceport on Brastos III, a dull gray world that mined gold, platinum, and a few exotic fissionable materials. Most of the mining was done by machines, and the population of the world was something less than a thousand, most of which lived in its sole Tradertown, which consisted of a hotel, a pair of restaurants, a general store, a bank, and an assay office.

It turned out that the ship really did need fuel, and Pretorius, after deciding that the two Kabori should remain on the ship, left Ortega and Pandora to see to the refueling and pay for it and the landing fees. He had Proto, who'd been working on his language, assume the appearance of a Kabori, though without a military uniform, and had him accompany Pretorius, Snake, and Circe to the bank, which looked solid and unimaginative.

"Snake," said Pretorius just before they entered, "your only function here is to prove that you started that account and then politely explain that I'm your advisor and I'd like to speak to the president, or some other officer, though I doubt that something this small has more than one or two officers. Circe, just nudge me when you sense that someone's lying."

She nodded, and they walked into the bank. Like the outside, it was far more functional than eye-pleasing. There was one teller of a race they hadn't seen before. Proto received less attention than the three Men, and Snake asked to see the president. A well-dressed

Tretoni female emerged from a back room and studied the four of them with narrow reptilian eyes.

"This is my advisor," said Snake, "and he wishes to discuss doing some business with you."

The Tretoni turned to Pretorius. "How may I help you?" she said in Terran.

"It's a private matter," replied Pretorius, "but if we can discuss it in your office, it could prove very lucrative to your bank."

"Certainly."

"This is my wife," he said, indicating Circe, "and this is my partner." He indicated Proto. "May they join us?"

"But of course," she replied, leading them to a small office while Snake remained behind. Once there she turned to Proto and said something in Kabori.

He paused for a moment, then responded.

She frowned and said something else.

"She suspects," whispered Circe. "Let's leave!"

"My partner is still recovering from a brutal incarceration by the Democracy," said Pretorius promptly. "Please address your questions to me."

"Your partner has never spoken a word of Kabori in his life," replied the Tretoni.

Pretorius promptly pulled a small laser pistol out of his pocket and put a hole between her narrow eyes. She fell to the floor without a sound.

"Did you have to kill her?" demanded Circe.

"You don't think she'd have let us walk out of here without sounding an alarm, do you?" He turned to Proto. "You flunked your first test. You'd better not flunk another. Now give me a hand stuffing her body in that closet."

Once the corpse was hidden Pretorius considered his options for a moment. "She spoke Terran to us, didn't she?"

"Yes," said Circe.

"All right," he said. "Proto, take her shape. You'll walk Circe and I back to the front of the bank, where we'll join Snake."

"What about—?" began Proto.

"I'm not done yet," continued Pretorius. "You'll explain that our Kabori companion is actually a Coalition auditor and will be in your office for the next few hours, and is not to be disturbed. Then Circe will offer to show you our ship and perhaps give you a keepsake for your kindness, since you can't return to your office anyway, and we'll all leave together. And with any luck, we'll be off the planet before anyone goes looking into the office."

"It's worth a try," agreed Proto.

"What about the security cameras?"

He shook his head. "No sense trying to destroy them now. Not only will the tellers start screaming for the authorities, but they already captured our images coming in, and we haven't got time to find out where they transmitted them to." He paused. "I wish we had time to pin the killing on a teller. The cops might just do it anyway, since nothing was stolen. Anyway, there's nothing we can do about it now."

They went out to the main area of the bank, Proto mimicked the Tretoni's voice and speech patterns, not perfectly but well enough not to arouse any suspicions on the part of the tellers, and a moment later they were on their way back to the ship.

"Shit!" growled Snake. "That's a million credits we'll never see again."

It took another hour for Pandora to return, but they were carefully monitoring all broadcasts and reports, and the body hadn't yet been discovered by the time they were out of the system.

They were still congratulating themselves on their narrow escape a day later when Pandora picked up a news item and flashed it on the holographic screen. It was the image of Snake, Pretorius, Circe, and Proto in his true form, all entering the bank, and a voice that the computer translated into Terran announced that these four beings were wanted for robbery and murder.

"Damn!" muttered Pretorius. "I forgot that Proto's image wouldn't fool the camera. Now they know what we're traveling with."

13

The entire team was assembled on the bridge, considering their options.

"We're probably going to have to steal another ship," said Pretorius. "They have to know which one took off after the killing."

"And they've got three phony IDs on file," added Pandora. She turned to Proto. "Did they get yours, too?"

In his human guise, Proto shook his head. "No, no one asked for one."

"Figures," said Pandora. "Visiting Kabori on a world that probably doesn't see a dozen Kabori a year. Okay, then, three more IDs."

"We'd probably better not set down on another world until we reach Petrus, either," added Circe.

Pretorius turned to her. "Why not?"

"They'll know we're traveling with *him*," she said, indicating Proto. "And you can't fool their security systems."

Pretorius shook his head. "What that means is that *he* can't leave the ship, not that we can't."

"They have holos of three of us," she persisted.

"Then we'll use makeup, or wigs, or whatever it takes to change our appearance, plus new IDs, of course."

"That'll work," said Snake.

"I can't help wondering, though," continued Circe. "If we blew it on a little backwater world like that one, what are our chances when we get to Petrus."

Pretorius resisted the urge to point out that they were never very good and instead said, "Not much worse than before. If we can find a way to sneak Proto past a security system, I'd say they're exactly the same as before."

"I admire your optimism," said Snake dubiously.

"No one said that it would be easy," responded Pretorius. "Just that it's possible." He turned to Proto. "I want you to keep learning the Kabori language, on the assumption that we *will* find a way to get you past a security system. Djibmet, keep working with him."

"I will," answered Djibmet. "And Michkag has learned everything I have to teach him. We'll keep going over it, but until we get there and see if anything's changed, he's as ready as I can make him."

"Okay. I just hope he doesn't get stage fright."

"I am Michkag," said the clone with a certain arrogance. "Nothing frightens me."

"Very good," said Pretorius.

"Thank you," said the clone. He paused for a moment. "I will not thank you or extend any small courtesies to any of you in the future. I must totally *become* Michkag if this is to work."

"I approve," said Pretorius.

"Well," said Pandora, "we have enough food and water to complete the mission and make it back home before we run out . . . but of course, that means nothing if we change ships again."

"We'll just have to find a way to transfer the food, water, and perhaps the fuel as well," said Pretorius. "Now, as for a ship, we're within the Coalition's territory, so that makes being approached by another pirate highly unlikely. That means we're going to have to land where there are other ships and appropriate one."

"I think they call that a spaceport," said Snake sardonically.

"Sometimes," agreed Pretorius. "But sometimes it's an agricultural world, where the farms are so vast that each landowner—I hesitate to call them farmers in the traditional sense—has a small landing field area for his own ships. And of course, there are probably half a dozen shipbuilding worlds between here and Petrus."

"They'll have more security than we can handle," said Ortega.

"Probably," agreed Pretorius. "I'm just pointing out that we have more options than spaceports. And of course, if we can get to a larger world, one with orbiting hangars, that makes our job even easier." He turned to Pandora. "See what you can do about new IDs, and then start checking out likely ports where we can dump this ship and borrow a new one."

"You know," said Circe thoughtfully, "maybe we don't have to borrow one at all."

"Oh?"

"We've got the equivalent of a few million credits. We could just *buy* one and have it registered to Felix's or Pandora's ID, or one of our new ones."

"That's not a bad idea," said Pretorius. "We ought to pick up something this size for well under a million. Then instead of hoping no one finds this ship, backtracks to Brastos III and anywhere else we may have been spotted, and figures out where we're headed, we transfer everything to the new, legit ship and crash this one into some uninhabited and uninhabitable world or moon." He paused, then smiled at Snake in amusement. "Don't look so downtrodden. You were never going to keep the money anyway."

"All right," said Pandora. "Just about every world that does any commerce at all will have ships for sale, either new or used. I'll start checking them out once I finish with the IDs, and hopefully I can find one that's properly small and off the beaten track."

"Okay," said Pretorius. "Any questions or observations?"

Nobody spoke up.

"Then go about your duties if you have any and grab some rest if you haven't. I'd suggest that you help Pandora, but no one can work those little machines but her."

The meeting broke up, and Pretorius walked over to the galley to grab a snack and a container of what passed for coffee. The galley responded instantly to his request, his artificial eggs tasted real and were cooked properly, and his *faux* coffee was indistinguishable from the equally *faux* coffee he'd become addicted to back on Deluros VIII.

Ortega soon joined him. "Hope you don't mind a little company," he said, "but the simple truth is that I can't stand to watch our Kabori eat, and I'm afraid to even think of what Proto eats."

Pretorius chuckled. "And they thought provincialism would end when we left the solar system."

"What is that you're drinking?" asked Ortega.

"Beats me. I pretend it's coffee, and then it doesn't taste quite so terrible."

"Yeah, I do pretty much the same with all the food on this ship."

Pretorius sat at a table, and Ortega joined him. They ate in silence for a few minutes, and finally Ortega spoke up.

"Just what are the odds of our pulling this off, do you think?"

"If everything goes smoothly, and as planned, there shouldn't be much of a problem," answered Pretorius.

"You ever had a mission where everything went smoothly and as planned?"

"Don't ask."

"I thought not," said Ortega. "Why not just have a goddamned all-out war and be done with it?"

"Why sacrifice tens of millions when they can sacrifice *us*?" replied Pretorius with a smile. "Besides, we've been *having* an all-out war, and after twenty-three years it's a stalemate."

"You're ruining my digestion," complained Ortega.

"Blame it on the food and don't worry about the mission," said Pretorius.

"I know: worrying won't help."

"You got it."

They finished eating, and since there are no days or nights aboard a small ship in space, Ortega went off to sleep, while Pretorius returned to the bridge to see how Pandora was doing on crafting new IDs.

"Got one," she said. "I'll have the other two in two or three hours. But let's not blow these. As we get close to the center of things, it's going to be harder to come up with IDs and passports that'll clear customs, let alone get us to wherever we're going on Petrus IV."

"While you're at it, get three or four for Proto, one as each of the more populous races in the Coalition."

"Whatever ID we give him, and however he appears, the security cameras and scanners will know his real appearance."

"Do it anyway," said Pretorius.

"You have something in mind?"

"Nothing spectacular. But if we can craft an alien dummy to fit over him until we're past security, then he can shed it and take on the appearance."

"You think a dummy can get past security on a world like Petrus IV?" she said dubiously.

"Not with what we know now," answered Pretorius. "But we have a month to learn. Besides, it'll only take you a few hours, and we've got the time to spare."

"Okay, but I'll need Proto to show me what he'll look like in each identity."

"Where is he?"

She checked another tiny computer. "Asleep."

"When he wakes up, have him impersonate the races, take your holographs or whatever you need, and work from that."

"We can't capture his image directly. I'll have to describe it in detail and have the computer come up with as close a set of approximations as possible." She stared at him for a long moment.

"Even if this works, can you trust him to carry out a believable impersonation?"

"He's been doing it all his life. Have you ever run into another member of his race?"

"No."

"What are the odds that he's the only one?"

She smiled. "Okay, so we've probably all been fooled by him or his brethren."

"It's clearly a survival trait," said Pretorius. "The fact that he's still alive means he's mastered it."

"Point taken," she replied.

"Okay, I won't bother you any further. Get to work on the IDs."

"Right," she said, turning back to the largest of her computers.

Pretorius decided to take a nap. When he was younger he was too restless to relax when on a mission, but years of experience had taught him that once the mission reached a certain point there would be no relaxing until it was over, no matter how many hours or days or even weeks that it took, and he knew he had to grab his sleep while he could.

He was awakened by a warning siren that rang throughout the ship. He'd kept his clothes on, so he had only to slip into his boots, and then he was out of his cabin and heading to the bridge.

"What's the problem?" he demanded.

"We've been hailed by a small military ship," answered Pandora, throwing an image of it onto a holoscreen.

"Kabori?"

"I think so."

"What do they want?"

She shrugged. "They haven't said. It might be just routine, or it might be that they've put two and two together and figured out this is the ship that took off from Brastos III an hour after the bank president was killed."

The others were now on the bridge and had heard what Pandora had said.

"What kind of armaments do they carry?" asked Ortega.

"Yeah," added Snake. "Do we fight or run?"

"Neither," said Pretorius.

"We just sit here and wait to be boarded?" demanded Snake.

"They've already had time to identify us," answered Pretorius. "If we shoot, the whole navy will know. And if we run from a navy ship, the whole navy will be after us."

"So what *do* we do?" asked Ortega.

"Hide."

"What the hell are you talking about?" demanded Snake.

"Snake, Pandora, Felix, Circe, go to your cabins." Pretorius turned to the Michkag clone. "You, too. You're the last thing we want anyone to see out here."

The clone and the four humans reluctantly followed his orders.

"Proto," he said, "become a Kabori. The same identity you showed me the last time I asked you."

Proto instantly projected the asked-for illusion.

Pretorius turned to Djibmet. "They won't bring a security system, or even a camera, onboard, but he still doesn't know the language enough to convince anyone he's Kabori, so you're going to have to do the talking."

"Me?" said Djibmet nervously.

Pretorius nodded. "If anyone asks, you found this ship abandoned on Questos II, that little world we passed last night, and you and your mute friend are bringing it back home to . . . to whatever planet you want to claim as home."

"I don't know . . ." said the Kabori.

"It'll work," said Pretorius. "They're looking for three Men and a lump, not two Kabori. Hell, it may even save us the need of stealing another ship. Let them come aboard, be friendly, be surprised but thrilled that you found such a nice ship sitting deserted on that little dirtball."

"I'll try," said Djibmet.

"You can do it." Pretorius turned to Proto. "Not a word, not a sound. You were born mute, or you lost your voice to a disease, whatever Djibmet says. You're not afraid of them. After all, they're your own race. If they need a loyalty salute or anything, just be guided by Djibmet and do what he does."

"Right," said Proto.

"That's your last word until they've come and gone."

Proto nodded his agreement.

"They'll be here in another ninety seconds," announced Pandora's voice over the speaker system.

"Okay," said Pretorius. "I'm outta here. Good luck."

He considered going to his cabin, then changed his mind and joined Pandora in hers, where her machines allowed him to see and hear what was happening on the bridge.

"Hail the ship!" said a voice in Kabori, which Pandora's computer translated into Terran. "Name and registration, please."

She quickly sent the registration data to the bridge computer, and Djibmet transferred it to the approaching ship.

"Prepare to be boarded, *Victor*."

Pandora handed Pretorius an earphone and plugged one into her own ear so they could continue monitoring the situation with no sound coming from her cabin.

A moment later three Kabori, all in military gear, burners in hands, boarded the ship. The leader stopped when he saw Djibmet and Proto.

"You are Kabori!" he said, surprised.

"Yes," said Djibmet.

"We were told this ship was the possession of three wanted Men and an alien."

"Perhaps it was," said Djibmet. "I cannot speak to that."

"Explain!"

"We found this ship half a Standard day ago on Questos II," said Djibmet. "It had been abandoned. I left my crew on my own ship and decided to take this back to my home planet to sell it."

The leader turned to Proto. "Is that true?"

"He is mute," said Djibmet quickly.

Proto offered a helpless and convincing shrug.

"What was your business on Questos II?"

"We had none," answered Djibmet. "We were passing through the Questos system on our way to Magtar IV, where I *do* have business. Evidently the previous owners were in such a hurry to leave the ship that they neglected to shut down all the systems. We detected a weak signal, and thinking it might well be a distress signal we landed as close to it as possible and found an empty ship. At first we thought the owners might be on the planet, but then we saw signs that they had transferred to a ship that had been kept nearby and departed. I felt that there was no sense letting a perfectly serviceable ship go to waste, so . . ." He left the sentence peter out.

"So you've no idea what direction the previous owners went, what their next port of call might be?"

"I do not even know who they were," answered Djibmet. "The ship had been stripped clean of all identification." He lowered his voice confidentially. "I do not believe they were Kabori, though. The chairs, the galley, even the lavatories were not created for us."

"They were not Kabori," confirmed the leader. "And you saw nothing of them?"

"No," said Djibmet. "I am not a thief. If they had been there, I would never have appropriated this ship."

"I commend your attitude."

Pretorius turned to Pandora, smiled, and gave her a thumbs-up gesture, mouthing the words *They bought it.*

The Kabori asked a few more questions, then returned to their own ship and headed away a moment later, as the rest of the team gathered on the bridge.

"You pulled it off!" said Pretorius enthusiastically as Proto resumed his human identity.

"I was frightened every second," admitted Djibmet.

"You didn't show it," noted Pandora.

"I have to sit down," said Djibmet, all but collapsing in a chair.

"What now?" asked Ortega.

"Now we figure out what we learned," said Pretorius.

"What we learned?" repeated Ortega, puzzled.

Pretorius nodded. "Pandora, once Djibmet's had a few minutes to relax, blow the whole scene up on the holoscreen and have him identify ranks on the uniforms and also tell you if the uniforms themselves have changed since he left the Coalition."

"Right," she responded.

"Circe, I assume you were monitoring it?"

"That's not quite the term I would use," she said.

"But they bought it?"

She nodded. "One was a little suspicious, but he was an underling and not inclined to argue with authority." Suddenly she smiled. "The overwhelming emotion came from Djibmet, poor baby."

"Okay," said Pretorius. "We've had our first serious confrontation. Let's hope all future ones will go just as well."

But somehow he knew that they wouldn't. He just didn't know how soon it would be.

14

"Shit!" said Pretorius.

"What is it?" asked Circe.

"There's a fleet of about a dozen ships headed this way, including one hell of a dreadnought."

"How far away?"

"A couple of days, but there's no way we can avoid them or even avoid being seen, not with the sophisticated gear the big one has."

"So what do we do?" asked Proto.

"We can't run," said Pretorius. "That'll just attract their attention." He paused. "So we have two options. We can keep going, as if we have every right to be here. Or we can touch down in this upcoming system. Seems to have seven planets, but I haven't checked any of them for oxygen yet."

"Why not go?" suggested Pandora. "After all, we've been inspected by the military. If they got the report, we're a harmless ship with a crew of two, both Kabori."

"I know," said Pretorius. "But if anyone checks for records or even traces of this ship on Questos II, we're in deep shit. So we're in one of three situations: they believed us and didn't check our story out, they believed us and checked it out anyway, or they didn't believe us. Given the odds, I'd say we're better off landing until the fleet passes by."

Snake shrugged. "You're the boss."

"Okay, we'll make for the nearest star. Pandora, start monitoring any messages they're sending. Let's find out what they're doing here and whether they plan to stay in this quadrant, or if they're just passing through."

Within an hour Pandora was able to report that the fleet was on a normal patrol route and would clear of the quadrant within two days.

"So they're not hunting for Men?" said Pretorius.

"I'm sure they'd love to find some, but no, they're not," she answered.

"All right. The fifth planet has an oxygen atmosphere, maybe a bit thin but breathable for a couple of days. And on the plus side, it's a smallish world, with about seventy percent Standard gravity, so at least we're not going to work up a sweat getting around. We should reach it in about six hours."

"Any sentient life?" asked Circe.

"Nothing native to the planet," answered Pretorius. "There's some animal life, and there seems to be a trading post, though what the hell they have to trade is beyond me."

"Got a name?" asked Snake.

"Just Mitox V," answered Pretorius. Suddenly he smiled. "We can dub it Sally Kowalski if you like."

"Make it Snake Kowalski and you got yourself a deal," she replied, returning his smile.

"Djibmet, how will you fare with the planetary readout I just gave?"

"I'll be fine with the gravity," answered the Kabori. "I think I may want weights in my boots, just to be on the safe side. Kabori legs are much more heavily muscled than yours."

"Okay, you have a few hours to make whatever adjustments you need."

"Good news," announced Pandora, looking up from the tiny computer in her hand.

"Oh?"

She nodded. "The dreadnought broadcasted its route to some other ship or fleet that's out of our range, but I was able to monitor it, and they don't seem to be stopping off at Questos II, so we can keep this ship, since it's on record that they've already inspected and cleared it."

"Good," said Pretorius. "The closer we get to the Orion constellation, the harder it will be to buy or even steal another ship."

"How are we going to land on Petrus IV?" asked Ortega. "I can't imagine we can just ask for coordinates and set the ship down in a military hangar, then hope no one's watching as we leave it and hunt for the fortress."

"I'm working on it," said Pretorius.

"Bullshit," said Snake.

"I beg your pardon?"

"You know exactly how you plan to get in," she said. "You improvise when you have to, but you never set out without a plan and a number of options."

"Like I said, I'm working on it."

"And we're not going to approach the damned planet in this ship, are we?" she continued.

"No, of course not."

She turned to Ortega with a triumphant smile. "See?"

They killed time for the next few hours.

"You know what I hate second-most about these damned covert missions?" said Ortega at one point. "It's all the goddamned waiting."

"What do you hate most?" asked Proto curiously.

"The part where we're not waiting anymore," answered Ortega.

"He hates everything," said Snake. "With an attitude like that, he should be in the regular army."

"Where do you think I got all these artificial limbs and eyes and such?" growled Ortega.

Pretorius walked over to stand behind Pandora's shoulder as she read one computer and listened to another. "How's it going?"

"Near as I can tell, no one's landed there in a week or more" was her answer.

"What the hell do they sell, or trade, or black market?"

"You want a shot in the dark?" she replied.

"Why not?"

"There seems to be a hell of a vicious fur-bearing animal living in the eastern hemisphere. Since there's no sentient native population and no colony, the only conclusion I can draw is that there are a few Kabori or other sentients roaming the hemisphere hunting for pelts. One small trading post would handle it, and it explains why there are only three ships there. No one wants to hike a thousand miles to find his prey, so they probably take their ships to where the critters are and then bring 'em back to the trading post."

"I believe Pandora has hit upon it," offered Djibmet. "There is a very rare, very valuable fur that comes from this general area of the Coalition. I confess that I don't know or recall what the animal is called."

"What does it look like?" asked Pandora.

"The animal?" said Djibmet. "I have no idea. But the pelt is an exquisite red-gold."

"That's probably it," said Pretorius. "At least it's as good an explanation as we're going to get until we touch down." He checked the navigation computer. "Which should be in about an hour. Djibmet, you'll go in alone. No sense letting them see that there are five Men and a Michkag on the ship. Tell them you were feeling sick, or lonely, whatever you think they'll buy, and that you don't want to inconvenience them and you'll take off in another couple of days." He turned to Proto. "Remember the bank president?"

"Yes."

"Take her form."

Instantly Proto was the female that Pretorius had killed.

"Pretty good. Do you speak her language?"

"No."

"Of course not," said Pretorius with a grimace. "Okay, these guys are pretty isolated, and Brastos III is quite a few light-years from here. Speak any language you know, and let them assume it goes with the female you're imitating."

"Why send both of us?" asked Djibmet.

"Because if for any reason they distrust you, I want one of you to go into hysterics or faint or something to take all their attention while the other presses the alarm button."

"Alarm button?" repeated Djibmet, confused.

"You'll each have a communicator. Pandora will rig it so that if you touch it in a certain spot or say a certain word, it alerts us on the ship that you're in trouble and need help."

They touched down in early evening, in the middle of a storm, and waited an hour until the worst of it had passed before sending Djibmet and Proto to walk the half mile to the trading post, a large but unimaginative building made of some alloy that could withstand all of the planet's weather conditions, some of which could be incredibly harsh.

"So how do you think they'll do?" asked Ortega after they'd shut the airlock.

"People out here in the boonies don't seem to want to make Kabori mad," answered Pretorius. "I can only assume they have good reasons not to."

"Their ships sure aren't much," noted Snake, looking at a viewscreen.

"These are the shopkeepers. The rich, or soon-to-be-rich, or hopefully rich hunters will have the best ships, and they'll all be parked out in the wilderness where the golden animals are," answered Pretorius.

"I was just hoping we'd find a nice one to steal."

"Forget it," said Pretorius. "This one's already passed inspection. Why get one that has to do it all over again. The next crew might not believe Djibmet and might want to inspect the whole thing. Besides, why do you care? You once told me that you don't like ships."

"I don't," she responded. "But I like stealing."

"Why am I not surprised?" he said.

"I don't know why I couldn't have gone with Djibmet," said Michkag.

"You're our treasure," answered Pretorius, "the reason for the whole mission. We can't risk you."

"But even if they identified me, we're well into the Coalition," continued Michkag. "Surely they wouldn't even consider harming me. The consequences would be cataclysmic."

"They thought no one would ever kill Caesar or Abraham Lincoln," responded Pretorius. "They tried to kill Adolf Hitler and Conrad Bland."

"I don't know any of those names," said the Kabori.

"No reason why you should. They were Men, and you're only two years old. But they've killed Kabori leaders in the past. Sometimes people don't care about the consequences, and you're too valuable to risk."

"I feel so useless on this mission!" complained Michkag.

"Wait until we reach Petrus IV and you convince a few hundred million countrymen that you're the original Michkag," said Pretorius with a smile. "I guarantee you'll feel useful in one hell of a hurry."

The Kabori remained silent, and Pretorius went to the galley for a snack. He was joined by Snake and Circe, and then Ortega. Finally they returned to the bridge and then, a couple of hours later, to their quarters.

Pretorius lay down on his bunk, an amused smile on his face as he marveled at how quickly they adjusted to day and night once again. He was awakened by an alarm that woke the whole ship. He went quickly to the bridge, where he found Snake and Pandora already there. Circe, Ortega, and Michkag joined them a moment later.

"Something went wrong," said Pandora. "That was the distress signal."

"Anything else?" asked Pretorius. "Do we know what happened, or how many people we'll be facing?"

She shook her head.

"Okay," he said, strapping on his weaponry, "Felix, Snake, you're coming with me."

"What about me?" demanded Pandora.

"And me?" added Circe.

"You have skills that are vital to this mission," he answered.

"But they don't lie in this area. If we're not back, or at least in contact, in half an hour, take off. I'll leave it to you to decide whether to abort the mission and get back to the Democracy, or to try to put our Michkag in place without Djibmet to guide and help him." He turned to Snake and Ortega. "Let's go!"

15

"You see anything out of the ordinary?" asked Ortega as they walked the half mile to the trading post.

"No," answered Pretorius.

"No ships have landed," noted Snake.

"You're the smallest of us," said Pretorius to her. "When we get close, circle around the building and see if there are any land vehicles.

"Land vehicles?" repeated Ortega.

"Yeah. If they're here for the whole hunting season, whenever and however long it is, they may keep their ship parked on their concession—or they may keep it hidden because they don't have a concession. For all we know, it's one hunter, he's armed, and he's got a grudge against the Kabori."

Snake shot out ahead of them at a slow trot and circled the building, then rejoined them when they were still eighty yards away.

"Nothing," she said. "Looks like some kind of super-hardened wood, and there are no windows anywhere on the building."

"Shit!" said Pretorius. "That means they've got to have some system to let them know when traders or buyers are approaching." He paused. "I should have brought Pandora after all. She might have been able to spot and negate the system."

"It's not that far," said Ortega. "We can go back and get her."

"I don't know how imminent the threat to Djibmet and Proto is." He stared at the building. "My first thought is that we can break into the building blind. Either a burner or a pulse gun should be able to get rid of the door almost instantly. My second is that even if she negates the system, that's exactly what we'll be doing anyway." He was silent for another moment. "Let's go. Snake, where's the door?"

"Around to the right," she answered "We're on the side of the building."

"It's tall enough to have a second floor. Any windows up there?"

"Not that I could see."

"Any handholds?"

She stared at him curiously. "You want me to climb the thing?"

"Can you?"

"Yes."

"Then yeah, I want you to. No sense all three of us walking in together, in case someone's got a weapon trained on the door. There's got to be a window, a vent, *something* up there." He gave her a reassuring smile. "You're the Snake. You can fit through anything. Start the instant we open the door. Their attention should be totally on us."

She nodded. "Right."

"And if we're in trouble, you know what to do."

He began walking forward again. As he and Ortega rounded the building and headed for the entrance, Snake went off into the darkness and was almost instantly out of sight.

"Shoot first?" asked Ortega.

"Secure Djibmet and Proto first, unless someone's shooting at you," answered Pretorius.

They walked up to the front door.

"Knock or enter?" asked Ortega.

Instead of answering, Pretorius grabbed the handle and pushed the door open—and found himself facing six armed aliens—short, golden, burly; armed with lasers, sonic weapons, and short-barreled rifles of a type Pretorius had never seen before. Djibmet and Proto were sitting on chairs that were too large for them, and a huge Torqual, clearly the proprietor, lay dead on the floor. The walls were covered with holos of hunters standing next to their newly slain trophies.

"Men!" exclaimed one of the aliens in Kabori. "There must be a reward for them."

"Don't worry about rewards," said another. "Just kill them."

"You kill us," said Pretorius in heavily accented Kabori, "and you'll never find the pelts we've brought to sell."

"How many?" asked the closest alien.

"That's none of your business," said Pretorius. "Unless you'd like to *do* some business. How many pelts will it cost to buy our lives?"

"All of them."

Pretorius smiled. "What if I told you we had only two?"

"Then I would say it's not worth the trouble and kill you right now."

"We have more than two."

"Of course you do," answered the closest alien. "Nobody comes away from the hunt with just two pelts. There are too many of these creatures. If they don't kill you, then you kill them—*lots* of them."

Pretorius nodded. "We killed lots of them." He indicated Djibmet and Proto. "Who are your friends?"

"Hostages or corpses, depending on our needs" was the answer.

"Don't kill 'em yet," said Pretorius.

"What are they to you?"

"Nothing," he replied. "I never saw them before. But you're going to need help carrying all the pelts from our ship."

"They stay here."

"Fine," said Pretorius. "We'll get 'em ourselves." He turned toward the door. "Come on, Felix."

"*Stop!*" commanded the alien.

"What's the problem?"

"If the two of you walk out that door, you'll never come back. How stupid do we look?"

"Fine. Get 'em yourselves," said Pretorius with a smile.

"What's so funny?"

"The ship's locked. It won't open until it reads either my DNA or my partner's here."

"He's mostly prosthetic," noted another alien. "Has he still *got* any DNA?"

"If he didn't, he'd be dead," said Pretorius.

"He soon will be anyway. What are two Men doing here?"

"I don't suppose you'd believe that we got lost?"

"Lie again and I'll kill you right now."

"All right," replied Pretorius. "We're smugglers."

"Just the two of you?" demanded an alien.

"Those are our partners," said Pretorius, indicating Djibmet and Proto.

There was a brief pause.

"Well," said one of the aliens, looking at his companions, "that explains why they're in Coalition territory."

"All right," said the alien that seemed to be the leader. "We're in the same business. It's just your misfortune that we got here first." He gestured to three of his associates. "You will accompany one of them to their ship and bring back the pelts."

"You don't think they're going to let us live, do you?" said Djibmet.

"We have to hope they'll honor their word," answered Pretorius. "If we don't agree to turn over the pelts, they'll kill us right now. If we do, there's a chance that they'll keep their end of the bargain."

"But . . ." began Djibmet.

You must know I'm lying, thought Pretorius, staring intently at him. *Just shut up and let us get on with this. Get him mad and he'll shoot you right now. He doesn't need you for the pelts.*

Somehow Djibmet understood his glare and fell silent.

"Okay, Felix," said Pretorius as three aliens walked to the door. "You know what to do."

Ortega nodded and walked out into the night with them, shutting the door behind him.

"You know," said Pretorius to the remaining three, "as long as we're in the same business, maybe we should join forces."

"I think not," said the leader. "Once we appropriate your goods, and my associates will go through your ship and appropriate everything of value, not just the pelts, you have nothing to offer."

"You're making a mistake," said Pretorius. "We could be very helpful to you."

"You're already being helpful. We'll not only appropriate your goods, but there's a standing reward for Men, so we'll claim two bounties as well. Now, since I'm going to know the answer in a few minutes anyway, how many pelts do you have?"

"None," said Pretorius, the hint of a smile playing across his face.

"Then I will kill you now," said the alien, aiming his weapon between Pretorius's eyes.

"I don't think so," said Pretorius—and as the words left his mouth there was a faint humming, and the alien, a puzzled expression on his face, pitched forward onto the floor, as Snake, who had appeared behind them, turned her burner on a second one. As the third turned to face her, Pretorius drew his screecher and knocked him flying against a wall with a barrage of solid sound.

Snake walked over and turned her burner on the third alien, putting a very neat hole in its forehead.

"I think he was already dead," said Proto, getting to his feet.

"It's the dead ones who get up and kill you," she replied.

"What kept you?" asked Pretorius.

"No windows. I had to slide in through a vent on the roof." She paused. "Will Felix need any help?"

Pretorius shook his head. "He hasn't got the quickest brain around, but from the neck down—maybe even the eyes down—he's all but invulnerable, and he's got more weaponry built into that body than you or I can carry between us." He paused thoughtfully. "Still, it never hurts to play it safe." He walked over to the nearest dead alien, grabbed it by its feet, and pulled it behind a counter. "Proto, impersonate him, just in case the wrong guys walk through the door." Proto immediately appeared as the alien. "And if Felix walks in, change into something else before he has a chance to shoot you."

Ortega was back in less than three minutes, and Proto changed his image back to the middle-aged man they were all used to before Ortega could fire his weapon. Pretorius gave an all-clear signal to Pandora, and she, Circe, and Michkag joined them a few minutes later.

"The Torqual had about a hundred pelts on hand," announced Pretorius after they'd performed a thorough search of the place. "If we can figure out how to find the black market in this sector, we can raise enough money to see us through any eventuality. Now, one of them mentioned that there's a bounty on Men, so we're going to have to be as circumspect as Michkag here about showing ourselves. Pandora, Proto's never going to learn Kabori fast enough to pass for one of them, so find out what race he *can* impersonate so we can unload the pelts."

"Right," she replied.

"Felix, dig a hole and dump all seven corpses into it."

"Seven?" said Ortega, frowning.

"The Torqual, too."

"Right." He smiled. "Never thought I'd wind up as a gravedigger."

"What *did* you think you'd be?" asked Circe seriously. "When you were just starting out, I mean."

He shrugged. "I come from a military family. It never occurred to me to be anything else." He frowned. "I lost my right arm on my second tour, an eye and a leg on my third. My other arm on one of Nathan's secret operations. Then one day I looked at myself in a mirror, didn't see much of a man left, and when my tour was up I decided not to re-enlist. I didn't know what else to do—my skills are mostly illegal in civilian life—so I joined a carnival. Didn't like it much, which is why Nathan didn't have much trouble talking me into coming along."

"I *never* wanted to be in the military," said Pandora.

"Oh?" said Circe. "What did you want to be?"

Pandora smiled sadly. "Beautiful. But by the time I got to my teens I knew that was a forlorn wish, so I concentrated on a career instead of on men. Turns out I was good with computers."

"An understatement," said Pretorius.

"And as I got better, I found that my very special computer skills were only of use to the military and the criminal element. So I joined the military. They not only paid and housed me, but they paid for my continuing education." Suddenly she smiled. "Of course, no one told me that I was going to wind up storming Michkag's fortress in Orion."

"Would you have joined if you'd known?" asked Ortega curiously.

"Yes, I'd have joined," replied Pandora. "I've got a unique skill. I might as well put it to use." She turned to Circe. "How about you? From what little I know—and I haven't used my machines to peek—you were very successful out in the business world. And you are stunningly beautiful. So what made you walk away from it all to wind up smuggling exotic animals' pelts and watching a mostly prosthetic man drag corpses out to bury on a nondescript little world in the Coalition?"

Circe chuckled. "If you'd put it in those terms, I might never have left." Suddenly the smile vanished. "I thank you for your kind remarks, but if I am beautiful, it is—as so many men have mentioned when they thought they were flattering me—an otherworldly beauty. My family underwent some mutations on the world they colonized a millennium ago, and while one of them is my appearance, the other is my ability as an empath. It's not quite the virtue you think, always knowing who is lying to you and why. But it's my ability, and I've used it to get ahead in the business world. The problem is that I felt so *useless* there. Who cares if this applicant for an executive position is lying or not? So when Nathan offered me the chance to come along, I jumped at it. Now I can finally do something that makes a difference. It's as simple as that."

"There's nothing simple about making a difference," said Pretorius. "And before this is over, every one of you will have a few chances to do so." He jerked a thumb at Snake, who sat by herself in a corner, her back propped up against a wall. "Even her," he added.

"Why did *you* agree to come along?" Circe asked her.

Pretorius grinned. "The alternative was to spend another couple of years in jail."

"Would you have come if you hadn't been serving time?" persisted Circe.

Snake shrugged. "I don't know. Probably."

Circe smiled. "I read that as 'Certainly.'"

"All right—certainly."

"Even though you knew you'd be putting your life at risk, perhaps more than the rest of us?"

"It's not much of a life," answered Snake. "So I can fold myself into a suitcase. Big fucking deal. I've been a thief since I was eleven, and I've spent as much time in jails as out of them. Our friend Nathan has a habit of surviving—I've survived two other missions with him—so he seemed like a good man to partner with."

Pandora turned to Pretorius. "How about you, Nate? You got a story or an opinion to share?"

"I've undergone a couple of decades of instruction on how not to share those details with anyone," he said with a smile. "I'd hate to see all that training go to waste." He got to his feet. "Okay," he announced. "It seems that damned near every time we touch down we take too many risks of exposure."

"And of death," added Snake.

"And of death," he agreed. "So I think our next step is to get to Petrus, even if we're a week or two early, rather than landing on any more worlds."

"Not in this ship, I assume," said Pandora.

"No, not in this ship—at least, not all the way."

"So some Samaritan is just going to transport us the last part of the journey?"

"In essence."

"How?" demanded Snake.

"I'm working on it," he replied.

16

They remained at the trading post for two days. On the first day they went out searching for the aliens' ship but couldn't find any trace of it.

"That means they have at least one other colleague, either well away from here or perhaps even in orbit," said Pretorius. "There are probably warrants out for them and the ship, and they didn't want to land it where it could be identified."

"So what do we do if it returns?" asked Ortega.

"If they actually land, we'll kill him or it or them and take whatever we need from the ship."

"*If* they land?" repeated Ortega. "Why wouldn't they?"

"They probably have an all-clear signal, and if they don't get it they won't approach," answered Pretorius. "We could just as easily be police or military." He paused. "Okay, why don't you and Proto start moving the pelts to our own ship? Just the ones that have been properly cured. I saw a couple that were starting to rot. We'll sell them along the way, and that should see us through the next few weeks."

Ortega nodded and went off to find Proto, who was exploring the various storage rooms with other members of the team, and as he did so, Pandora approached Pretorius.

"We have to talk," she said.

"Privately?"

"That's up to you. We're all a team, and I don't much care who's listening."

"Follow me," he said, leading her to a private office and closing the door behind them. "Okay, what's this about?"

"You made a major blunder, Nathan, and I don't want you to make it again."

"Oh?"

She nodded her head. "Yes. You told me to stay behind when you came over here last night."

"It was a proper decision," he said firmly.

"It was not."

"I'm sorry if it hurt your feelings, but I'm not concerned with feelings, only with the success of the mission."

"It has nothing to do with my feelings," she replied. "You fucked up."

"Look," he said, "you are the best computer and cypher expert I've ever met, surely the best in the Democracy, maybe the best there's ever been. But that doesn't mean you can handle yourself in a fight. I've never even seen you with a weapon, and if you come at me right now I'll have you pinned flat on the floor in two seconds."

"Pull your weapon, Nathan," said Pandora.

"Burner, screecher, or the little pulse gun I've got tucked in the back of my belt?"

"Makes no difference."

He withdrew his burner.

"Point it at me."

He did as she said.

"Now fire it."

He frowned. "I don't know what this is about, but I'm no good at playing games."

"All right," she said, holding out her hand. "May I see it for a moment?"

He passed it over to her.

She switched off the safety and pointed it at him. "This is why you blundered," she said, pressing the firing mechanism.

Nothing happened.

"What the hell's going on here?" he said, frowning.

"I disabled all your weapons while you were speaking to Felix," she said. "And I could have done it to the aliens' weapons last night if you'd had the foresight to invite me along."

"You can do that without knowing the nature of their weapons?"

"I can negate just about any weapon except a projectile one—an old-fashioned bullet gun—within fifty meters."

"Son of a bitch!" he said. "You never told me that!"

"You never asked."

"One question: would it have disabled our weapons too?"

She nodded her head. "The trick is for there to be more of you than of them . . . but in a little building like this, with no ship in the area, there didn't figure to be many of them. And once all the weapons were disabled, all you had to do was send in Felix with that remarkable artificial body of his."

"You were right," he admitted. "I won't leave you behind again."

"Okay," she said. "I just wanted you to know that you weren't making use of all your assets."

"No hard feelings?" he asked.

She reached forward and shook his hand. "None."

"All right," he said. "I've got another task for you."

"What is it?"

"Proto is never going to learn Kabori in time to pass for one by the time we get to Petrus. Find out what races don't draw any attention in the Orion constellation, see what they speak, and see what languages he knows. He's got a remarkable ability, but it's going to be hard enough to hide him from security systems without having him give himself away the moment he opens his mouth."

She nodded her head. "I'll start researching it here, and when I've narrowed it down to the likeliest races, I'll have the ship's computer produce life-sized holograms so he can study their physiques and modes of dress. Then it'll just be a matter of which language, if any, he's comfortable with."

Pretorius grimaced. "Don't say 'if any,'" he said wryly. "He's supposed to be an asset, not a liability." He paused. "It's amazing that his race didn't rule the whole damned galaxy before security systems became this sophisticated."

"I asked him about that a few days ago," said Pandora.

"And?"

She smiled. "They only developed light speeds about two centuries ago."

"Yeah, that'd explain it," said Pretorius, returning her smile. "Damned good for the rest of us."

They went to the primitive kitchen, where they were joined by the other team members, ate a minimal meal—none of them cared for Torqual food, and that was all there was—and then continued their inventory.

"Not much worth appropriating except the pelts," announced Circe after another hour. "The poor Torqual couldn't have led much of life, living all alone here in these primitive surroundings."

"So what's our next move?" asked Snake.

"I think the closer we get to Petrus, the more we're going to be stopped, probably boarded, certainly questioned," said Pretorius. "If that happens enough—and for all I know, once is enough—we're incarcerated at best and killed at worst. So I think we'll stop doing it in small jumps and go straight to the Petrus system."

"In our ship?" said Ortega. "It'll never work."

Pretorius shook his head. "Definitely not in our ship. We need to transfer one last time."

"Just what kind of ship do you plan to approach Petrus in?" asked Snake.

"Something large," answered Pretorius.

She frowned. "Like a battleship?"

He chuckled. "They'd blow it to pieces."

"Then I don't understand."

"Outside of one of Michkag's military ships, what ship is most likely to approach and land on Petrus without raising any eyebrows—not that the Kabori have any—and without incredibly detailed security inspections?"

"Oh, shit!" said Snake. "We're going to stow away on a supply ship!"

"Not just any ship," said Pretorius. "It's got to be one that definitely supplies the fortress."

"How many ships do that?"

"I don't know," he answered, "but our information back at headquarters is that the fortress has a standing army of close to ten thousand, and since most of them aren't native to Petrus IV, they import most of their food, as well as their weaponry and ammo."

"Okay," said Snake. "Which ships go there?"

"We don't know yet," said Pretorius. He turned to Pandora. "But someone is going to find out for us, isn't she?"

"I can probably track the larger ones," she replied.

"We need to know their routes as well," continued Pretorius. "We've got to choose the best place to create a diversion while we're sneaking aboard, and we don't want to be stuck on it for more than a week."

"I'll get on it as soon as we're back on the ship," said Pandora.

"You might as well start now," said Pretorius. "There's nothing for you to do here." Suddenly he smiled. "Besides, the food'll be better on the ship." He turned to Djibmet. "I know we've packed a couple of uniforms for you and Michkag, but I want you to check daily newscasts and make sure that it hasn't changed, that he hasn't given himself four or five more medals, that he hasn't put on or lost a lot of weight."

"I will do so," agreed Djibmet.

"Michkag, you monitor those broadcasts as well," continued Pretorius. "I know you've been schooled in all his gestures and speech patterns, but make sure he hasn't picked up any new ones or that he hasn't fallen in love with some new expression since Djibmet left the Coalition."

Michkag nodded his acquiescence. "It will be a pleasure to finally have something to do."

"Something important," confirmed Djibmet. "This, after all, is what you were created for."

"Circe," said Pretorius, "I know you're feeling like a fifth wheel, but we're getting near the point where your talents are going to be essential. If any Kabori becomes even the least bit suspicious of our Michkag, we've got to know that before he can act on his suspicions."

"I know," replied Circe.

"Okay," said Pretorius. "Anyone who wants to return to the ship is free to do so. But we've been confined to ships for so long, we can take an extra day here to just stretch and relax. It's up to each of you."

Snake, who had no problem with close quarters, elected to go back to the ship and indulge in some human food. The rest of them remained, not in the trading post but in the immediate vicinity of it, walking, exercising, and just relishing having the room to move freely.

It was during twilight of their second day on the planet that Pretorius, who had moved a chair out past the front door, heard an ear-shattering bellow that startled him into immobility for a few seconds. When he finally stood up, he found himself confronting one of the gold-pelted creatures, six-legged, perhaps eight feet at the shoulder, sporting a quartet of long, razor-sharp horns.

He immediately pulled out his screecher, set it on half-power, and fired point-blank. The creature jumped as if electrified, emitted one last, shaky bellow, and raced off.

"What happened?" asked Circe, rounding the corner of the building just in time to see the beast running away.

"One of the creatures they come here to hunt," replied Pretorius, returning his screecher to full power and holstering it.

"Why didn't you kill the damned thing?" asked Ortega, joining them.

"Why bother?" responded Pretorius. "We have enough pelts. Besides, who the hell wants to skin one of those? I gave him a hell of a blast of sound. He won't be back." He looked at the setting sun. "I think we'd all better get back to the ship. *He* won't be back, but I can't speak for his brothers and sisters, and I don't think any of us want to run into them in the dark. Felix, hunt up Proto and the Kabori and tell them."

Ortega nodded and headed off to find them.

"You know," said Circe, "it occurs to me that we'd better sell the pelts quickly and spend the money quickly as well. I don't imagine Men are free to walk around Petrus, let alone spend money there."

"We're not going to need it before we get there," said Pretorius.

"Then why even take the pelts we have with us?" she persisted.

"Because we may need the money to get back to the Democracy once we're done here."

"I'm glad *someone* thinks we're going to be going home at the end of this."

17

The ship was twelve hours out of the Mitox system when Pretorius woke up from a nap, stopped by the galley for a few minutes, and then approached Pandora at her workstation.

"How's it coming?" he asked.

"I've found seven supply ships that stop at the fortress every five to ten days," she replied.

"Big ones?"

She nodded. "Quite large. Definitely big enough for our needs."

"How many are between us and Petrus right now, and how many are on the far side?"

"Three on this side, two on the far side."

Pretorius frowned. "That's only five."

"Two are docked at the fortress right now."

"*At* the fortress? Not in some orbital hangar?"

"*At* the fortress," said Pandora. "I assume their loads are so big that it would take a dozen shuttles to carry the stuff down, so the fortress seems to have four towers that serve as docks, maybe half a mile high, to accommodate them. One may be for military ships—and of course they'll have an orbiting hangar for the really big troop transports—but at least three of the towers are for supply ships."

"Better still," said Pretorius. "That means we don't have to find a covert way onto the planet and into the fortress. I didn't like the thought of transferring to a shuttle. This solves the problem."

"You still have the problem of how all eight of us are getting onto a supply ship."

"Find out where the three cargo ships that are between us and Petrus are touching down on their regular routes, and we'll work it out."

"Give me another eight or nine hours."

"Take twenty."

She looked at him curiously. "Twenty?"

"Yeah," he said "And get me blueprints of the ships."

"That might be difficult."

"They're not combat ships or military of any kind. Some ship-builder made them and had to file the plans somewhere." He smiled at her. "Hell, find me one with an all-robot crew that you can control, and take twenty-one hours."

"You're all heart, Nate," she said, and turned back to her computer.

"Oh . . . and hunt up a couple of worlds along the way where we can unload the pelts."

"Actually there's one coming up in about an hour," she replied. "A single planet circling Pordeli, a class-G star. Seems to be a trading outpost. Hard to believe they haven't seen these furs before."

"Radio ahead, make sure someone on the planet buys pelts, and if they do, make an appointment and set us down there."

She did so, got a positive reply, and they landed a little more than an hour later. Djibmet got off the ship, met the proprietor of the shop that dealt in such goods, got a pair of robots to help, and while they were making the trips carrying the pelts Pandora wiped all knowledge of the ship's human crew from their memories.

They found another world five light-years away that bought the rest of the pelts. Djibmet offered to turn all the money over to Pretorius, but the latter shook his head.

"I can't show myself or spend your currency anywhere within the Coalition," he explained, "and by the time we get to where I *can* spend it, this currency's no good. So you hang onto it. You're the only one who can spend it where it'll be accepted."

Pretorius then declared that all the preliminaries were over and it was time for the main event: reaching and entering the fortress.

"So what do we *do* once we're inside it?" asked Snake, as she and Ortega joined Pretorius at Pandora's station on the bridge.

"Wait for Michkag to arrive," said Pretorius.

"Just like that?" she said sardonically.

"Come on, Snake. You've been on enough missions to know."

"Tell me—*us*—anyway," she replied. "Maybe someone can make a suggestion."

Pretorius shrugged. "Okay. We sneak in, we find a secure room, we find a way to monitor what's going on, we capture their Michkag and replace him with our Michkag, we escape with him if we can or kill him if we can't, and then we make a beeline for home."

"Sounds simple when you put it that way," said Ortega.

"You think so?" said Snake derisively. "How are we going to sneak into the fortress past armed guards that are there to make sure nothing gets unloaded except the goods they ordered? If we're in a room that's so secure their security system can't penetrate it, how is Toni going to monitor them without telltale emanations from her machines?"

"Toni?" said Ortega, puzzled.

"That's Toni," said Snake, pointing. "Nathan calls her Pandora, but her name is Toni."

"I didn't know."

"That's the least of things you don't know," continued Snake.

"How are we going to kidnap the best-protected Kabori in the whole damned Coalition—and if we pull *that* off, how do we escape the planet with him in tow?"

"You sound like you want to quit," said Circe.

"No," said Snake. "But if we pull it off, I sure as hell want a raise and a bonus."

That broke the tension and brought general laughter.

"I assume you *are* doping out all these problems?" said Circe.

"That's what they pay me for," answered Pretorius.

Snake chuckled. "They only pay if you survive."

"Our friend Nathan has survived a hell of a lot," noted Circe. Ortega turned to Pretorius. "What was it like on Benedaris IV?" he asked.

"Where's that?" said Snake.

"Our stalwart leader's last assignment," said Pandora without looking up from her keyboard. "The record is absolutely fascinating."

"Oh?" said Ortega. "What was his mission?"

"I have no idea," answered Pandora. "It's still classified."

"Then what's so fascinating about it?"

Pandora smiled. "He was given a posthumous Medal of Valor—and then they brought him back to life."

"You were really dead?" asked Ortega.

"They say I was, for maybe a couple of minutes," answered Pretorius. "I don't remember a damned thing."

"Just as well," said Snake. "Who wants to spend the rest of their life remembering hell and stocking up on burn lotion?"

"Thanks for that vote of confidence," said Pretorius dryly.

"We're all going there," said Snake. "Well, all of us except maybe Proto." She turned to him. "Hey, Proto—you ever kill anyone?"

"No" was the answer.

"Cheer up," said Ortega. "You'll have plenty of opportunity on Petrus IV."

"Please do not joke about this," said Djibmet. "After all, these are my people."

"We're only talking about killing the bad ones," said Snake.

"They are not bad, only misled," answered Djibmet. "That is why *our* Michkag will make a difference." He paused and looked at each of them in turn. "I have read and viewed some of your history. You have had many tyrants—Caligula, Adolf Hitler, Conrad Bland. Once they were gone, was it necessary to perform genocide on their followers, or were they incorporated back into a civilized society?"

"Point taken," said Pretorius. "And we'll take your concerns into consideration from this point forward." He looked at each of his crew. "There will be no more joking or making light of the more repugnant things we may have to do to accomplish this mission. Is that understood?"

There was a unanimous nodding of heads, even from Proto, who in actuality had no head of his own to nod but understood and mimicked the gesture.

They fell silent then. Snake and Circe went off to the galley to eat, Proto joined Djibmet and Michkag in their connected cabins for more lessons in the language, Ortega went off to take a nap, and Pretorius, as he did in almost every spare moment, concentrated on all the problems that Snake had outlined.

Finally, after a few hours of relative silence, Pandora got up, stretched, and announced that she had pinpointed the ship they wanted.

"You're sure?" asked Pretorius.

"It fits your criteria, and it'll be the easiest to approach," she answered.

"Okay, tell me about it."

"I can't pronounce its name—doubtless Michkag or Djibmet can—but it translates as *the Wayfarer*. It's the second-largest of the three ships between here and Petrus, but it has three advantages over the others."

"What are they?" asked Pretorius.

"First, it's due to land on Nortiqua II six days from now, and we're only four days away. Second, it's to unload all its cargo at the fortress nine days after that, and from what I can tell, that puts us on Petrus two days ahead of Michkag, maybe three."

"I see the trace of a smile," he said. "What are you holding back?"

"The third advantage."

"I'm all ears."

She grinned. "It's a totally automated ship. The entire crew consists of six robots, nothing else."

"You know, it makes sense," said Pretorius thoughtfully. "What the hell do they need a living crew for when all they're doing is transporting inanimate goods, and every port has machines to do the loading and unloading."

"I thought it would please you," she said, still smiling. "I should be able to access the security and robot override codes in another hour."

"You were right. It pleases me."

"Anything else?"

"You need me to tell you?" he said. "Lay in a course for Nortiqua II."

18

Pretorius had called the entire crew to the bridge to explain their next assignment.

"We're going to touch down on Nortiqua II during the middle of its night. There's no sense landing at the spaceport that's our ultimate destination. There's simply no way we could avoid being identified."

"But the ship has been inspected and cleared," said Snake.

"Yeah, but it's a ship with two Kabori and no one else, as far as the records show. We're not in the Democracy; this close to Orion, they'll shoot Men on sight."

"We could pose as Djibmet's prisoners," continued Snake.

Pretorius shook his head. "We've got someone they haven't seen who is even more instantly recognizable than a Man, and that's our Michkag," answered Pretorius. "If anyone reports seeing him, they'll lock up Petrus IV tighter than a drum."

"So what *do* we do?" asked Circe.

"Once we get close enough, Pandora will pinpoint the spaceport—and if there's more than one, she'll find the one we need—and then she'll have the computer map the roads around it and at least an hour from any city that may be attached to it or surrounding it." He turned to Pandora. "You can do that easy enough, right?"

She nodded. "Not a problem."

"All right," said Pretorius. "We touch down, hopefully unseen, hijack the first vehicle to come along that will hold the lot of us—

hopefully it'll be a truck or their equivalent of one, something we can drive right to a loading dock—and take it to the spaceport."

"Somehow I suspect that's the easy part," said Circe.

Pretorius smiled. "There are no easy parts, or I wouldn't have selected you to come on this mission."

"So what comes next?" asked Ortega.

"If Pandora can pinpoint which warehouse supplies the ship that's going to Petrus, we'll find a way to get into it, hide inside whatever's being shipped, and just wait to be loaded into the ship."

"That sounds too easy," said Ortega.

"We'll probably have to kill our way onto the vehicle, and if it isn't permitted to pull into the storage building, we'll almost certainly have to kill our way in and eliminate any eyewitnesses. That means *you*"—he indicated Pandora—"are going to have to rig something that'll screw up their security system. Killing our way in is just half of the problem; not being seen on some screen half a mile away is the other half."

"I'll do what I can," answered Pandora, "but I can't guarantee it'll work until I find out what kind of system they're using and how it works."

"They must all have certain things in common," suggested Pretorius.

"I'm told if you go to Earth," she replied, "you'll find a variety of insects called spiders. They have many things in common—but some can kill you with a bite or a sting, and others can't even break your skin."

"Do what you can," said Pretorius.

"And if it doesn't work?" asked Djibmet.

"Then we're going to have to kill one hell of a lot of people before they kill us," answered Pretorius. "There are a couple of other things, basic but essential."

"Okay," said Snake. "What are they?"

"I know you hate alien food, but there's a limit to what we can take with us. The ship will either be carrying food to Petrus, or it will have once been run by a live crew of whatever race and will have a galley. Same with water. Once Pandora's got the override codes, she'll make sure there's food and water to be had somewhere on the ship. If she can't, that's when we'll worry about an alternative."

"There's a small galley leftover from when the ship had a live crew," said Pandora, studying her computer. "We won't like it, but it'll keep us alive."

"And the other thing?" asked Circe.

"Somewhere in our own storage unit are a bunch of unmarked, nonreflective black outfits with matching boots and weaponry. You're practically invisible in them. I want everyone wearing them before we touch down on Nortiqua II. Not Proto, of course, since he'll just be casting an image"—he turned to the alien—"but try to match the color and texture. I don't want a headlight, a spotlight, or any kind of light sensor spotting you on the road or at the spaceport."

"What about our heads?"

"I've brought hoods."

"Sounds uncomfortable," commented Ortega.

"If Snake can stay locked in a drawer for half a night, you can stay in a hood for the same length of time." He paused. "The second we know they're obeying our orders, you can take off your hood and let the ladies admire your face."

"What about us?" asked Djibmet.

"You're Kabori. The closer we get to Petrus, the less suspicions you'll arouse." Pretorius turned to Proto. "You're not going to fool any camera or sensors, but you might as well appear as a Kabori. If they just look at you, they'll accept it. And if not, well, you're a life-form they haven't seen before, but you're traveling with two Kabori, so that might convince them."

"All right," said Proto. "Though of course if the situation calls for me to appear as anything else, just let me know what and when."

Pretorius nodded, then turned to Michkag. "Now we come to another problem. We're going to have to change your appearance, and I don't know enough about your race to make any suggestions, so that will be Djibmet's job, though everyone will pitch in and help once he decides what needs doing."

"If Proto can't fool a security system," said Michkag, "what makes you think makeup or a false limp or some such thing will?"

"It won't," agreed Pretorius.

"Then why bother?" asked Snake.

"If he appears as Michkag, it'll set off alarm bells from here to Orion," said Pretorius. "They *know* where Michkag is, they know where he's going and when he's arriving, they know how many medals he has on his uniform and how many subordinates surround him whenever he appears in public. We let *our* Michkag appear as he really looks, and we've got a life expectancy, not to be too pessimistic, of maybe two minutes."

"Then I don't understand," persisted Snake.

"If he is heavily disguised, then if the security systems pick up his true appearance, there's only one conclusion: he's traveling incognito, inspecting various worlds and their security, and woe betide anyone who gives his identity away."

"I don't know . . ." said Snake.

"Neither do I," admitted Pretorius. "But I *do* know what happens if we let him appear as Michkag."

Circe nodded her agreement. "A telling point."

"We can't count on having makeup facilities aboard the cargo ship, so I suggest that Djibmet start practicing when this meeting breaks up, and I want a couple of you to help him." He turned to Ortega. "Felix, I think we can assume makeup isn't your specialty, so when I'm through speaking, go into the cargo hold and start pulling out the black uniforms."

"I hope you remembered night-vision goggles," said Snake.

Pretorius nodded. "For everyone but Felix. You can't improve on the vision he's got with those artificial eyes."

"So I am initially a Kabori?" asked Proto.

"Probably," said Pretorius. "We'll have to play it by ear."

"Whatever that means."

"It means we'll adapt to the situation as required. But if you have to be a Kabori, I want you to appear as a low-ranking officer—enough to get obedience from the local citizenry and some of the spaceport employees, but not enough to make them wonder what a commander or general or their equivalent is doing here."

Proto nodded his assent.

Suddenly Pretorius turned to Djibmet. "I've got a question."

"Yes?" said the Kabori.

"If we're properly identified—not suspected, but identified—once we get to Petrus, we may need a few seconds' confusion to escape or establish a defensive position."

"Yes?" repeated Djibmet, frowning as he tried to see what Pretorius had in mind.

"On Earth, and even on some worlds that have been colonized by Men, some members of my species still retain, even at this late date, an instinctive fear of and revulsion toward snakes."

"What is a snake?" asked Djibmet.

Pretorius turned to Proto. "Do you know? Can you show him?"

An instant later a glistening black snake was slithering toward Djibmet, hissing and baring its fangs.

"This is a snake?" asked Djibmet.

"Yes," answered Pretorius.

"And Men have an instinctive fear of it?"

Pretorius nodded an affirmative. "Okay, Proto."

Proto instantly appeared as a middle-aged man.

"We have no instinctive fear of it," answered Djibmet. "Or at least *I* don't." He turned to Michkag. "Do you?"

"No," answered the clone.

"I didn't think you would," said Pretorius. "But is there something, anything, that can elicit an instinctive fear or revulsion in a Kabori?"

"*Ah!*" exclaimed Djibmet, finally comprehending. "Yes, indeed there is."

"What is it?"

"A *crosthion*."

"Can you describe it?"

"Better still," said Pandora. "Give me a minute and I'll pull up a holo."

She went to work on her computer, and some forty seconds later the image of a long, lean, low-to-the-ground alien animal with glowing golden eyes and flaring nostrils appeared on the bridge.

"That *is* just an image, right?" asked Djibmet nervously.

"Right," said Pretorius.

"I've never seen one before," offered Michkag. "But it makes me very nervous. The thought of making any kind of physical contact with it is . . ." He concluded his thought with a shudder.

Pretorius turned to Proto. "Can you do it?"

"Let me study it a little more" came the answer. "I need to see it move some more."

Djibmet and Michkag backed away and gave the image a wide berth.

"All right," said Proto. "I'm ready."

"Wait," said Pretorius.

Proto looked at him curiously.

"Djibmet and Michkag, close your eyes. Nothing will harm you, I promise."

The two Kabori did as he asked. Then he turned and nodded to Proto, who immediately took the form of a *crosthion.*

"Okay, open 'em up," said Pretorius.

The two Kabori opened their eyes and quickly backed away from Proto and the holo.

"Can you tell which is which?" asked Pretorius. "Take your time."

The answer, after a full minute, was negative.

"Okay, we've got at least one way to buy a little time. Proto, put that one in your repertoire. If you've any doubts, practice it out here where Pandora can compare it with the image."

"Right," said Proto, returning once again to his human image.

Ortega returned a few minutes later, loaded down with the black, light-killing outfits and weapons for the human contingent.

"Okay," said Pretorius. "I've provided backpacks for each of you and for our two Kabori too, though I want them in their military uniforms tonight. Proto, you'll start out as a Man, but of course you won't be wearing one of the outfits. Just study them and make a duplicate that'll pass visual inspection. Just add it to your image." He paused. "Okay, that takes care of today's session. We reach Nortiqua II in three days. By then Pandora will know a lot more about the landscape. In the meantime, just stay healthy and be ready for surprises, because I've never been on a mission that didn't have its share of them."

19

Three and a half days had passed, and they were now within an hour of Nortiqua II. Luck was on their side, at least so far. The spaceport would be on the nightside of the planet, and the cargo ship was approaching at such a rate that, as best as Pandora could calculate, it wouldn't land for five hours.

"Okay," said Pretorius as he assembled his team. "There's a pair of major roads leading to the spaceport from the north. We'll approach from a hundred miles north of them, see which one has more traffic, and decide where to land based on what we can observe. Proto, they're not going to have security out where we plan to get transportation to the spaceport, so you might as well appear as a Kabori. They may be suspicious, but there's no way in hell they're going to shoot a Kabori in the dark, and if three of you signal them to stop, I think they will." Suddenly he laughed aloud. "Oh, shit! We've got a better way to use you!"

Proto looked at him nervously. "Oh?"

"All you're doing is projecting an image, right?" continued Pretorius. "There's no limit to its size?"

"Well, I can't appear to be a seventy-five-story building or a stadium teeming with spectators," said Proto carefully.

"But you could appear to be a disabled vehicle, couldn't you?"

"Yes."

"That makes this a lot easier," said Pretorius. "By the time we land, Pandora will be able to supply holos of the local vehicles. We'll wait by the roadside, and when our instruments tell us that a truck or the Nortiquan equivalent is coming down the road, you'll convince them you're a truck that's broken down, and Djibmet and Michkag will signal the oncoming truck to stop. The driver won't say no to a pair of Kabori, not this close to Orion."

"I thought you didn't want anyone to see me," said Michkag.

"It'll be pitch-dark on this side of the planet. Nortiqua II's got no moons. We'll have Djibmet change your face a bit, and that should do the trick. No one's going to be looking for Michkag next to a broken-down vehicle in the middle of the night on a minor dirtball like Nortiqua."

"Makes sense," agreed Circe.

"What do we do when we get to the spaceport?" asked Snake.

"Djibmet will tell them he's got a load for whatever the hell the name of the cargo ship is and ask whoever's in charge to direct him to it."

"Just like that?" said Snake dubiously.

"In theory," agreed Pretorius.

"And if it doesn't work?"

"Then we improvise."

"Surely you have *some* alternative plan?"

"I've got half a dozen," answered Pretorius. "It depends on the situation."

"Give me a for-instance, just so I'll be less edgy," said Snake.

"Okay. The guard says no, we can't approach the ship. Maybe it's our papers, maybe someone's found the real driver's body, maybe it's some other reason. We invite him into the truck, show him Michkag, ask if he knows who he's facing, and explain that he's on his way back from a very private conference with a turncoat representative of the Democracy, and he has to get to Petrus for the much-ballyhooed meeting. That ought to convince him to help us every way he can."

"And if it doesn't?"

"Then we'll use one of my five other contingency plans or just wing it."

"Maybe if you had more reasonable plans, you wouldn't keep winding up in hospitals," said Snake.

"By the time they send *me* out on a job, the enemy has seen every variation of every reasonable plan in the book," said Pretorius.

"Getting one," announced Pandora suddenly.

"One what?" asked Felix.

"You haven't been listening," said Pretorius. He turned to Pandora. "Okay, let's see it."

"Here it comes," she replied, and an instant later the holograph of a truck-like alien vehicle appeared in the middle of the bridge. "This is about twenty percent of its actual size, but I couldn't fit a full-sized one in here."

"Damn!" said Pretorius, studying the image. "I don't know what the hell those wheels are made of, but they don't look like it's even possible for them to ever go flat. What fuels it?"

"I can't tell," said Pandora.

"But nothing combustible?"

"When's the last time you heard of a vehicle that ran on combustible fuel?"

Pretorius stared at the image for another minute.

"They got any wildlife on this section of the planet?" he asked.

"Probably," answered Pandora. "It's an outpost world. Probably doesn't have a population of more than half a million. That's a lot of unsettled, unbuilt world." She stared at her computer. "Ah! Here it is!" She projected a holograph of a large, fur-bearing animal, a third the size of the vehicle.

"Herbivore?" asked Pretorius.

"Yes."

"About how much would this one weigh?"

"Maybe three tons," said Pandora.

"Okay, that'll do it. Proto, can you project both the truck and the animal?"

"Yes."

"All right," said Pretorius. "Once we're on the ground, we'll wait for a truck of the proper size to come down the road. Before it gets within a mile or so, you'll project an image of another truck on its side, with the front end caved in, and right next to it one of these animals, looking like it was hit and killed by the truck. Can you do it?"

"Yes," answered Proto.

"Let's see it."

"There's not enough room here."

"Give us a smaller picture. Pandora did."

"Okay, but it won't feel right."

"To us or to you?" asked Pretorius.

"To you. I'll be doing an approximation; I can't get every detail right unless I make it the right size." He paused. "Trust me. I've seen the vehicle and the animal. I can cast those images." Another pause. "I have to warn you, I cannot *aim* them. You will see exactly what the driver sees."

"Not a problem," said Pretorius. "We'll know the difference." He turned to Pandora. "Do we know the precise spot the *Wayfarer* is landing?"

"Not yet, but we will shortly."

"We damned well better. We're out of here in a few minutes."

"I'll be bringing my computers along. If we don't know before we leave, we'll know by the time we've . . . ah . . . *arranged* our ground transportation to the spaceport."

Pretorius nodded briskly. "Good enough." He walked over and stared at Michkag. "Damn!" he said. "You still look like yourself."

"Only to your eyes," said Djibmet. "No native Kabori will mistake him for the original Michkag."

"You'd better be right."

"I am," replied Djibmet. "For example, were it not for their hair color, I would have difficulty distinguishing between Pandora and Circe, yet I am sure they look very different to you."

"That may be the nicest compliment ever paid me," said Pandora with a smile.

"Okay," said Pretorius. "I get your point." He checked his timepiece and turned to Pandora. "Might as well start."

She nodded, selected the location that she deemed was optimal for encountering the kind of vehicle they needed, and began approaching the planet, always keeping it between them and the spaceport. When they were within fifty thousand feet she turned it over to the automatic pilot.

"All right," she said. "We're below the range of their security scanners."

"It seems too easy," remarked Ortega, frowning.

"Almost nothing but cargo and supply ships ever come here," said Pretorius. "We couldn't pull this kind of stunt on Petrus IV or anywhere near it. That's why we're going to let a cargo ship take us the rest of the way."

They touched down in a heavily wooded area, did what they could to camouflage the ship, then walked a mile to the road.

"Now we wait," announced Pretorius.

"How much warning will we have?" asked Ortega.

"At least five minutes," answered Pandora, constantly checking the smallest of her computers.

"Okay, we might as well set it up right now, just in case they speed up. Proto, become that truck you saw on the ship, but lay it on its side, half on the road and half in the ditch."

Proto instantly created the image.

"I wish we could have some flames and a bunch of smoke, but we don't know if there's anything combustible in the damned machine." He stared at the image for a few seconds. "Now give us the dead herbivore and put its head and neck at an impossible angle."

Proto complied, and Pretorius turned to Michkag. "We want to make sure they stop, so sprawl out on the road as if the collision has thrown you there."

Michkag did as he was instructed.

"Looks convincing," said Snake.

"Djibmet, kneel down next to him as if you're trying to revive him or stop the bleeding. The instant the truck we're waiting for pulls into view, jump to your feet and flag him down."

"Flag him down?" repeated the Kabori uncomprehendingly.

"Signal for help and make it look extremely urgent."

"What about the rest of us?" asked Circe.

Pretorius looked around the area. "Circe and Pandora, get behind the shrubbery. On your bellies." He turned to Snake. "You're better at hiding than anyone I know. Make yourself scarce but close enough to where the vehicle stops so that you can signal me if there's anyone still inside it once the driver stops and gets out to help."

She nodded her agreement.

"What about me?" asked Ortega.

"Stand behind the image of the truck for a minute," replied Pretorius.

"Okay."

As Ortega was walking, Pandora called out, "Thirty seconds, maybe a little less."

"What now?" asked Ortega.

"Just stay there. I wanted to make sure I couldn't see you through this image Proto's created."

"Just stay here?"

"Right," said Pretorius, walking over and joining him. "And when I tell you to, start shooting."

"Kill 'em all?"

"If we were just a day from Petrus, I'd say disable them and tie them up. But we're nine days away, they won't stay immobilized for that long, and this is war."

"Just checking," said Ortega.

"I hope the situation doesn't arise, but if you have to, remember that you can shoot right through the truck here," said Pretorius. "It's just an image."

"I can't see through it."

"I know," said Pretorius. He raised his voice. "Djibmet!"

"Yes?"

"If you hear me yell 'Hit the dirt!' I want you to instantly drop to the ground and flatten yourself out on it."

Before the Kabori could answer an alien vehicle came into view. Djibmet got to his feet and began jumping and screaming and pointing at the prone Michkag.

The vehicle came to a halt about ten yards shy away from the image Proto had created of the capsized truck, and two aliens emerged from it.

Ortega raised his weapon and took aim at where the alien voices were coming from, but Pretorius held up a hand, signaling him to wait.

He scanned the darkness, looking for Snake, and finally he saw her squatting in a depression about fifteen feet from the truck. He gave her a questioning gesture, and she raised her fist in the air once.

He silently mouthed the words "Be ready!" to Ortega, then yelled, "*Hit the dirt!*"

As Djibmet dove to the ground Ortega started firing at where the alien voices had been.

"Proto, kill the image!" hollered Pretorius.

The disabled truck vanished, and they found themselves looking at four bodies on the ground, two of them the Kabori, one a dead alien, and one a barely twitching alien.

"Pay the insurance," ordered Pretorius.

"I don't understand," said Ortega.

"Kill him."

"But he's almost dead already."

"It's the almost dead ones that cause problems," said Pretorius. "Dead ones never do."

Ortega shrugged and aimed his burner at the back of the twitching alien's head.

Pretorius, burner in hand, carefully approached the back of the vehicle.

"Well, you certainly took your time getting here," said Snake, who was leaning against it.

"Any aliens?" asked Pretorius.

She pointed to a dead body on the ground, her dagger protruding from its chest.

"He came racing out when he heard you yelling, so I didn't see any sense waiting for you." She smiled. "A girl has to take care of herself when she goes out on a date with you, Nathan."

Pretorius had Ortega bury the three bodies, and then his crew climbed into the vehicle.

"Wouldn't it be funny if, now that we've killed them all, we found that no one knew how to drive this damned thing?" said Snake.

But that was not the case, and in another minute they were on their way to the spaceport.

20

"Check that stuff in the back," said Pretorius as Djibmet drove them to the spaceport, while Proto, in the guise of a Kabori, sat next to them and the rest all hid in the back. "Maybe we lucked out and waylaid a truck that was bringing a shipment of goods to the *Wayfarer*."

"I can't read this shit," said Snake from the back of the vehicle.

"I saw it when we were all preparing to climb in," said Djibmet without taking his eyes from the road. "And it's a shipment for . . . well, it translates into Terran as *The Morning Star*."

"Damn!" muttered Pretorius. "I guess we have to do it the hard way."

"There's an easy way to steal the real Michkag?" said Snake with a laugh.

"No more of that," said Pretorius firmly.

"I can't make a comment?" demanded Snake.

"You can't call or think of the being we're replacing as the *real* Michkag. The Michkag who's in this vehicle is every bit as real, and I never want anyone making the mistake of calling him the false Michkag or the Michkag clone or anything like that. Got it?"

"Yeah, yeah, I got it," said Snake.

"So what do we do when we get to the spaceport?" asked Circe.

"Well, we sure as hell don't hang around waiting for the ship to land," said Pretorius. He turned to Djibmet. "Slow down."

The vehicle halved its speed.

"Pandora, how long until the *Wayfarer* is due to touch down?"

She checked her computer. "About thirty minutes, if it's on schedule—and if it was very much behind schedule, more than ten or fifteen minutes, it would have signaled ahead."

"Is *The Morning Star* on the ground?"

She stared at her computer. "There's one ship on the ground, but I can't read the name."

"Can't read it or can't see it?" asked Pretorius.

"Can't read it."

"Hand your computer to Michkag and let him read it."

"Damn!" said Pandora. "I should have thought of that. I guess I'm a little tense."

"Just because we killed some locals and are about to sneak aboard a ship bound for our enemy's stronghold?" said Snake with a chuckle. "I can't imagine why."

Michkag looked briefly at the computer. "I cannot read it," he said. "I guarantee Djibmet cannot either."

"Good," said Pretorius.

"Good?" repeated Circe.

"They could read *The Morning Star*. If they can't read this ship, that means it's not *The Morning Star*, and that the *Star* is still approaching."

"Why is that a good thing?" asked Ortega.

It's a damned good thing you're such a perfect killing machine, thought Pretorius, *because I'd hate to depend on your brain.*

"Because if *The Morning Star* was parked at the spaceport, we wouldn't have an excuse not to go directly to it," explained Pretorius. "This way we'll at least have a chance to approach the *Wayfarer* in the truck instead of on foot. They'll figure we just got anxious, made a mistake, and approached the wrong ship."

"And then what?" asked Snake. "We still have a shipment of goods for the other ship."

"We'll see," answered Pretorius. "Maybe seven of us will hop out in the darkness and climb aboard the *Wayfarer*, and the eighth can drive to *The Morning Star*, wait until they start loading it, and then make his way back to the *Wayfarer*."

"*His* way?" repeated Snake.

"Got to be a Kabori, which means it's got to be Djibmet, and Pandora has to show him the override codes," said Pretorius. He turned to Pandora. "Where's *The Morning Star* now? Is it going to land ahead of the *Wayfarer*?"

She uttered some low commands into her computer, then looked up. "It's not due for another two hours."

Pretorius seemed lost in thought for a moment. Suddenly he smiled. "Perfect!" he announced.

"I don't understand," said Circe. "Someone's got to position this vehicle so that the robotic crew of *The Morning Star* can unload it. What if the *Wayfarer* takes off before it lands?"

"It'll probably be best if it did," answered Pretorius.

Circe frowned. "Explain, please?"

"If we hadn't waylaid the truck it would have arrived three hours before *The Morning Star* landed. We didn't pass the equivalent of a restaurant or a bar anywhere along the way, so they knew they were going to get here a few hours early. They also knew that they wouldn't have to handle their cargo, that the ship's robots would do that. So it stands to reason that they planned to eat or drink or visit some very short-term ladyfriends, or the equivalent, at the spaceport while waiting for the ship to land." Suddenly he smiled. "And *that* means that when the ship *does* land and they're not there, no one's going to suspect foul play. They're just two guys who are eating or enjoying themselves and lost track of the time."

"And when they never show up?" persisted Circe.

"They figured they were going to be fired anyway, so they just left."

"I don't know," she said. "That's awfully far-fetched."

Pretorius shrugged. "Okay, arrest them and question them."

Even Ortega laughed at that.

"I bow to your devious mind," said Circe, inclining her head.

"Spaceport in about two minutes," announced Pandora.

"Dark as hell," remarked Ortega.

"Everything's done by instruments," said Pretorius. "They don't need lights, and it'll make it easier for us to move around."

"I still like the spaceports on Ballanchyne III, my home planet," said Ortega. "They're lit up all over, and you feel as if all kinds of commerce is going on. This place feels deserted."

"Yeah," said Pretorius, "but your spaceport handles spaceliners, and thousands of travelers, and it provides services for them. This is just a little cargo port on a mostly uninhabited planet."

"I didn't say I don't understand the difference," replied Ortega, "just that I prefer the one to the other."

"Not when you're on a covert mission, I trust," said Pretorius as the vehicle entered the spaceport's grounds. "Okay, just follow the signs to the cargo-loading area."

They drove another quarter mile and came to a single ship that was totally dark, with its doors and hatches all shut.

"Obviously they don't take off until tomorrow," noted Proto.

Pretorius turned to Pandora. "How's *our* ship coming?"

"About five minutes."

"Okay. Djibmet, pull over to a building, a tree, *something* that the *Wayfarer* will know not to hit as it lands."

Djibmet drove the vehicle a couple of hundred yards to what looked like an empty warehouse and turned it around so that it faced the landing area.

"There it is!" said Circe, pointing at a rapidly moving object in the sky.

"Let's see where it lands and work from there," responded Pretorius, looking to where she pointed. "You gave Djibmet the override codes for the ship and the robots, right, Pandora?"

"Right," she responded.

The ship came in lower and lower, and finally it gently touched down on its tail, its nose pointing up. Two ramps extended to the ground, hatches opened, and the ship began to glow a very dull silver.

"What's going on?" asked Ortega.

"That's so everyone knows it's there and no one runs into it," said Pretorius. He looked to his right, then his left. "Damn!"

"What is it?" asked Circe.

"It's not here for *us*," answered Pretorius. "I was hoping whatever cargo it's picking up would be here already, so we could just climb into it."

"I don't see anything approaching," said Pandora, checking her computer. "It's quite possible that whatever they plan to load won't be here until dawn."

"We can't wait that long," said Pretorius. "It's going to be hard enough to pull this off in the dark." He paused and considered their options. "Okay," he said at last. "Everyone out!"

All eight of them—the five Men, the two Kabori, and Proto—emerged from the vehicle.

"What now?" asked Circe.

"I've decided which of two harebrained approaches to try."

"I just love the way you give us confidence in your judgment," said Pandora.

"One is to board the ship in the daylight, and that's just suicidal. So the other is to board while it's still dark. And since whoever has the ship's legitimate cargo isn't here and isn't approaching, it makes sense that they won't get here before daybreak, so we can't sneak into whatever they're loading. Probably couldn't anyway, if whatever they've got is sealed."

"So what's left?" asked Snake.

"You're none of you going to like it," answered Pretorius.

"Probably not," agreed Snake. "But tell us anyway."

"We're going to walk right up to the ship, climb up the ramps, and make ourselves comfortable."

"Just like that?" she said disbelievingly.

"Not quite, but close. The five Men will disarm themselves. Put your weapons in your backpacks. Either this works or it doesn't, but what they see in your backpacks won't matter. Djibmet and Michkag, you've captured us and are taking us to Petrus IV, so draw your weapons and train them on us."

"What about me?" asked Proto.

"That's the tricky part," answered Pretorius. "You *could* remain in the guise of another Kabori, but two of them with weapons ought to be enough. I'd really like you to appear as the kind of robot they've got on the ship, and I'm sure after you get a look at one of them you can become his physical double. Problem is, if they have some electronic means of communicating with each other, they'll know you're a fraud the first time they ask you something."

"Then I suppose I'd better be a Kabori," said Proto.

"Not necessarily," answered Pretorius. He paused briefly. "As I say, having three instead of two doesn't give us any kind of additional edge. But you got a good look at the ones we killed when we took over the vehicle. What if you appeared as one of them, and Djibmet explained that you were the one who discovered us, informed on us, and are going to Petrus to give testimony, collect a reward, have a medal pinned on you, something like that?"

"Why?" asked Proto. "What purpose does that serve?"

"If you're not a Man, you're not the enemy. And if you're not a Kabori, you're not required to keep an eye on the enemy. That *might* give you some freedom to wander around the ship. You're not a prisoner, you're not responsible for watching the prisoners; you're just some guy they're bringing along to Petrus."

"I *like* that idea!" said Pandora.

"So do I!" said Snake.

"All right," said Pretorius. "Pandora, stick your computers in your backpack. Snake, Circe, put your weapons away. Ortega, I know you're a walking weapon, but at least *try* to look cowed and harmless. And I want all four of you out of your black outfits and into street clothes. No sense looking like a unit." Pretorius put his own burner and pulse gun into his backpack and began changing clothes. "Michkag, let Djibmet do the talking. We don't want any record of your voice in the ship's memory, just in case there's some secret memory capture that Pandora's computer hasn't found yet."

Michkag gave the Kabori shrug that was the equivalent of a head nod.

"Okay, Proto, time to bring the dead driver back to life."

Proto instantly changed his appearance.

"What do you think?" Pretorius asked the others. "Is that the way he looked?"

"It's close enough," said Circe. "It's unlikely the robots have ever seen him. He just has to look the part."

"Point taken," said Pretorius. He looked at the *Wayfarer.* "Okay," he announced. "Let's go."

21

They approached the ship, with Djibmet and Michkag training their burners on them, and Proto walking nervously alongside—*so* nervously that Pretorius wondered if he was acting.

When they reached the ship a robot—two-legged, upright, but definitely not shaped like a Man—appeared at the top of the ramp.

"We have been told your ship is bound for Petrus IV," said Djibmet. "These five Men are spies and we have been ordered to transport them to the fortress there. This one"—he gestured at Proto—"was our source of information. We have been instructed to bring him along, though whether for his testimony or for some reward I do not know. Now step aside and let us aboard."

He nudged Pretorius with his burner, and Pretorius began walking up the ramp, hands in the air, followed by the others.

"Do you speak?" asked Djibmet in Kabori as he neared the top of the ramp.

"I speak," responded the robot.

Djibmet quickly uttered the override codes. "You will not report that you are carrying us to Petrus IV," he continued. "These are very important prisoners, and if word reaches Petrus IV before we arrive, there is serious concern that they may be assassinated before they can be interrogated. Do you understand?"

"I understand."

"And you will tell the other robots?"

"They already know," answered the robot.

Djibmet looked around. "Where are they?"

"Inside the ship. I have transmitted your message to them."

"Good. You will tell them to clear a private area for my companion and myself. We will be responsible for our five prisoners and this local, and should any problem arise you will not be held responsible, and we alone will deal with it."

"Yes."

"It must have a door that can be closed and locked, and you will instruct the other robots that neither you nor they will be permitted to overhear anything we may say."

"By 'we' do you mean the two Kabori?"

"I mean any of the eight of us," said Djibmet. "Is that understood?"

"Yes."

"And will it be obeyed?"

"Yes."

"All right," said the Kabori. "Lead us to our private area and then leave us alone. If we need anything, I will seek you out."

The robot turned without another word and led them through the large ship, past huge rows of boxes and containers, until they came to a clear area that was perhaps forty feet on a side.

"This is not private," said Djibmet.

The robot seemed not to hear or move, but an instant later the area was surrounded by walls of a bronze-colored alloy, and there was a door right where they had walked through to enter the area.

"This will be acceptable," said Djibmet.

Before the robot could turn and leave, Pretorius cleared his throat noisily. Djibmet turned to look at him, and he silently mouthed the word *Food*.

"Also," added Djibmet before the robot could leave, "we have not brought any food for ourselves and the prisoners. Have you a galley, or will I have to appropriate some foodstuffs from your cargo?"

"We have a galley. It is long-unused, but is in working order."

"Good. You will prepare two meals a day for each of us, after your scanners and computers determine what each of our species eats. If there are not the necessary materials for the preparation of meals in the galley, take whatever is needed from you cargo, and you will be reimbursed."

"Yes."

"Finally, is there a trash atomizer nearby, one where we can dump uneaten food?"

The robot answered, using its own measurements. The nearest trash atomizer was twelve *somethings* straight out the door and then fourteen *somethings* to the left.

"Thank you," said Djibmet. "I have one final order. I want the ship to delete all record of our ever having been aboard."

"Yes."

"Good. Leave us now."

The robot left, and the door slid shut behind it as Djibmet leaned against a wall, looking like a runner who had just completed a marathon.

"Well done," said Pretorius. "You're a born martinet."

Djibmet slid slowly down the wall until he was sitting on the floor. "I have never been so tense in my life."

"You did fine," said Circe, reaching over and patting him on what passed for his shoulder.

"What next?" asked Snake.

"I know it's impolite to discuss toilets in mixed company—and it doesn't get much more mixed than right here," said Pretorius, "but it's even more impolite not to use one, and we're going to be stuck in this room for nine days." He turned to Djibmet. "Go out and get one of the robots to rig a toilet somehow, one all of us can use."

Djibmet approached the door, which slid open for him and closed again as soon as it sensed no one else was going to follow him.

"Well, so far, so good," said Circe.

"You really think the robots won't report their extra cargo, meaning us?" asked Snake.

"It said it wouldn't," responded Pretorius. "And why would it lie, especially to a member of the ruling race?"

"I suppose you're right," she said.

"Damn!" enthused Pretorius. "That was easier than I thought."

"Getting aboard?" asked Proto.

"Well, that too," answered Pretorius with a smile. "But I was referring to getting Snake to agree with me."

She glared at him but remained silent.

"And getting aboard was a hell of a lot easier too," admitted Pretorius. "As for getting off, there are certainly enough containers to hide in."

"Won't they be full of things?" asked Proto.

"Not by the time we choose the ones we want and empty them out," answered Pretorius. "We'll want eight identical ones. The last thing we want is to get separated before we know our way around the damned fortress."

"If you've got nothing else for me to do, I'm going to get some sleep," said Pandora. "I've been up almost a full Standard day."

"Not a bad idea," agreed Snake, walking to the farthest end of the room. "This corner's mine."

Djibmet returned twenty minutes later, just as Pandora and Snake had fallen asleep.

"Well?" asked Pretorius.

"It is done," he answered. "There is no privacy, but since there is only one toilet only one of us will be using it at a time."

"You did well," said Pretorius. "I have one more chore for you. Go hunt up a robot—any one of them will do, as long as they transmit everything instantaneously or nearly so—and explain that if they see any member of our party walking to or from the atomizer we are simply fulfilling a biological need. They are not to harass us, report us, or hinder us in any way."

"I will," said Djibmet. "I hope they believe me."

"You're a sentient entity, and they're machines that have been built to serve sentient entities—especially Kabori in military uniforms," said Pretorius. "No reason why there should be a problem."

Pretorius noticed that Circe was smiling at him.

Well, it sounds good and it calms him down, he thought as he smiled back at her. *But it'll never work on any robots we encounter inside the fortress.*

22

On the fourth day they found the containers they wanted and very carefully emptied eight of them, bit by bit, carrying what they removed to the atomizer. It took them two days.

On the sixth day they were close enough for Pandora to tie into the ship's even more powerful computer and pull up the current security around the spaceport's loading docks. It seemed that the containers would pass muster, that the weight of the Men and Kabori almost equaled the weight of the items they had removed. Proto, in his true form, didn't begin to weigh as much, and Snake was too light as well, but they simply left some of the original contents in their containers.

On the seventh day Pandora was able to study the fortress, looking for possible means of escape once they'd accomplished their mission. She pulled up floor plans of three levels, but the fortress was composed of seven levels, not counting its huge towers, and four of the levels were just too highly classified for her to access. She determined that the easternmost of the towers was the dock for military transport ships, and the other three for supply ships.

On the eighth day the *Wayfarer* was assigned the dock at the southern tower, and Pandora was able to cast images of the tower's interior into the room so they could study it—although, as Pretorius pointed out, it made no difference until they knew where their particular containers would be deposited. The main objective, he pointed out, was to get down from the tower once they'd gained access to the fortress and then determine where their quarry was, how best to approach him, and how to hide until that opportunity arose.

On the ninth day Pretorius had Djibmet summon a robot to the room.

"I have been given new orders," said the Kabori as the robot appeared in the doorway. "I am to return the prisoners and the being who witnessed their brutality to Nortiqua II."

The robot, which had been asked no question and given no order, offered no response.

"My superiors do not want anyone to know that the prisoners are aboard this ship, for fear of public unrest and anger. Therefore, in accordance with their instructions, I am ordering you and all other robots aboard *The Morning Star* to eradicate all trace of us, to restore this room, the atomizer, and the galley to the condition they were in ten days ago. You are to completely forget that we were ever aboard the ship, and should you see any of us between now and when the ship takes off from Petrus IV again, our images are not to register. You will proceed with your duties as if we are not present, and you will mention this to no one. Is that clear?"

"Yes," said the robot.

Pretorius caught Djibmet's eye and mouthed the words he wanted spoken.

"Is it understood and obeyed?"

The robot seemed frozen for about ten seconds. "Yes," it said at last.

"Good," said Djibmet. "Now go away."

Pandora told them when they were within thirty minutes of docking, and they left their room, sought out their containers, and climbed into them.

They docked almost half a mile above the ground at the southern tower. A team of robots began unloading the cargo, they felt themselves being moved, and the preliminary stage of the operation was finally over.

Now the fun begins, thought Pretorius wryly.

23

Pretorius waited until he was sure the robots were through moving cargo to the storage area where the containers had been placed, then opened his and stepped out. He found himself in a large circular room, perhaps one hundred feet in diameter. The room was filled with crates, containers, and boxes, and the portal leading to the ship was closed. He looked out a window and saw that he was perhaps half a mile above the ground. He walked by the seven crates that held his team and tapped gently on each. One by one they emerged, and he gave them some time to look around and get their bearings.

Finally he walked over to Pandora.

"The tower's just for cargo, right?"

"And defense against land attacks, though I don't imagine there have been any in centuries," she replied.

"How many towers are there?" he asked.

"Four. One at each corner."

"But the fortress itself is seven rectangular levels?"

She nodded. "That's right."

"It looks like stone," he said. "At least the part I could see from the window."

"No, Nate. It's much stronger than that. The stone is just a decorative surface laid on over the super-hardened metallic structure."

"Okay," said Pretorius. "Do they use the tower for anything besides defense and storage?"

"I don't think so," she replied. "What did you have in mind?"

He shrugged. "I don't know. Prison, laundry chute, anything."

"Like I said, I don't think so."

"Djibmet?" he said, turning to the Kabori.

"Yes?"

"Would I be correct in assuming that no one comes up here unless they're after something that's stored here or the place is under attack?"

"I assume so."

"You 'assume' so?" repeated Pretorius. "Why don't you *know*?"

"I have never been to Petrus IV," answered the Kabori. "I am on this mission as Michkag's coach and teacher."

"Have you heard anything about it?"

"Very little," said Djibmet. "Just that it has this impenetrable fortress."

"We've already penetrated it," said Pretorius. "So much for myths." He put his hands on his hips and slowly surveyed the room. "I guess we'll make this our headquarters at the start, at least until Michkag shows up. They're a lot less likely to do a spy check up here rather than down on one of the levels that we can assume are constantly in use."

"So we just sit here and then hope we can find Michkag?" demanded Snake.

"I didn't say that, Snake," replied Pretorius. "This is where we'll eat and sleep, and where we'll come back to after making our excursions into the parts of the fortress where Michkag and his bodyguards will be." He paused. "We've got to get Pandora access to some of their security systems if it's at all possible, so she can rig them to let us pass. And we need a place to hide Circe where she can still contact us, because she'll be the one who knows if they're buying the impersonation or not."

"And the rest of us?" asked Ortega.

"The rest of us are foot soldiers," said Pretorius. "Or, more accurately, foot saboteurs. The three who definitely have predetermined functions are Pandora, Circe, and of course Michkag, who is the object of the exercise. The rest of us will work at harassing, misleading, and confusing the enemy enough so that we can pull off this masquerade and make our escape with our prisoner."

"How will we escape?" asked Proto. "We don't have a ship."

"I'm working on it," said Pretorius.

"You're not much for sharing your plans with your comrades," complained Djibmet.

"You swear in blood—always assuming you have some—that no one more than thirty feet away can hear me, sense my presence, or read my lips, and I'll consider being more open with you."

"I apologize," said the Kabori. "I am not a warrior or a saboteur or a kidnapper. I am just a businessman who is appalled by what my home planet and our Coalition have become."

"No hard feelings," said Pretorius.

"You have to understand," said Circe gently, "this is new to you and relatively new to most of us, excerpt perhaps Snake, but Nathan's been doing it just about his whole adult life. That's why we trust him as our leader, and we also don't question him when we're in enemy, or even neutral, territory."

Djibmet turned a dull shade of purple—the Men assumed it was his equivalent of a blush—and stared at the floor.

"Well, we might as well get started," said Pretorius. "Or at least *one* of us might." He turned to Pandora. "I see a door off to the left. It looks too small for any machine that would be required to take these containers out more than one at a time, so I assume it's for Kabori to enter and exit. Is it wired?"

Pandora checked the tiny computer in her hand, then took another off her belt to double-check.

"Yes, but I can negate it."

"Without sounding any alarms?"

"There won't be any alarms even if I screw up, Nate. It'll show up in their security headquarters, but they won't want whoever's using the door to know that he's alerted them."

"And you can negate that?"

She checked her two computers again. "Almost certainly."

"Ninety percent chance or better?" he persisted.

She nodded her head.

"Good. Have the robots move six—no, make that seven—containers in here, containers that can hold a Man or a Kabori—and line 'em all up on that wall, just in case we should have any use for them in the days to come." He turned to Djibmet. "All right. You'll be our advance scouting party of one." He stared at him. "Get out of that officer's uniform. I don't want anyone talking to you, mentioning things, or asking questions you don't know the answer to. I know you packed a grunt's uniform too. No one ever talks to them."

"A grunt?" asked Djibmet, confused.

"An enlisted soldier," said Pretorius. "Someone who can ask certain questions I want answered without arousing any suspicions."

Djibmet walked over to his backpack, opened it, and uttered a very alien growl.

"What is it?"

"It's gone."

"Gone?" repeated Pretorius.

"One of the robots on the ship offered to clean my goods for me when I was in the bathroom. Somehow it neglected to put it back." He growled again. "But I never told it to clean *that!*"

"Could he have put it back in Michkag's backpack?"

Michkag quickly inspected it. "No," he said.

"I am so humiliated!" said Djibmet.

"No sense worrying about it now. We have work to do. Snake?"

"Yeah?" she replied.

"You can hide in more uncomfortable places than anyone I've ever met. Go out the door, find out how we get down to the main body of the fortress, and note any possible places we can hide for more than a few minutes once we're down there, or as we're getting down there."

"We can do better than that," said Pandora. She took a tiny machine off her belt and attached it to the front of Snake's belt.

"What is this?" asked Snake.

"Our eyes," said Pandora. "It'll see what you see—or it will if you remember to turn or pivot so it's facing whatever you're looking at—and it'll send a tri-d video back to us."

"Sounds good," said Snake, heading for the door.

"Just a second," said Pretorius.

"What else?" demanded Snake irritably.

"Pandora, show her where the on-off switch is."

Pandora did so, and Snake frowned. "Do you want me to transmit images or not?"

"Of course I do," said Pretorius. "But if you wind up hiding in the equivalent of a file drawer for five or six hours, I want you to remember to turn the damned thing off or it'll be useless to us once you're on the move again."

Snake walked to the door, which slid open the instant it sensed her presence.

A moment later the image that was being sent by Snake's computer materialized near them, and they all watched intently as the small woman made her way to an airlift, stepped onto it, and began descending.

"I hope she's bright enough not to ride it all the way down," said Pretorius. Even as the words left his mouth Snake uttered an order to the airlift.

And nothing happened.

"Can I speak to her quickly?" asked Djibmet.

Pandora made a quick adjustment to her computer. "Go ahead."

"*Kydosh!*" he said, and the airlift came to a stop, suspending Snake in midair.

"That was the word in my language for 'stop,'" said Djibmet. "Can you pronounce it?"

Snake did so, and Djibmet turned to his companions. "All of you."

They all repeated the word a few times.

"Good," said the Kabori. "The word for 'start' is '*Lobeesh*.'" As the word left his mouth, the airlift began transporting her down again.

"Good words to know," said Pretorius. "Especially on this world. If there are any others you think we need to know, teach them to us before we leave here."

"I cannot know what situations we'll find ourselves in," replied Djibmet, "but I will supply you with a dozen words that one or more of you will probably have to use sooner or later."

"Good," said Pretorius. "Start with her," he added, indicating Pandora. "She can capture your voice and pronunciation on one of her computers and play it back when we need it."

He made the Kabori equivalent of a nod of his head, then walked over and began speaking into one of Pandora's machines, uttering first the Terran word or term and then the Kabori equivalent.

Pretorius sat down with his back propped against a gleaming metal crate and watched the video transmission.

"Where is she now?" asked Proto.

"Looks like a far end of a corridor," answered Pretorius. "On the seventh level, I hope."

"Why is that preferable?"

"If she has to run, she's already on the top level. All she has to do is make it to the airlift and up to our level of the tower."

"By the way," said Circe, "what *is* our level?"

"I saw some symbols when the door was open," said Pretorius. "I'll copy them into Pandora's computer when she's done."

"There's no need to," said Michkag. "I of course read my own language. We are on the sixty-third floor or level, but I do not know if the numbering started at ground level or just above the seventh and last level of the main fortress."

"Makes no difference," said Pretorius.

"Oh?"

He smiled. "I just want to make sure we all know how to get back here. Once they see the symbols and can interpret them, that problem's solved."

"We got one that isn't solved," said Ortega suddenly, staring at the transmission.

Snake was coming up to a cross corridor, and she—and they—could hear footsteps of what seemed like a party of from four to six Kabori walking down the corridor. She looked in each direction, saw a small container in the corridor, something that had clearly been left out for a service robot to transport or dispose of.

"Oh, come on!" muttered Pretorius. "You couldn't fit in that thing if it was totally empty! Turn and run back to the airlift!"

She raced to the container, which was no more than two feet high and perhaps that wide, turned it upside down so that its minimal, neatly wrapped contents fell out, pushed them a few doors away with her foot, and began climbing into it.

Suddenly the picture went black. Not vanished, but black, since that was all the computer could see. They could hear the Kabori walking by; one of them said something, another replied, they uttered the semi-roar that passed for Kabori laughter, and their footsteps grew fainter.

"What did they say?" asked Pretorius.

"It was a joke about sending the service robot back to training school," replied Djibmet.

"And that's funny?" asked Ortega.

"Robots don't go to school," explained Djibmet.

Suddenly the video feed showed the corridor again rather shakily at first as Snake climbed out of the tiny container.

"You should have run to the airlift," said Pretorius. "You were lucky this time, Snake."

"Lucky, hell!" she grated. "I was good."

"That too," agreed Pretorius.

"I don't know what you're paying me, Nathan," she said, "but if I have to climb into anything like that again on short notice, I want a raise."

Pretorius smiled. "That's my Snake."

"Well?" she demanded as she began walking down the corridor again.

"If you survive, you've got it."

24

Snake spent another ten minutes exploring.

"Nothing's going on this level," she said at last. "I think most of the action's going to be on levels three and four."

"Why those?" asked Pretorius.

"No sense putting it on six. This floor is pretty solid, but it can be breached. And you'd never put your most valuable asset on the ground floor, or even the second level. So it figures to be three, four, or five. And five is the least likely, simply because it's the most bother to reach."

"Makes sense," agreed Pretorius.

"Why not five?" asked Ortega. "He'll be one level safer there."

"This isn't enemy territory, Felix," said Pretorius. "Once he makes whatever deal he's making, he'll probably want to make a speech from a balcony or the equivalent, and why make him even harder to see? He'll probably have a couple of hundred spotters and snipers positioned around the area."

"*We* got in," said Ortega stubbornly.

"We got in because he's still a few days away," replied Pretorius. "Even up in the towers you can figure security will triple by the time he arrives."

"So do you want me to go down to one of the more likely levels?" asked Snake.

"I think it's too dangerous," said Pretorius. "Come on back."

"Sooner or later we have to learn what the layout is on the operative levels," she said.

"If I have to send you back again, I will," said Pretorius. "But we've got a few days, which gives Pandora time to try to tie in to their computers and get the layout."

"Okay," replied Snake. "And for what it's worth, I've found two empty offices where we can hide if we have to."

"No cameras or security devices?" asked Pretorius.

Snake smiled. "Cameras, yes. Sensors, no."

"Then they'll see us walk in," said Ortega.

Snake grinned. "There's one of us they won't see, and he can disable the cameras."

"Sonofabitch!" said Ortega. "I never thought of that!"

Pretorius turned to Proto. "*Can* you do it? The real you isn't a hell of a lot taller than that box Snake hid in."

"I can do it," Proto assured him. "My body absorbs my limbs when I am not using them. I can reach to a height of five feet."

Pretorius shook his head. "That's not enough. The ceilings in that corridor look to be ten feet high."

"Then fashion me a tool I can use."

"Yeah, I suppose we can do that," said Pretorius. "Tell Felix what you need, show him how you'll handle and manipulate it, and let's see what he can come up with."

"So you really don't want me to go any farther?" asked Snake.

"Not unless I'm your beneficiary in your will," said Pretorius. "Come on back."

"Okay, coming back," she said.

"I confess that I feel useless," remarked Djibmet.

"In a few hours you'll wish you were feeling useless again," said Pretorius. Djibmet looked at him questioningly. "We have five Men who can't be seen, Proto's not going to fool any sensors, and the one member of the party who absolutely cannot be seen is Michkag. That leaves you."

"Leaves me for what?" asked Djibmet, looking confused.

"Once Pandora gets us a better picture of the lower levels, you're the only one of us who can go down there without being shot or arrested on sight. We need to know, or at least have an idea, where they're going to be keeping *their* Michkag: where he eats, where he sleeps, where he conducts private business. There's no way we can make the exchange in front of an audience, in a huge meeting room or a balcony or anything like that. Remember: this is a *covert* operation."

"I see," said Djibmet.

"All right," said Pretorius. "Circe, Michkag, start going through some of these boxes and see if there's anything useful—weapons, food, anything. Snake'll help you when she gets back."

They began checking the containers while Ortega worked on a device that Proto could manipulate that would gently kill the power to a certain camera or sensor, rather than blow it away in a manner that would bring an instant response from the security forces.

Snake returned in another ten minutes, gave her video equipment back to Pandora, and promptly began helping them search through all the stored boxes and containers.

"Any progress?" asked Pretorius, walking over to where Pandora was working with her computers.

"I just need the right code," she answered.

"How long is that likely to take?"

She sighed. "If the machine, fast as it is, has to go through a near-infinite progression of symbols and numbers, it could take days, or more likely weeks or months."

"Which we haven't got."

"Which we haven't got," she agreed. "So what I'm doing is trying to focus on breaking into one of their less-sophisticated machines. Like most militaries, including ours, once they have something that works, they tend not to upgrade it until they need it to do more things. Some of the more sophisticated machines could take days, weeks, or even months for me to access all their security codes and systems, but there are a few that I should be able break into in less than a day."

"Well, get some food and some sleep. I need you to be sharp once you *can* access them."

"I'm not going to be sitting here all day and night, Nate," she said with a smile. "What I'm doing now is ordering my machines to break through their defenses and take one or more of them over. I'll be done in another ten minutes, fifteen at the outside, and then they'll alert me when they've accomplished their task."

"Serves me right for not being a computer scientist," he said with a smile.

"From what I hear," replied Pandora, "if you *had* been one, you'd still have your original spleen, liver, pancreas, left foot, and what else?"

"Nothing important."

She nodded. "Right. You can always grow another brain."

He wandered over to where they were inspecting all the crates and containers.

"Nothing yet," announced Circe. "Not even any weapons."

"But there are enough foodstuffs to make you think they're feeding a division or two," added Snake.

"Anything we can metabolize?" asked Pretorius.

"Most of it is processed, and we can't tell what the hell is in it until Djibmet or Michkag reads the label," said Snake, "but there's enough fruit and veggies to keep us going. Nothing we'll like, but it doesn't look like it'll kill us."

"Good," said Pretorius. "The alternative was to chop you up into steaks."

"There's not enough of me," replied Snake. "You chop anyone up, it should be Felix."

"There's not enough of the original Felix left to supply even one meal," said Pretorius with a smile. "Anyway, hand me a fruit and let's see what the hell it tastes like."

She walked to an open box, pulled out something mildly round and mildly purple, and tossed it to him.

He took a bite and made a face. "Kind of bitter," he said.

"But edible?"

He nodded his head. "But edible."

"Good," she said. "Because once we pull this swap off, they're probably going to be so hot on our tail that we won't have time to stop off and get anything more palatable to eat at least until we hit No Man's Land and probably not until we reach the Democracy."

Pretorius ate the rest of the fruit and tried not to think of how it tasted. He looked around, and saw Ortega with Proto, in his true form, working on some gadget off in a corner.

"How's it coming, Felix?" he called out.

"Getting there," came the answer.

"You need any tools?"

Ortega laughed and held up his left arm. Instruments instantly extended from it and then began rapidly spinning. "I *am* a goddamned tool kit!" he laughed.

Within another hour Proto had his tool, a plastic extender—it was difficult to think of it as an arm—with a laser, a pincer, and two or three other functions, and Ortega joined in the search through the boxes.

"So who goes out next?" asked Circe.

Pretorius considered her question for a moment. "If we want to check out a more populated level, it makes sense to send Djibmet," he answered. "He's a Kabori—but we still have to pass him off as a grunt, and that's going to take a little work." Suddenly he smiled. "Or maybe not."

They all stared at him. "What did you have in mind?" asked Snake at last.

"Right now," said Pretorius, staring at Djibmet, "you're an officer. Not a very high-ranking one, but an officer, and that should be enough."

"Enough for what?" asked the Kabori nervously.

"Enough to commandeer the first grunt you see," replied Pretorius. "Go down to the sixth or seventh level, walk along the corridors as if you had a purpose, and when you finally see an enlisted soldier, tell him you have a job for him up in the south tower."

"What if he tells me he's already working?" asked Djibmet.

"Pull rank on him. You're an officer, he's not. He helps you right this minute, or he goes on report. This is a military fortress. Believe me, he'll come."

"So I just go down to the sixth or seventh level, stop the first enlisted soldier I find, and order him to come up to the tower with me?"

"That's right," said Pretorius.

"And then what?"

"Then stand clear."

Djibmet uttered a little sigh, approached the door, waited for it to slide open, and walked to the airlift.

"Can we track him?" asked Pretorius.

"Take a look," said Pandora, as she uttered a brief command and had various security cameras cast his image between them.

Djibmet walked down a corridor without seeing anyone, then stood still as an enlisted Kabori, carrying something over one shoulder, began approaching him.

"You there!" said Djibmet.

The soldier stopped and stared at him.

"Yes, you!" continued Djibmet. "I have need of you."

"But . . ."

"Do you intend to disobey me?"

"No," said the soldier promptly.

"Good. I have a job in the south tower. It won't take long, but it's essential that it be done before Michkag arrives."

The soldier snapped to attention at the sound of Michkag's name. "I am yours to command," he said.

"Good," said Djibmet. "Follow me."

He led the soldier to the airlift, and they ascended to the tower, got off, and approached the door.

The soldier turned to Djibmet with a puzzled frown. "In here?"

Djibmet nodded. "I'll be right behind you."

The soldier entered, Ortega pulled him all the way in, and Pretorius hit him with a burst of solid sound at point-blank range. The soldier staggered and collapsed.

"Check him and make sure he's dead," said Pretorius.

Snake knelt down next to him. "No breath, no heartbeat," she announced after a moment.

"Good. A burner would have been even surer, but I didn't want to get any blood on the uniform. Okay, Snake, strip it off him. Give her a hand, Felix. And Djibmet, as soon as they're done, put it on. You look pretty much the same size, but if it sags or is too tight, we may have to alter it."

It was indeed too loose, and Circe volunteered to spend the next few minutes adjusting it.

"I want you to learn your way around the place," said Pretorius as Circe was working on the uniform. "You're going to have to get a good look—a good *close* look—at Michkag when he arrives."

"Why?" responded Djibmet. "We already know what he looks like." He pointed at the clone. "There's his double right there."

"With all due respect, that's his *genetic* double. And maybe they looked exactly alike two years ago, and for all I know maybe they still do. But maybe they don't. If something doesn't match when they're seen together, which one will have the immediate authority? The one with the right scars and identifying marks."

"I hadn't thought of that," said Djibmet.

"You weren't being paid to," said Pretorius. "But speaking of uniforms, we also need to know exactly what Michkag's looks like. What new medals he's given himself since the last holos we have of him. What new patches and ribbons. And along with preparing a one-of-a-kind Supreme Commander's uniform for our Michkag, one of the first things we do with their Michkag is remove his uniform. Hard to give orders when you're standing there in the Kabori equivalent of your underwear and telling people that the identical guy in the uniform they all recognize is a fake. Especially when *our* Michkag claims that the other is an imposter, brought here to do exactly what *we* are doing, and orders him immediately incarcerated." Pretorius allowed himself the luxury of a smile. "You know how brutal their Michkag is. They may have their suspicions, but do you think anyone's really going to disobey the one in the uniform?"

"No, of course they won't," replied Djibmet.

"We hope it doesn't come to that," continued Pretorius, "that we can pull this off in secret. Because if we can't, he'll have to order their Michkag instantly put to death, before he can convince anyone that he *is* Michkag . . . and we want him back in the Democracy, where we have drugs and other less pleasant means of extracting vital information from him."

Pandora got up from her computer.

"Figure another thirty minutes on your uniform. Perhaps an hour, just to be on the safe side," said Circe to Djibmet. "I haven't done this kind of work in a *long* time."

"Pandora ought to have some kind of info on Michkag by then," said Pretorius. "Then we can get to work."

The Kabori looked at him. "You frighten me, Colonel Pretorius," he said. "You act like this is all just business to you."

"It *is* my business," answered Pretorius, "and for what it's worth, the feeling is mutual."

"I don't understand."

"You frighten me too," said Pretorius. "Because it's *not* business to you, and in a couple of hours seven lives are going to depend on your becoming a damned good spy in a hell of a hurry."

"How's it coming?" Pretorius asked Pandora.

"It's coming," she replied. "Slowly, but coming."

"How much longer?"

"For the whole castle? Maybe a Standard day."

"Just one level," he said.

"I've got the seventh—that's the top level—just about done, but I thought you wanted something we hadn't seen yet, something with a little more activity."

He nodded. "And how soon can you give us one of them?"

"Well, you certainly don't want the ground level. This isn't Michkag's home planet, so there'll be more security there than anywhere else. And I believe we're assuming most of the business will take place on levels two, three, four, and possibly five. I can bring up six in about two more hours; five will take a little longer."

"We're just talking blueprints or floor plans here," said Pretorius. "They're all the same size, so why should any one of them take longer than any other?"

"I'm accessing *their* floor plans," she said. "And the more security they've built into a level, the longer it's taking to pinpoint it and break through their codes. Of course, if you'd like to just go down there and hope you'll be lucky . . ."

He didn't respond, and she went back to work.

"Now what exactly am I trying to do when I climb into the uniform and descend to the main fortress?" asked Djibmet.

"See if you can find out exactly when Michkag's arriving," said Pretorius. "Try to find out where his sleeping quarters are, and if he's sleeping alone. Find out how to access his quarters when he's awake and elsewhere."

"To lay a trap for him?" asked the Kabori.

Pretorius shook his head. "He'll have better security than that. I just want you, or one of us, to steal one of his uniforms so *our* Michkag isn't walking around naked while trying to convince them all that he's *their* Michkag."

"But he already *has* a uniform!" protested Djibmet.

"He has a military uniform. If he'd had to walk around on one of the planets we touched down on while we were on our way here, he might have gotten away with it. But not a general's uniform. Wearing it would be like waving a red flag and saying 'I'm an imposter!' Michkag's not here yet, but they have to have *some* generals quartered here. We can probably create facsimiles of the medals, but we've got to have the basic uniform."

"I'm not military," said Djibmet. "I won't even know what to look for."

"I just told you: a general's uniform."

"No," said the Kabori. "I mean now. I don't know where to look for security devices and systems."

"Not a problem," said Pretorius. "I'll be with you."

"We'll both be killed on sight!" protested Djibmet.

"Oh, I won't be there in the flesh," answered Pretorius. "We'll rig you with the same kind of camera Snake had, and we'll plant a tiny receiver in your ear so I can speak to you and no Kabori, or even any device, can pick up the sound."

"You're sure nothing will be able to pick it up?" asked Djibmet.

"Pretty sure."

"You don't give me an overwhelming sense of confidence."

Pretorius smiled again. "It'll help keep you on your toes."

"Kabori don't have toes," said Djibmet.

"Okay, spend the next two hours figuring out what I meant."

"This is *boring*," complained Snake. "Did we have to get here this early?"

"No," answered Pretorius. "We could have arrived the day after Michkag gets here. I guarantee it would have been less boring."

As she was speaking to him, she practically curled herself into a pretzel.

"My God!" exclaimed Circe. "What are you doing?"

"Stretching exercises," answered Snake.

"No one stretches like that!" said Circe. "It's like you don't have any bones or joints, or at least they're all in the wrong places."

"No one's born a contortionist," said Snake. "If I go a week without stretching, it'll take me another week before I can curl myself into this kind of ball again. And if I go a month, that's the end of it; I'll never be able to do it again."

"How did you become a contortionist?" asked Circe.

"Seriously?"

"Yes, of course."

"I had a drunken, abusive father who tried to beat the hell out of me every time he was liquored or drugged up, so when I heard him coming home I used to hide . . . and as I got bigger, I couldn't fit into the usual places in the usual way. But since the alternative was getting my head split open, I found new ways to fit, and that was the start of it."

"I'm sorry," said Circe.

"Don't be," answered Snake. "Hell, if I wasn't a contortionist, I don't know what the hell I'd be. Made me a much better thief, and I've been on my own since I was eleven. I'm not bright enough to work with computers like Pandora here, I was never pretty enough to be a stripper, I can't sing, I can't dance, and as Nathan's fond of pointing out, I left my manners in my other set of clothes. So I'm doing the one thing I'm good at doing."

"And even then she could be better," added Pretorius.

"Bullshit!" snapped Snake.

"Where did I find you this time?" he asked with a smile.

She frowned and sighed deeply. "Okay, that one time I could have been better." She turned to Circe. "He got me out of jail."

"Got it!" announced Pandora.

"Which level?" asked Pretorius, getting to his feet and walking over to her.

She shook her head. "Sorry. No level—yet. But I've got Mich-kag's arrival time. He lands in fifty-three Standard hours."

"At the eastern tower?"

"No. It looks like he'll touch down about a mile from here and have a triumphant parade to the fortress, surrounded by tens of thousands of cheering subjects." She smiled. "They're rounding up his spontaneous applauders right now and carting them in to the city."

"Has this city got a name?" asked Pretorius. "So far all we've referred to is the planet and the fortress."

"I can answer that," said Djibmet. "It's Turrobage. Named for a local hero of the indigenous race."

Pretorius frowned. "All I've seen on any screens are Kabori. What does the native race look like?"

"I don't know," answered Djibmet. "We wiped them out a millennium ago and colonized it ourselves."

"Nice people," remarked Ortega.

"Come on, Felix," said Pretorius. "We've done the same thing on dozens of worlds. And we have the temerity to say that we've pacified them."

"If you feel that way, why are you fighting for the Democracy?" asked Michkag.

"Because I believe in our stated ideals, even if circumstances are such that we don't always live up to them. And because I believe the Coalition wants to annihilate us, and I truly don't think we want to do the same to the Kabori."

"And if we would," added Snake, "at least we'd rather be on the winning side."

"I wonder if the two sides can ever live in peace," said Djibmet.

"We're here to see that they have a chance to," replied Pretorius, walking back to his chair. "It all depends on our Michkag." He turned to the clone. "If we do our job right, you're going to be in charge not just of this world or the Orion constellation but about a thousand more worlds. It'll be your job to tone down the rhetoric, start dealing even-handedly with the Democracy, and give peace a chance."

"*Now* you sound more idealistic," commented Djibmet.

"Every soldier, whether overt or covert, puts his life on the line for a cause," answered Pretorius. "There's no sense risking it if he didn't believe in the eventual goal, however much he disapproves of the immediate one."

"You disapprove of our mission?" asked Ortega.

Pretorius shook his head. "I was making a general statement."

"I've even got the parade route," announced Pandora. "Looks like there's a moveable ramp somewhere on the grounds, and he'll be marching up it to the second level, where he'll make some kind of speech from a balcony there."

"And when does whoever he's meeting arrive?"

She shook her head. "No exact word yet, but I'd say it's about a week away."

"That gives us five days to make the switch and get away clean," said Pretorius. "If we can't do it by then, we're in the wrong business."

"I'll vouch for that," said Snake. "I'd just like the rewards to be a little greater."

"Sell your autobiography if you live through this."

"You're all heart, Nathan."

"My job is to keep it—and everyone else's—beating." He looked over at Pandora. "How's it coming?"

"You just asked five minutes ago," she said irritably.

"I assume that's a 'No progress,'" he said. "I'll ask again in another five minutes." He looked over at Djibmet, who had finally donned the uniform. "How's it feeling? Comfortable?"

"Yes. A bit tight, but not enough to cause any comments or questions."

"And the gun is loaded?"

"Gun?" he asked, frowning.

"The laser pistol," said Pretorius. "The burner."

"Yes, it's fully charged. I never heard it called a gun before."

"All right. I assume you know how to salute, or respond to salutes?"

"Certainly."

"And you don't speak Kabori with a noticeable accent, so once we know where we're sending you, you should pass muster."

"Unless you send me to a proscribed area."

"I wouldn't think there'd be many of them until Michkag arrives," answered Pretorius. "Now, we certainly don't want any trouble this early, and we don't want you killing anyone—but I assume you know how to use your burner if you have to?"

"Yes, though I've never killed anyone with it."

"Hopefully you can make that statement on Deluros VIII in a month," said Pretorius. He turned to the clone. "Michkag, I especially want you watching and listening to Djibmet as we track him. If you see anything you can incorporate in your bearing or behavior, make a note of it. Same for anything that's said."

Michkag nodded his massive head. "I will."

"Getting nervous at all?"

"Excited," said Michkag. "This is what I was created for."

"Good attitude," said Pretorius. "Anyway, as soon as Pandora can access some of their security devices, I want you to spend every waking moment watching and studying them. I like your confidence, but the fact remains that Djibmet is the only member of your race you've ever seen until today, the only one you've interacted with, and I want you to feel as comfortable as possible with your people—because that's just about *all* you're going to see for at least the next year."

"I fully understand."

"And if you do it right, no one currently on this planet or in the Democracy will think of the Coalition as the enemy in a few years' time."

"This is my goal," Michkag assured him.

"I've got level five!" announced Pandora.

Pretorius got to his feet. "Blow it up and cast it in the middle of the room here," he said.

A moment later they were staring at an incredibly detailed holograph of the fifth level of the fortress.

"Where are the security devices?" asked Pretorius.

"Cameras in blue, sensors in red, scanners in yellow," she announced, and tiny well-concealed lights of all three colors began blinking.

"Okay, what's the big room in the center?"

"Looks like a lobby or a gathering area," answered Pandora. "I suspect on one of the lower levels it's an auditorium, probably a bit larger than this. Note the corridors around it front and back. That means if it *is* an auditorium on the second or third level, it could extend all the way to the fifth, since people can easily walk around it."

"What would you guess the fifth level's function is?"

"Mostly small offices," she said.

He shook his head. "A fortress doesn't have that much office work."

"What do *you* think it is?"

"Probably enlisted men's quarters, or enlisted Kaboris, if you prefer."

"I don't think so," she said. "None of these rooms have the Kabori equivalent of a bathroom."

Pretorius chuckled. "These are enlisted men. Dog soldiers, we used to call them. They'll have one communal bathroom on the whole damned level, or at most one at each end."

Pandora smacked her forehead with the flat of her hand. "Of course!"

"Anyway, that's what it's likely to be." He paused. "And as such, there's no sense sending Djibmet to the fifth level. They'll expect him to know where his quarters are, and when he doesn't, he'll be arrested at best and shot at worst."

"Then what shall I do?" asked Djibmet. "She's already said she can't pull up another level right away."

"The sixth, maybe," said Pandora.

"Forget the sixth," said Pretorius. "Work on the second through the fourth."

"To which I repeat," said Djibmet. "What do *I* do while she's trying to access more floor plans?"

"I'm thinking about it," said Pretorius. He shut his eyes for a few seconds, then opened them and stared at Djibmet. "Do you have a friend who died young, or at least moved away, one you've lost contact with for at least fifteen years?"

"Yes."

"What was his name?"

"Drelsung."

"All right," said Pretorius. "We'll rig you with a well-hidden camera and the speaker in your ear, and send you down to the third level."

"The third level?" Djibmet asked nervously.

Pretorius nodded. "Yeah. You're going to look nervous anyway, so we'll give you a reason."

"I don't understand."

"You're looking for Lieutenant Drelsung," said Pretorius. "He ordered you to report to him, but he's not where you thought you were to meet him. Look nervous and confused, which ought to come easily in this situation. Ask any officer you see if they have seen a Lieutenant Drelsung. Of course they won't have, but if you ask half a dozen or more of them, it gives you an excuse for wandering up and down the corridors, and perhaps even getting up to the fourth level."

"Ah!" said Djibmet. "I see!"

"If anyone who seems to be in charge orders you to go to your quarters and that he'll send Drelsung there, protest that you don't want him to think you didn't try to report to him. If it becomes too tense, agree and go to the airlift. If he doesn't accompany you, stop off at the fourth level and do it all over again. Pandora will be capturing everything you see and hear."

"What if he demands to know my room number so he can send Lieutenant Drelsung there if he shows up?"

"You just arrived and it hasn't been assigned yet."

"He'll never believe that."

"He will if you're so nervous and apprehensive about whatever terrible thing Drelsung has to say to you that you simply put everything else, including getting a room, out of your mind."

"I don't know . . ." said Djibmet.

"Fifty-fifty the situation will never arise," said Pretorius.

"And if it does?" persisted Djibmet.

"Then at the last second you'll remember that whatever it is he had to tell you is private, and you were to meet him on the seventh level, not the third or fourth."

"And if the officer accompanies me to report me to the mythical Lieutenant Drelsung for misremembering the meeting place or for some other real or imagined shortcoming or violation?"

"We'll be monitoring you every step of the way," said Pretorius. "If you bring him up to seven, Felix and I will be waiting for him, and we'll have yet another uniform for Michkag, even if it hasn't got enough rank or medals."

Clearly Djibmet felt more comfortable with Pretorius's answer. "All right," he announced. "I'm ready to go."

"Not just yet," said Pretorius.

"Oh?" The Kabori frowned. "Why not?"

"We've got to fit you with a camera and earphone first, unless you'd like to wing it."

"Wing it?"

"Go down there with no video or communicative devices."

"I most certainly would *not* like to do that!" Djibmet assured him.

"All right," said Pretorius. "Pandora and Circe, will you outfit our expeditionary force, please?"

In five minutes Djibmet was ready, and a moment after that he was floating gently down the airlift to the third level.

"What now?" asked Circe as they sat around the images that Djibmet's microcamera was transmitting.

"I don't know about you," said Pretorius, "but personally, I sure as hell hope there's not a Lieutenant Drelsung anywhere in the fortress."

Nobody laughed.

26

"What the hell is *that*?" exclaimed Snake.

They all looked at the creature that was approaching Djibmet as he walked down the corridor of the third level. It was tall, almost eight feet in height, with two sets of eyes, one set looking straight ahead, the other positioned over each ear. It didn't seem to have a nose, but then it turned its head, and they could see a pair of broad slits on each side of its neck.

"Male or female?" asked Pretorius.

"Who knows?" said Circe.

"Whatever it is, it's well-armed," added Pandora.

"I think it's an advance party from the group Michkág's here to negotiate with," said Pretorius. "It's not paying Djibmet any attention. See? It's walking right by him. No salute, no indication that it even sees him. And no questions about what he's doing on that level. Snake, what the hell kind of weaponry is he carrying?"

"It looks like a variation on our pulse guns," she answered. "I think it's also got a dagger tucked into a belt, but if that's what it is, it's just for show."

A Kabori officer walked out of the room about forty feet ahead of Djibmet and began walking in the opposite direction.

"Put me through," said Pretorius, and Pandora made a quick adjustment to the computer she was holding.

"Djibmet, go into that office that was just vacated."

"What if there's still someone in there?" whispered Djibmet nervously.

"Then you're looking for Drelsung, and this is where you think he told you to meet him."

"But—"

"Just do it."

They could almost feel Djibmet swallow nervously as he approached the room in question. He stopped and stood in front of the door as it read his presence and slid into the wall. He entered, and it slid shut behind him.

"It's empty," he announced.

"We can see that," said Pretorius. "Which doesn't mean you're not being watched, so let's make this fast. Look once around the room—walls, corners, windows, floor, everything. Make it look like you're confused. Call out Drelsung's name once or twice, as if you're very nervous."

"I am," whispered Djibmet.

"Don't let your gaze linger. Pandora's capturing it all. Do what I tell you and be out of there in thirty seconds."

Djibmet followed his instructions, even managed to back up to a closet that slid open, which allowed him to jump back and spin around nervously so that Pandora was able to analyze what was inside it. Then he hesitantly called out the name, shook his head in puzzlement, and went back into the corridor.

"Well done," said Pretorius.

"What now?" whispered Djibmet.

"This long corridor you're in is intercepted by half a dozen cross corridors. As you come to the first of them, look to your right and left and see if anyone's leaving one of the rooms. If so, perform the same routine. If not, go to the next corridor, and so on, all the way to the last of them."

"You want me to enter an office in *each* corridor?"

"No, just one more. If the security is identical, we'll assume it's pretty much the same throughout the fortress."

"All right," said the Kabori. "Proceeding."

A Kabori officer began approaching from the opposite direction.

"Salute, damn it!" snapped Pretorius.

Djibmet saluted, the officer glared at him for a moment, then kept on walking.

"Try to remember," said Pretorius, attempting to keep his anger out of his voice. "You're an enlisted man—well, an enlisted Kabori—and that means you salute everything that moves. Got it?"

"Yes. I hadn't thought of that. I won't forget."

"You'd better not," said Pretorius. "We'd all like to see you again."

Djibmet continued walking, came to a cross corridor, looked down to both ends of it and didn't see anyone emerging from any of the rooms, and continued walking. Another Kabori officer approached him, and he snapped off a salute.

"Just a minute, soldier," said the officer.

"Oh, shit," muttered Snake.

"I don't believe I've seen you before," continued the officer. "Where's your station, and what are you doing on this level?"

"I have just been transferred here," replied Djibmet nervously, "and I do not yet know my duties. I am supposed to report to Lieutenant Drelsung on the third level."

"He's shaking like a leaf," noted Ortega.

"That's okay," replied Pretorius. "He's lost, and he's being questioned by an officer. He's allowed to be nervous."

"I assume he gave you an actual location," said the officer.

"Zab 23," answered Djibmet.

The officer shook his head. "This corridor is Luj. You were doubtless heading to Luj 23." He turned and pointed. "Zab is three more corridors down from here."

"Thank you, sir," said Djibmet. "I appreciate the help, sir." He saluted so nervously that he almost poked his eye out. "I'm sorry to have bothered you, sir."

"Just go!" said the officer wearily. He continued on his way, and Djibmet began walking toward the Zab corridor.

"That was terrifying!" he whispered.

"No problem," said Pretorius. "He was satisfied with your answer."

"You've been trained for this," continued the Kabori. "I have not."

"Then you're going to get some valuable on-the-job training."

Djibmet muttered something the machine couldn't translate and kept walking.

"Hey!" said Pretorius as the Kabori passed a cross corridor. "Where the hell are you going?"

"To Zab," answered Djibmet.

"Why? The officer's gone, and you weren't really going to try to enter Zab 23 without knowing it was empty, were you?"

"I'm . . . I'm sorry," stuttered Djibmet. "I'm so terrified I'm not thinking clearly."

"All right, I'll direct you," said Pretorius. "No, don't turn and go back to the corridor you just passed. That'll draw attention. Go to the next one. That's right. Here's another officer. Salute him. Smile at him if you can. Two more. Salute them. Good! Corridor coming up. Come to a stop in a few seconds . . . now. Okay, look to your right. Anyone leaving?"

"No," said Djibmet.

"I know. We can see everything you see. Now look to the left. Damn! Empty."

"What now?"

"No one's coming. No one's behind you. Just stand there with a puzzled or thoughtful expression on your face."

"For how long?" asked Djibmet.

"Until someone leaves a room, or soldiers start coming down the main corridor."

"I feel very open and unprotected like this."

"That's because you *are* open and unprotected," said Pretorius. "After all, you're a member of the military, safe in the best-protected building in the Coalition . . . just a minute. There, off to your right! Seven or eight doors down!"

"Yes, I see."

"Don't move yet. Wait until he comes up to your corridor and turns one way or the other. We don't want him seeing you entering his office."

"Right."

"And salute him."

Djibmet saluted the officer, who returned the salute, gave him the Kabori equivalent of a smile, and turned to his left.

"Wait . . . wait . . . okay, now turn into the corridor and go to his door."

Djibmet did as Pretorius instructed, the door slid open, and he gave the office a thorough but brief inspection, looking into every corner and crevice on the assumption that Pandora could freeze and enhance any image at her leisure.

"Anything else?" he whispered as he turned and faced the door.

"No, that should do it."

"Now what?"

"How brave are you feeling?" asked Pretorius.

"Not very," admitted the Kabori.

"All right," said Pretorius. "Go on back to the airlift and come up to the seventh level."

"I'm not feeling brave," repeated Djibmet, "but I will do what must be done. Where shall I go next?"

"Just stay where you are for a minute. I need to think." Pretorius signaled Pandora to kill the sound system. "Okay, I can't send him down to two, which is clearly the operative level on this place. I mean, hell, three is almost as deserted as six was."

"Then you have no choice," said Snake. "Like it or not, you have to send him down to two and hope he doesn't faint."

"I don't think so," said Pretorius.

"What are you getting at?"

"We're all in agreement that it's obvious two is the main level. As Michkag and his fleet get here, the other levels will get a lot busier, but the mere fact that they're so empty now means that no one's preparing a meeting or a celebration on any of them. There may be some minor meetings between lesser officers on both sides on the higher levels, but clearly two's where the major speeches and business will take place."

"So two is where he's got to go," insisted Snake.

"No," said Pretorius firmly. "We plan to snatch Michkag, but preferably not in front of a few thousand armed followers."

"Maybe we can get both sides shooting at each other," suggested Snake.

He grimaced and shook his head. "Not until they've finished shooting at *us.*"

"Then what the hell do you have in mind?"

"If we're going to make the switch," he explained, "we are sure as hell *not* going to do it in front of an audience."

They all turned to look at him, curious as to what he was thinking.

"There's one group in the fortress who already know where Michkag's room will be, and that's the service robots. And I think Djibmet will cause a lot less suspicion if we give him a reason to question the robots than if we send him down to inspect where Michkag will be speaking and working and maybe even eating on the second level."

"Makes sense," agreed Circe.

"Yeah, I suppose so," said Snake grudgingly.

"All right," said Pretorius. "Give me sound again."

Pandora flipped a switch. "It's on."

"All right, Djibmet," he said. "New assignment. Ask some low-level soldier—*not* a general, commander, or captain—where the service mechs are stationed."

"You mean the service robots?" replied Djibmet. "They're everywhere."

"You want their headquarters, the room they keep their supplies in. You're recovering from an injury inflicted by Men in some minor border action, and you need something—an extra pillow, a heating pad, I'll leave it to you—to ease your pain when you're trying to sleep. If anyone suggests that the robots just put it in your room, you're still looking for Drelsung, who's got your orders and knows what room you've been assigned, but you're in enough pain that you want to make sure you get whatever it is you need now and don't have to demand it in the middle of the night."

"I can do that," replied Djibmet after a few seconds' silence. "Then what? I assume you want me to find out where Michkag will be quartered?"

"Yes, but you're going to have to do it very indirectly. After all, you can't just ask for the room number of the most important leader of a totalitarian society."

"So what do I do?" asked the Kabori.

"Cause a little problem for them," said Pretorius. "Accidently lean against a pile of something—towels, sheets, water pitchers, whatever.

Then, while they're cleaning up—and they won't blame you for your clumsiness; they're robots, and their function is to clean up—find a place to hide the microcamera you're carrying. If you can aim it at a computer screen, so much the better."

"And if I can't, or it's covered up by a pile of something, anything, then what purpose will this serve?"

"The sound will still be operative. An order concerning Michkag's room may be announced, or one robot may say something about it to another, or a Kabori officer may enter the place to request or demand something be taken to his room. Now, the robots will certainly know where his room is, but my guess is that the officer will state it anyway."

"All right," said Djibmet. "I will do my best."

"Good," said Pretorius. "And remember to salute every Kabori officer you see. Come back here when you're done." He signaled Pandora to turn the sound off again.

"Well, we should know soon where we're making the switch," said Ortega.

"We may even get down there unnoticed, though I have no idea how," said Snake, "and actually make the switch. But how the hell will we get back out and off the planet?"

"I'm working on it," said Pretorius.

"Oh, fuck your 'I'm working on it' shit!" snapped Snake. "Have you any idea at all of how we even get back to this room with Michkag?"

"Oh, course I do," said Pretorius. "And if you think about it, so do you."

She frowned. "Can't you just out-and-out *say* it?" she demanded.

"There's a member of the team who hasn't pulled his weight yet, but that's going to change very soon now."

Pretorius grinned and turned to look at the member he was referring to, and suddenly all eyes turned to the Michkag clone.

27

Djibmet made it back to the storage facility an hour later.

"All right," announced Pretorius. "From this moment on, someone is going to monitor that transmission every second of every day until we find out where Michkag will be sleeping."

"Have you figured out how we're going to get to wherever it is?" asked Circe.

"I'd tell you I was working on it, but it would just set Snake off on another screaming fit," he replied with a smile.

Snake glared at him but said nothing.

"All right," continued Circe. "Once you've got him and brought him up here—I assume you're bringing him back here—how do we make our escape?"

"That's a little easier," answered Pretorius. "There'll be ships docking here at the southern tower once Michkag lands, because they'll be feeding four or five times as many mouths and supplying whatever else Michkag and his party needs. Our best information back on Deluros is that we can expect upwards of ten thousand military, mostly Kabori, to accompany him, and probably more. That's going to take a lot of daily supplies."

"This isn't the only tower, you know," she said.

"I know. But it's the one we're in, they're only using three for shipping, and we'll make sure a ship is docked here when we go into action. Pandora, how many ships are on their way in?"

"Give me a minute," she replied, putting the question to

the proper computer. "More than two hundred in the next four days."

He shook his head. "I asked too general a question. How many supply ships?"

She checked again. "At least six, possibly as many as eight, during that same four-day span."

He turned to Circe. "There you have it. Three towers, six ships. We'll get at least two, maybe three."

"But they unloaded the one we came in on in just a few hours," she noted.

He smiled. "But we weren't planning on hijacking it."

"How do we plan to do it?" she persisted.

"As soon as we know which one or two will come to this tower, we'll have Pandora's computers dope out the best way to take one over. The only problem will be if it comes *before* Michkag arrives. We might get it to stay moored for eight or ten hours, but we'll never get away with keeping it in dock for, say, two days."

"Then what do we do?"

"We find another one to steal."

"Out there?" she said, waving a hand in the general direction of the city that surrounded the fortress.

He shook his head. "No, it won't be that easy. But once we make the switch, we can have *our* Michkag arrest us and order Djibmet to fly us to some location that Michkag won't share with his staff. He thinks there's a traitor among them, that we're working with him, and he's not about to let anyone know where he's stashing us until he can question us."

"Why wouldn't he just stash us in a room here?" asked Ortega.

"Only one reason," said Pretorius. "But a very telling one."

"What is it?"

"Michkag has a reputation for killing people who question his orders," answered Pretorius. "That goes for planetary populations all the way up to long-time trusted officers."

"Someone will still follow us," said Ortega.

"Probably," agreed Pretorius. "But at least we'll be off the planet and out in space."

"That's not much comfort if we're facing a dreadnought."

"No, but it's minimally less uncomfortable if we're evading it rather than facing it."

"I don't like it," said Ortega.

"Welcome to the club," said Pretorius.

"So do we just sit here until Michkag lands?" asked Circe. "No more sending anyone out in the corridors?"

"If you can think of anything we can learn that's worth the risk of sending them out, I'll send them," answered Pretorius. "But until then, we've found out pretty much all there is to find out until we learn where Michkag's quarters are and exactly when he's due to land."

"I can help you a bit on that," said Pandora, staring at yet another of her computers. "They just issued a directive that they're not allowing any commercial traffic tomorrow afternoon, so my guess is that's when he's coming in."

"But no one's said so officially?"

"No," said Pandora. Suddenly she smiled. "Who can blame them? There's always a chance the Democracy will send in a highly skilled team to kill or kidnap him."

"You never can tell," replied Ortega.

"Strike 'kill' from our lexicon until the switch is made," said

Pretorius seriously. "We kill him in front of anyone, and the whole purpose of this mission is destroyed."

"So we've got until tomorrow afternoon," said Ortega. "What do we do until then?"

"You might consider sleeping," suggested Pretorius. "I want everyone alert and ready to put in maximum effort and some very long hours."

"And eating," added Snake. "You may not have a chance for another meal until we're in space." She made a face. "Undoubtedly on a Kabori ship whose galley doesn't cater to Men's tastes."

They spent the next few hours eating, loafing, and napping. Then one of the computers beeped, and a moment later Pandora called out: "Got it!"

"Where he's staying?" asked Pretorius, suddenly alert.

She nodded. "Fourth level, corridor Zab, rooms 42 and 43."

"Check the floor plan," said Pretorius. "Are they connecting rooms, totally separate, or what?"

"Give me a sec," responded Pandora. "Connected by a standard doorway."

"So he may have bodyguards in the other room," said Pretorius.

"Or maybe a girlfriend," suggested Snake.

"Or maybe he just likes a lot of room," added Ortega.

"It shouldn't be that hard to figure out," said Pretorius. "Pandora, how did you know what his room numbers were?"

"I intercepted a message to the robots."

"Did it say to deliver the same stuff to both rooms?"

"Bedding to 43, foodstuffs to 42," she answered.

"There you have it," said Pretorius. "He's turned it into a suite. He'll lounge and maybe have visitors in Zab 42 and do his sleeping in Zab 43."

"And maybe leave a bodyguard in 42," added Circe.

"Anything's possible," agreed Pretorius.

"You don't seem especially worried about it," continued Circe. "It sounds damned dangerous."

"It *is* damned dangerous," agreed Pretorius. "But look at it this way. Two months ago we were on Deluros VIII, hatching an impossible plan to kidnap the most powerful general of the Coalition and put our Michkag in his place. Today we're actually inside his fortress, we know what room he'll be in, we're all still alive and unharmed, and we're maybe a day or two from making the switch. What odds would you have given on even getting this far?"

"It's right that an optimist should be in charge of an operation like this," replied Circe with a smile. "But it's not a bad idea to have a pessimist pointing out potential pitfalls."

"You start counting pitfalls on a mission like this one," said Snake, "and you could run smack-dab into eternity."

"Back to business," said Pretorius. "Let's assume he adjusts to Petrus IV's hours, which is to say he's awake in the daylight and goes to sleep a few hours after dark. That means if he lands here in, say, midafternoon tomorrow, we probably don't approach him for perhaps ten to twelve Standard hours after that."

"You keep making it sound easier than I think it's going to be," said Circe. "Who says there has to be a bodyguard in Zab 42? What if there are half a dozen posted in the corridor outside the two doors?"

"We'll distract them, mislead them, or kill them," answered Pretorius. "I know that's not a comforting answer, but I've been on half a dozen of these missions, and my only observation is that whatever you expect, you're likely to be surprised—usually unpleasantly. You just have to plan for every eventuality and take advantage of every opportunity, because the enemy—*any* enemy—isn't inclined to give you too many."

"I don't mean to be argumentative," said Circe. "But unlike you, I *haven't* been on half a dozen missions like this. In fact, I doubt that there have ever *been* half a dozen missions like this. I've been on one minor one, and even that was a lot more dangerous than any of us were led to expect."

"No offense taken," said Pretorius. "But if we based our entire plan on one presumed set of circumstances and found at the last minute they were different, we'd be in more trouble than if we go in with open minds, following a general scenario but prepared to improvise on a second's notice."

"I apologize," said Circe.

"Forget it." Pretorius got to his feet. "Anyway, barring anything unforeseen, we can assume we'll be going after Michkag about a dozen hours after he arrives here—and that's always assuming there's a cargo ship docked here. Pandora, let me know if a troop carrier or a dreadnought docks at the military tower, but only if you can ascertain that there's no one left aboard except maybe some robots or androids that one of your computers can override."

"Right," she said, nodding her head.

"So we'll plan on late tomorrow night, always on the condition that we have at least one potential means of escape." He turned to the clone. "This is what you were created for. I hope you're up to it."

The clone offered him an arrogant glare. Then, after a moment, he spoke. "Was my response acceptable?"

Pretorius smiled. "I don't think you're going to have any trouble at all."

"Good. I really have spent half of my waking hours since my birth studying my other self."

"Just remember," said Pretorius. "Once we're in the room, even before we subdue him, *you're* Michkag and *he's* the imposter. You can pass any DNA test or any other physical test there is. Just act like you know who you are and of course you're in total command, and you should be able to pull it off." He turned to Ortega. "But if there are any other Kabori around, your first job is to knock their Michkag senseless. Ours can pass every physical test there is, but he can't tell them what he had for lunch or what joke he told at the dinner table a few hours earlier."

Ortega nodded his head. "Got it."

Pretorius turned to Circe. "We finally have need of your special talent," he said. "If we're with him when our Michkag has to speak to any of his soldiers, you've got to let me know instantly if anyone has any doubts, not about his judgment but his identity. If we have to make up any lies . . ." He stopped, then started over. "We're Men. Of course they won't believe us. But if Djibmet has to lie about why we're here, or in his company, or why a clearly senseless Michkag is with us, you have to let me know who's buying it and, more important, who isn't."

"Of course," said Circe.

"You seem suddenly less nervous," he remarked.

She smiled. "You're asking me to do what I'm good at," she replied. "I'm not at all good with weapons and sneaking around."

"You'd be surprised how many people of just about every race aren't good at that," replied Pretorius.

It was four hours later, while Snake, Circe, and the two Kabori were sleeping, that Pandora walked silently over to Pretorius, who was lying on his back, hands folded behind his head, staring at the ceiling some thirty feet above him.

"You awake?" she whispered.

"Yeah."

"The *Moonbeam*—that's a cargo ship—docks here late afternoon tomorrow."

"Here?" he repeated. "You mean the fortress?"

"No, I mean this tower," she replied with a smile. "While everyone was sleeping or eating, I finally managed to find out the names of the towers."

"Which one is this?"

"You couldn't pronounce it. But it jibes with the floor plans."

"Then we're in business."

"If you actually make the switch and get back up here intact and we can take control of the ship and they don't blow us out of the sky."

He sighed deeply. "Yeah, always assuming that."

28

The ships started arriving the next morning, dozens of them, then hundreds.

"He sure likes to make a splash," noted Ortega.

"Got to be ego," agreed Snake. "This is a secure planet, deep in their stronghold. There might be one assassin lurking, but he's come prepared for a huge invasion—or a lot of publicity."

By noon cargo ships had docked at two of the other towers.

"Any way to tell if we're next?" asked Pretorius.

Pandora shook her head. "I know that the *Moonbeam* is landing at our tower, but there's no way to be sure which lands next. They have a dozen warships directing traffic up there. It seems to be on schedule, so I'd say it's still docking in midafternoon."

"Real crew or robot crew?"

She checked her computers. "Robot. They're programmed to load and unload, and the flight pattern is controlled from . . ." She peered at the screen. "From Galladra VI. I would guess that's the corporate headquarters or the equivalent."

"Good. You'll be able to tap into their programming, order them to keep our existence secret, and do what we tell them to do."

"Within reason," she replied. "I can't, for example, order them to fire on the military. They'll have certain inviolate commands embedded in them."

"They won't have any weaponry anyway," said Pretorius. "The *Wayfarer* didn't."

She shook her head. "You're not following me. I'm not worried about them blowing up a city. You wouldn't have them do it even if the ship had the capacity to do so. We're going to be trying to escape, not get into a shooting contest."

"Okay, what am I missing?"

"I think there's a real likelihood that they'll instantly obey any orders our prisoner gives them. Not knowing who he is would be like not knowing who Hitler or Conrad Bland were during *their* eras."

"We can find out easy enough," suggested Ortega. "Just have Proto appear as Michkag when they land and see if they listen to him."

"They're machines with sensors, not eyes," replied Pretorius. "They'll see a lump on the ground."

"Damn!" said Ortega. "I forgot."

"Maybe it's about time you laid out your plan for us," said Circe.

"Those are not very big rooms down on the third level," said Pretorius, "and there are seven of us that have to move covertly, even if Djibmet approaches the rooms openly." He paused. "I think it would be counterproductive for all of us to go down there together. We'll just get in each other's way—and more to the point, we'll attract too much attention along the way."

"Just how the hell do you propose to get down there *without* attracting attention?" demanded Snake.

Pretorius walked over to three containers and pointed at each in turn: "Michkag, Circe, me."

"No way you're leaving me behind!" snapped Snake.

"I'm going too," added Ortega. "I've been rebuilt for the kind of trouble you're going to be facing."

"It'll attract too much attention," replied Pretorius. "We're not going to fight him, so I don't need all your built-in weaponry, Felix. And we're not entering stealthily, so I don't need your skills to get in or out, Snake. You've gotten us this far, and we'll need you on the way home, but seven crates would attract too damned much attention."

"And three won't?" demanded Snake.

"One won't."

"Even *I* couldn't fit three of me in one container."

"We'll have a robot take 'em down one at a time, so no one ever sees three large crates going down the corridor at once," said Pretorius. "I'll be in the first, so that if Michkag shows up before we're all there, I'll disable him."

"He outweighs you by a hundred pounds," said Ortega.

"His size won't help him against *this*," said Pretorius, holding up a small, thin box.

"What is it?"

"Something that'll knock him out for a day and a night," answered Pretorius. "And I've got nine more if we need them."

"Why *her* and not me?" demanded Snake, pointing at Circe.

"Because she has an essential talent that no one else here has. She's an empath."

"So what?"

"We're not here just to kidnap or kill *their* Michkag. We're here to replace him with *ours.* The whole purpose of this operation is to put an ally at the head of the Coalition. He looks the part. He'll pass any DNA or retina or any other physical test they can devise. But with all due respect to him, the only member of his race he's ever been in contact with is Djibmet. We *hope* he's got the other Michkag's inflections and mannerisms down pat—after all, he's been studying holos of him for a long time now—but until we know that his closest associates accept him, we can't leave him behind without any protection. As I say, our entire purpose is to replace the current Michkag with ours. It's a matter of no importance to me, and not even much to the Democracy, whether their Michkag dies or returns to Deluros as a prisoner. The important thing is that our Michkag can convince them he's the Michkag they've been following, and if there are any immediate doubts the only member of our party who will know is Circe."

"So what you're saying is that you plan to *stay* in his rooms until he speaks to some subordinates and she can vouch that they're buying it?"

"She tells me she has to be in proximity, that she can't do it off a hidden video or sensor," answered Pretorius.

"That's correct," said Circe.

"How long do we give you before we mount a rescue operation?" asked Snake.

"I don't believe you've been listening at all," replied Pretorius with a grimace. "Djibmet will have his microcamera with him. You can watch whatever he's transmitting. But if we get into trouble, your job is to get the hell out of here and get word to General Cooper that the switch didn't work, that the Michkag in charge is the one who's always been in charge."

"He'll figure that out soon enough," said Ortega.

Pretorius shook his head. "Michkag didn't get where he is by being stupid. If this thing falls apart, he's bright enough to pretend it worked, send a message of condolence to Cooper that his troops killed us before he could call them off, and offer to meet with him."

"I hadn't thought of that," said Ortega.

You're a hell of a killer, thought Pretorius, *probably the best we've got here. But we could fill a few dozen encyclopedias with things you haven't thought of.*

"All right!" growled Snake. "You're the boss."

"I'm glad someone remembers that," said Pretorius. He turned to Michkag. "Now, on the assumption that Michkag lands about the same time as the *Moonbeam*, or probably even earlier, we can assume his personal effects will be in one of his rooms by the time we get down there. The first thing we've got to do is get you one of his spare uniforms. Once we make the switch, check and make sure you're wearing every insignia he's got. I don't suppose they hand out duplicate sets of medals here, any more than they do in the Democracy's military, so once we subdue him, remember to appropriate all his medals and anything else that's not on the uniform you'll be wearing."

Michkag nodded his agreement.

Suddenly there was a huge cheer from beyond the fortress, and they looked out various windows.

"There he is!" said Djibmet, pointing to the original Michkag, who was walking up to the fortress at the head of a column of his troops.

"He's not going to look so cocky this time tomorrow," said Snake.

"Look at those medals," said Circe. "He must work out in the gym just to be able to carry them all."

Pretorius turned to the clone. "What do you think?"

"It's like looking at myself in a mirror, only my reflection's acting independently of me."

"Okay," said Pretorius. "Let's give it maybe two hours. Then . . ."

"Isn't that awfully soon?" asked Circe. "He won't be going to sleep for another eight or ten hours."

"I just want to grab something from storage here—any small thing—and sent Djibmet, or even a robot, down to Michkag's room with it. That way we'll know that you've got the right security code for it and we can get into it whenever we want, and also it may give us an opportunity to swipe a uniform for our Michkag."

"There won't be any problem opening the door," Pandora replied.

"I hope not. But they may be putting him in those rooms precisely because the locks are more complex."

She manipulated her computer for a moment, then looked up with a smile. "I've locked it and unlocked it. Not a problem."

"Good," said Pretorius. "There's no sense drawing any attention to Djibmet—I don't want anyone seeing him go in there twice in one day and start asking questions—so you'll program one of the robots to do it."

"Just take some trivial gift down, steal a uniform if it can find it, and come back up?"

"With the uniform in whatever container it carries down there. For all I give a damn, it can throw the gift into the atomizer."

"All right," she said. "I can do that."

A little more than two hours later, when Michkag was addressing an enormous crowd from a long, ornate balcony on the second level, a robot made its unobtrusive way down to the third floor, carrying a small, artfully wrapped container. It went to Zab 42, fed in the proper code, and entered the room as the door slid open and then shut behind it.

It unwrapped the package, found the trash atomizer in the

bathroom, emptied its contents into it, walked to a closet, opened it, and found that it was empty. It stood still, awaiting Pandora's instructions, received them, walked through to Zab 43, opened the closet in that room, appropriated a military uniform, picked up a pair of boots from the floor of the closet, closed the door, and carefully folded the uniform, placing it into the box. Only one boot would fit. It loaded it, then waited for more instructions.

"Go to the bathroom," ordered Pandora.

The robot did as ordered.

"Pick up a towel."

The robot picked up a towel.

"I see a number of cleansing lotions on a shelf. No, to your right. Choose the one that is the least translucent and pour two ounces on the towel. Now rub the towel against itself, smearing the stain. Good. Now wrap it around the boot, so that it looks like a cylinder."

The robot made three attempts, but finally got the shape she wanted.

"Good. Now leave the room through the door at Zab 42, walk to the same airlift you used to get there, and bring what you are carrying to me in the tower's storage area where you were given the package. If anyone questions you, the box contains something that an officer—you don't know his name—is shipping out on the *Moonbeam.* And the towel is dirty, and you have been ordered to dispose of it."

The robot was back in the tower's storage area in four minutes, without being stopped or questioned along the way. Pretorius took the uniform and boots from it and handed them to Michkag.

"One thing we can he sure of," he said with a smile. "They'll fit."

"It will look naked without the medals," said Djibmet.

"With luck, no one will see it without the medals," answered Pretorius. "Except maybe the guy we're borrowing the medals *from*."

29

Then it was just a matter of waiting, the part of a mission that Pretorius hated the most. He tried to take a nap, wasn't sleepy, and soon found that he wasn't hungry or thirsty either. He wasn't even nervous, just annoyed that all the preparations were done and that he still had to wait a few hours.

Michkag tried on the uniform. "How do I look?" he asked.

"Like you belong in it," said Pandora.

"Like the leader of the Coalition," chimed in Circe.

"Like someone stole your medals," said Snake.

"We'll get them before anyone sees him," said Pretorius.

"Are you sure you don't want me to accompany you?" asked Djibmet.

Pretorius shook his head. "Too dangerous. If someone sees you and remembers that you were wandering around before, looking for your room and your missing officer, and now you *still* don't know where you're quartered . . ."

"I see," said Djibmet, who actually looked relieved. "I hadn't considered that." He paused, then added reluctantly: "I'm in my officer's uniform. I could wear it and accompany you."

"To what purpose?" replied Pretorius. "Hell, I wish I didn't have to have Circe along, that it was just me and Michkag, but we have to know if they're buying it without question."

"I hadn't asked," said Djibmet, "but how will she know? I assume she'll overhear, if that's the word, their thoughts or reactions, and once she's satisfied the two of you plus their Michkag will be carted up here in the containers. But how will our Michkag know when the time comes?"

"*Their* Michkag will be carted up, hopefully within a minute of his entering the room," answered Pretorius. "But we can't leave *our* Michkag in his place until we know that they accept him. Which means Circe and I will have to hang around for a while."

"They'll kill you on sight," said Michkag.

"Not if you tell them not to," said Pretorius.

"And they think he *is* Michkag," added Snake.

"So what exactly do I do?" asked Michkag.

"You improvise," replied Pretorius. "I wasn't going to mention this until we had maybe half an hour to go, so you didn't spend any time worrying about it. Just remember: you are an absolute dictator. You can tell them we're turncoats and spies in your service, or that we're prisoners. Either way, you want us taken up to this tower and shipped out of here. No one will dare disobey you."

"And if one of my officers offers his own ship?"

Pretorius shook his head. "We don't want to split up. You'll find a reason not to accept the offer."

"A *valid* reason," replied Michkag, frowning. "I hope I'm up to this. I am not afraid, but when all is said and done I am less than two years old. There may be answers that will give me away."

"We're going to supply you with a tiny earphone. I'll whisper into it when no one's looking—and if they *are* looking, I'll pretend to cough and cover my mouth with my hand. Just remember: anything you say is absolute law."

"I assume I won't be sending you back to the tower without armed guards. What happens when they get there? They won't just open the door and shove you inside, and then go back down."

"They'll turn us over to two of your officers who are waiting for us there," answered Pretorius.

"Two?" said Michkag, surprised. "There's just Djibmet."

"Proto, become an officer," said Pretorius, and instantly Proto appeared as a uniformed Kabori officer, the equivalent of a colonel.

"But they'll know it's not real," protested Michkag. "He can't fool any of the devices."

"So what? They'll only see him at the doorway, with no scanners or sensors trained on him. Then the door will slide shut, they'll be on the outside going back to the lower level, and that's the end of it."

"They may insist on entering this area."

"That'd be against your orders," replied Pretorius. "And if they're foolish enough to disobey orders, Felix and Snake will be happy to demonstrate the consequences of disobedience the second the door slides shut."

"Well," said Djibmet, "it *sounds* foolproof."

"Nothing's foolproof," answered Pretorius. "The trick is to be prepared for just about anything that can go wrong, because something always does."

Pandora handed the earphone to Michkag and gave the tiny speaker to Pretorius. "You got any false teeth, Nate?"

"All but four or five," he answered.

"Good," she said, walking over and standing in front of him. "Open up." He opened his mouth. "Yeah, there's a nice molar on the lower left. Too damned clean and unmarked to be an original. We'll remove it and insert the transmitter there."

"Be my guest."

She reached into her pocket, brought forth a number of tools, chose the one she wanted, and replaced the others. She then reached into his mouth, clamped the instrument on the molar in question, and gave it a yank.

"Goddamn, that hurt!" muttered Pretorius, rubbing his lower jaw.

"Of course it hurt," she replied. "It was anchored in there. Now let me stick this in. There'll be a couple of pins on the bottom that'll keep it from moving around, so prepare to curse again."

She fastened and adjusted the transmitter. He grimaced but made no sound.

"Now," said Pandora, "run your tongue over the top of it." She paused as he did so. "Do you feel a little extension or ridge at the top?"

"Yes."

"Press it forward with your tongue, and Michkag will hear every word you whisper under your breath. And since most of what you have to say isn't worth listening to, or is shouted at the top of your lungs, just switch it off with your tongue when you're not trying to secretly feed him answers or instructions."

"Okay, let me try it out," said Pretorius. He flicked the switch with his tongue. "Can you hear this?" he whispered.

"Perfectly," said Michkag.

"Michkag and I can both hear it," said Pandora, "but no one in your proximity can." She inserted a tiny receiver in his left ear. "And now you can hear me when I activate my transmitter."

"Good," said Pretorius, switching it off. "We'll test it one more time before we leave here and once more in Zab 42." He turned back to Pandora. "Only one thing can screw us up." Suddenly he smiled. "Well, lots of things can, but the one I have in mind is the *Moonbeam*. I haven't seen any robots unloading anything."

"We're okay," she replied. "It's due to dock in"—she checked one of her computers—"eighteen minutes, and I've already taken control of their robots."

"No live staff at all?"

"None. Who needs them on a cargo ship? You'd just be paying them to sit around for days between stops, and they can't lift or carry anything or work any machine a robot can't lift or work cheaper and better."

"Dumb," muttered Pretorius.

"Why?"

"They're at war. *We're* at war. I hope to hell the Democracy knows to leave at least one Man on each ship. I mean, hell, look at us: five Men plus Proto plus a clone of their ruler came in on a ship run totally by robots, and except for the clone we'll be leaving the same way."

"No one else would try a stunt like this," offered Snake with a smile. "Where else are you going to find five people this crazy? General Cooper knows a madman when he sees one."

A computer beeped, and Pandora turned to it. "The *Moonbeam*'s entered the atmosphere," she announced.

"And the robots know we'll be here and they're not to report seeing us?" said Pretorius.

"I just told you that."

"It's worth making sure of," he replied. He turned to Michkag. "This is a hell of a time for me to think of asking, but I really should know: if it gets a little wild down there, do you know how to use your weapons?"

"I have practiced every day prior to joining you," answered Michkag. "The original Michkag is proficient with all weapons and is especially fond of this one." He patted his pulse gun where it sat in his holster. He paused. "I have also memorized the names and faces of his closest friends and most trusted officers. Hopefully I'll be able to address them all by name when we finally confront them."

"Good," said Pretorius. "Let's hope 'confront' isn't quite the word that fits, and that you don't have to use your weapons." He stood up, paced around the room once, and sat back down. "I can't think of another thing to tell anyone."

"Just as well," said Snake. "The damned ship's due to start unloading in a few minutes."

"All right," replied Pretorius. "Let's see if they have any comfortable crates."

"The next comfortable crate anyone makes will be the first," replied Snake. "Except maybe for coffins, and I think their tenants are beyond complaining."

"Now, *that's* interesting," said Pretorius. He turned to Djibmet. "How do you bury your dead?"

"Pretty much the same as you do—in coffins," answered the Kabori. "Well, when we have time for it. In the aftermath of a battle, we usually bury the slain right where they've fallen, after confiscating their IDs so we can report their deaths." Suddenly he frowned. "At least, that's what I've been told. I've never actually been on a battlefield."

"Since you're the only one here, probably including Michkag, who knows what a Kabori coffin looks like, see if we have one anywhere in this entire storage area, and if not, check the two other shipping towers as well. If we can pack their Michkag in a coffin, we might not have to explain anywhere along the way why we don't want to open it."

"He'll suffocate."

"We'll drill some breathing holes in it. If anyone wants to take a peek, we say he's been dead a month and his religion forbade us to do anything to preserve the body. *That* ought to keep them from asking us to open it."

"I'll look," said Djibmet, "but it seems unlikely that anyone would ship a single coffin to Petrus IV."

"Probably," agreed Pretorius. "But it beats sitting around doing nothing, and you're the only one who can walk the seventh-level corridors between the towers without getting arrested or shot."

"I might as well start now," said Djibmet, getting to his feet and starting to go through the accumulated objects in the tower.

A few minutes later the *Moonbeam* docked, and a minute after that a sextet of robots began unloading tons of cargo, helped by the robots that were already stationed in the tower. It took them almost an hour to finish.

"Okay," said Pretorius to Pandora. "Not only don't they remember us, but they don't hear us unless we're directly addressing one of them but using the word 'Robot' at the start of a sentence."

She nodded, fiddled with her computers for almost a full minute, and looked up at him. "Done."

"Good," he said. "Now you're going to keep the ship docked here until we've finished making the switch and all of us are aboard, right?"

"At least that long."

Pretorius frowned. "At least?" he repeated.

"It won't take off before I give it permission," she replied. "But if I tell it to take off before it's programmed to, it'll set off every alarm in the fortress."

"I see," he replied. "When is it due to leave?"

She checked. "That's still undetermined. Probably tomorrow. They don't want it to fly home empty, so they're still trying to arrange a couple of stops along the way."

"I suppose we'll just have to live with that." He paused. "Is there anything on Michkag's schedule for the rest of the day?"

She checked. "Just a banquet in two hours, always assuming he's through giving his speech by then."

"Okay," said Pretorius, leaning back uncomfortably. "We wait."

30

When the banquet was an hour old, Pretorius summoned a pair of robots. When they arrived he led them to a large cylindrical container and had them open it up.

"Once I step into this, you are to take me to Level 3, Zab 43. If anyone asks you, this contains some of Michkag's belongings, you don't know what kind, and he ordered you to take it to Zab 43. Do you understand?"

"Yes," said each robot.

"Good. Now, once we're in the room and the door is closed, you will immediately open the container and let me out of it. Then, unless I tell you otherwise, you will return the container to this room and take *this* person"—he indicated the clone—"back down to Level 3, Zab 43 in the same container. If anyone should question you, you will offer the same answer you would have answered before—that it contains the private property of Michkag, you don't know what kind of property, and he personally ordered you to bring it to his room. Is that understood?"

"Yes," replied the robots simultaneously.

"Good. You will let him out of the container the moment the door shuts behind you, and then unless I order you otherwise, you will return to this room with the container, take *this* person"—he indicated Circe—"down to Level 3, Zab 43 inside it. If anyone asks what you are doing, you will offer the same answer as before. Once there, you will help her out of it and await my further instructions. Do you understand?"

"Yes," said the robots.

"All right," said Pretorius. "Open the container."

One of the robots unlocked it; the other opened the door. Pretorius stepped into it, found it awkward to let his arms dangle down at his sides, and crossed them across his chest.

"There'd damned well better be enough air," he said.

"It should be good for forty Standard minutes, maybe a little more," replied Snake. "Of course, with my breathing techniques *I* could make it an hour."

"Close it and take it to Level 3, Zab 43," ordered Pretorius.

The robots closed the door, leaned the container back, and began wheeling it out the door. He couldn't feel when they came to the airshaft, but he could hear it—or rather, he could no longer hear the container's wheels. They got off after descending almost half a mile, took him down the long corridor, turned at Zab, and a moment later stopped.

"Goddamn it!" growled Pretorius from inside the container. "Give them the code to open the door!"

A moment later they wheeled him into room 43, waited for the door to slide shut, and opened the door—and he found himself facing a Kabori in an enlisted soldier's uniform.

"What are you doing here?" demanded the Kabori.

Pretorius instantly drew his screecher and fired it, and the solid wall of sound hurled the Kabori back against a wall. As he bounced off, Pretorius fired again, and he fell like a stone.

Pretorius turned to the robots. "Wait here," he ordered them. Then he walked to the door leading to Zab 42, screecher in hand, and waited until the door slid open.

He stepped into the room, prepared to fire at any movement,

however slight, but there was none. He checked the closet and the bathroom, then holstered his screecher and relaxed.

"You two," he said to the robots. "Load this Kabori into the container, lock it, and take it back up to the tower. If anyone asks what's in it, you don't know, you were just ordered by Michkag to store it in the tower until he needs it. Do you understand?"

"Yes," replied the robots in unison.

"Okay, load him and leave."

The robots lifted the dead soldier, carried him to the container, stood him upright in it, locked it, and wheeled it out into the corridor.

"Pandora, you still there?" said Pretorius. "And I assume Michkag is too?"

"Right," she said.

"The robots are on their way back up."

"Well, that went smoothly enough," remarked Michkag.

"Not as smoothly as you think," replied Pretorius. "There was a low-level soldier, probably some kind of orderly, in the room. I had to kill him. At least, I *think* he's dead. He's certainly unconscious. When they get up there, I want Michkag to climb in and get down here as fast as possible. Who the hell knows how many other orderlies or even officers have access to this damned room?"

"And the orderly you're sending up?"

"Have Felix and Snake kill him. Chop him into pieces and toss 'em in the atomizer. Same with anything he bleeds on when they're subdividing him. I don't want any trace of him to remain."

"We may be taking off tomorrow," said Pandora. "Can't we just keep him incapacitated until then?"

"No," answered Pretorius. "We're not *all* leaving, tomorrow or any other time. Michkag is staying here, and I don't want him to have to answer any awkward questions in the near future. Besides, even if you doped him and tied him up, you'd still have to hide him just to be on the safe side, and the likelihood is that he'd starve to death before anyone found him. Just do as I say."

"All right," said Pandora. "I'll pass the word to Felix and Snake." There was a moment's silence, and then she said, "They're here now."

"Okay, get Michkag loaded and moving fast. I want him down here before there are any more surprises."

Pretorius waited for a count of 90, then whispered softly: "Can you hear me?"

Utter silence.

"Shit!" said Pretorius. "We just made this a one-way system between me and you. When you get here let me know if my voice came through to you."

It took the robots another three minutes to arrive. They waited until the door lid shut behind them, then unlocked and opened the container. Michkag stepped out, stretched his arms—they were longer than Men's arms, and he'd clearly felt uncomfortable—and turned to Pretorius.

"I heard you," he said.

"Good," replied Pretorius. He turned to the robots. "All right, go back to the tower and get the last person. If anyone stops you on the way there, you're just service robots moving an empty container to a storage area, and if they demand to see what's inside, open it and show them that it's empty. But once you've put Circe into it, you'll give the same answers you would have given on your last two trips from the tower to this room—that you'd been ordered by Michkag to move some of his personal property inside this container to Level 3, Zab 43, and you will refuse any order to open the container until I personally issue that order. Is that understood?"

"Yes."

"Okay, go."

The robots wheeled the empty container into the corridor, and the door slid shut behind them. Michkag began pacing through the two rooms, past the couch, chairs, and table in Zab 42, around the bed and chair in 43. He stopped and stared at the bottle, filled with what he had been told was his favorite intoxicant. It was surrounded by exquisite crystal goblets, and be began rearranging them on their platinum tray.

"Nervous?" asked Pretorius.

"A little," answered Michkag.

"Don't be," said Pretorius. "You'll almost certainly be dealing with officers. Take it from me, they're a lot easier to fool than the average enlisted man."

Michkag smiled. "But you yourself are an officer."

"I've been trying to get busted down to sergeant and inherit a desk job for years," answered Pretorius. "One of these days . . ."

Michkag laughed. "Thank you. That was just the relief from tension that I needed."

"Good."

"So what do we do now?"

"Hope that Michkag comes in alone," said Pretorius. "We've got to incapacitate him almost instantly, before he can call for help or leave the room. And we have to get his medals onto your uniform. If anyone's with him, we'll have to kill them before they can escape or let anyone know there's a problem."

They waited in silence for a few more minutes, and then the robots returned with the container. Pretorius opened it and helped Circe out.

"Nobody's shown up yet?" she asked.

"No one but the orderly I sent up a few minutes ago." He turned to the two robots. "Take this container and put it in Zab 43's bathroom, then order the door to close and return to me."

The robots moved the container, then turned to Pretorius, awaiting further instructions.

"Can you both fit, upright, in the closet?" he said. "It'll be tight, but I think you can manage it without damaging the uniforms."

They walked to the closet and briefly inspected it. "Yes," they replied.

"Zab 42's closet is empty," noted Michkag.

"Yeah, but you're going to be entertaining there, and we don't want anyone getting warm and opening the closet there so they can hang up a coat and finding the robots." He turned to the robots. "Once you're in, order the doors to shut, and stay there until I order you to come out."

The robots entered the closet, which shut behind them a moment later.

"What now?" asked Circe.

"Now we wait and hope to hell that the next guy through the door is Michkag, since he's the only one we won't have to kill on sight."

"And if it *is* someone besides Michkag?" she persisted.

"I don't know about you," he replied, "but I, for one, will be very unhappy."

"Seriously, Nathan."

"Seriously, if there's just one, and he's alone, I suppose we can hide him in Zab 42's bathroom for a while. If there are two, there's going to be a lot of shooting on both sides. Our job is to stay alive and make the switch in the confusion. Let's hope we don't have to." He paused. "Let's assume it goes the way we hope it does. You and I can stand over here"—he indicated the wall beside the door—"so that the first thing Michkag sees is his double. We totally hide, but if the first thing he sees is his double, he may take a step forward out of curiosity or because he can't believe his eyes. If we're the first thing he sees, he's just as likely to back out and call for help."

"Why don't we hide in the connecting room?" she asked.

"I don't know which *is* the connecting room," said Pretorius. "Is he coming to bed, or is he coming to relax and maybe chat with some officers? If the latter, he'll almost certainly go to Zab 42, which is set up for that and hasn't got a bed in the middle of it. Which means if he comes here, he's more likely to be alone, and if he goes there, at least we'll have a chance to hear if he's got company before we show ourselves and the shooting starts."

"You sound like you do this all the time," said Michkag in admiring tones.

"Only between stints in the hospital," said Circe.

"Probably going to happen again this trip," muttered Pretorius. "I think the odds are that he goes into the other room first. Unless he plans to come right in and go to sleep."

"Then why aren't we waiting there?" asked Michkag.

"Like I said, our best chance is if he comes in alone, and he's more likely to come into this one if he's alone."

"Well, we might as well stand by the wall as you suggested, since the food was probably served close to an hour ago," said Circe.

"But if he likes to visit at the table or make long speeches, we could be waiting for a long time."

Pretorius pulled the tiny dart gun out of a pocket, checked the firing mechanism to make sure it was charged, checked the rest of it to make sure it was loaded, put the small case back into a pocket, and held the gun in his right hand.

"How quickly will that work?" asked Circe.

"They tell me it's instantaneous," answered Pretorius. "I'll settle for it knocking him out before he thinks of yelling for help."

They remained standing for another half hour.

Suddenly Pretorius whispered so softly that Circe, who was standing next to him, wasn't aware of it. "Get ready. Someone's at the door."

Michkag adjusted his position by the bed so that he was bathed in the brightest light.

Pretorius touched Circe on the arm, held a finger to his lips when she looked at him, and handed her the dart gun. He had just finished doing so when the door slid open.

Michkag—the original Michkag—stood there frowning at the clone.

"What is going on here?" he whispered—and as he did so, Pretorius stepped over, grabbed his arm, and jerked him into the room.

He took the weapon back from Circe and fired a dart into Michkag's neck, all in one motion. Michkag began reaching for him but collapsed before he could take a step.

"Damn, that stuff works fast!" said Pretorius, impressed.

He opened the closet door. "Robots!"

"Yes?" they replied.

"There is a Kabori officer lying on the floor. Remove all of his medals and put them in exactly the same places on the uniform of the Kabori who is standing. Do the same with any other insignia."

It took them about five minutes to move everything from one Michkag to the other.

"All right. Now bring in the container from where you put it in the bathroom, lift the fallen officer, and place him in it."

They did so.

"Now lock it."

They locked it.

"Good. Now take him up to the storage facility in the East Tower. If anyone should stop you and ask what is in the container, you don't know. All you know is that Michkag himself told you to take it there and not to open it for anyone. If anyone has any questions, Michkag is in Zab 42 of Level 3 and will be happy to answer them. Once you get to the storage area, wait until the door shuts behind you, then open the container, but leave him in it unless one of the three Men up there gives you a contrary order. Then go into standby mode."

"Yes," said the robots, wheeling the container into the corridor.

"Well," said Pretorius. "That takes care of Step One."

"I can't believe we made it!" said Circe.

He looked at her and said, "That was the easy part."

31

A minute passed, then another. Pretorius frowned.

"I think you'd better summon some of your officers. For all we know, you don't like to be disturbed at night, and no one's going to come in here."

"I *do* know them," answered Michkag. "I have been studying them all my life."

"If a few of them don't show up pretty soon, I think we'll have you summon them."

"Have you decided whether we're spies or turncoats?" asked Circe.

"We'd better be turncoats," answered Pretorius. "If we're spies, sooner or later someone's likely to take a shot at us or wonder why the hell we're still here and not in irons. But if he's given us our instructions, and we're going back to the Democracy to feed them false information, they'll be less likely to interfere—and of course Michkag will make them understand that they disobey his orders concerning us under pain of a very slow, very painful death."

Another ten minutes passed.

"I think I'd better precipitate the action," said Michkag.

Pretorius nodded. "Otherwise we could be here 'til morning, and I think Pandora's the only one who *won't* mount a rescue operation by then."

"You two wait here," said Michkag. "I'll call some of my officers into Zab 42 and explain that you're working for me, then introduce you. If they see you before I can explain your presence, they'll almost certainly try to kill you."

"Okay," said Pretorius. "Might as well get started."

He and Circe sat on the bed while Michkag walked through the door to Zab 42 and waited for it to slide shut behind him. A moment later they heard his voice on a fortress-wide speaker system summoning half a dozen officers by name. They soon heard them enter Zab 42, and the clone began speaking to them.

Pretorius turned questioningly to Circe, who seemed lost in concentration, though her eyes were open.

"So far, so good," she whispered.

Michkag spoke for a few more minutes, and then the door slid open and he motioned Pretorius and Circe to join him. The Kabori officers, who had been seated, were instantly on their feet, and two of them actually pulled their weapons.

Michkag held up a hand. "Calm yourselves," he said sternly. "These are my operatives. You may ask them any questions you want, but when this meeting is over they are to be treated with the upmost respect and courtesy, and I want the word passed to everyone in this fortress."

"I know of *this* one," said a Kabori, indicating Pretorius. "He brought down an entire empire in the Albion Cluster."

"And now he's here," said another. "How do we know he doesn't plan to do the same to *our* empire?"

"One Man, against thirty billion Kabori?" snorted an officer contemptuously.

"You," said the first officer, pointing at Pretorius. "Why have you suddenly turned against your own people?"

"It is not as sudden as it seems," answered Pretorius in heavily accented Kabori. "I don't know how it works in your society, but in the Democracy a man with my military accomplishments would reasonably expect to be commanding his own division by now. He would expect the money and honors due him for his service to a society that is no better or worse than any other but is simply the one into which he was born." He paused. "I am not a young man anymore. If I am ever to receive my just rewards, it must be soon—and while my own Democracy has made it clear that such rewards are beyond my reach, your General Michkag has made it clear that we see risk and reward in the same light. I ask for no special treatment, just what we might call, in some other field, an honest day's pay for an honest day's work."

"And what *is* this work to be?" asked another.

Pretorius rubbed his hand briefly across his jaw and mouth, whispered, "Secret!" as he was removing it, and looked at his questioner.

"There may come a day when I will confide in each of you, and of course General Michkag can tell you anything he likes whenever he wishes to, but right at this moment I am a covert operative for the Coalition, and I trust no one but my partner"—he indicated Circe—"and Michkag."

"We know about Pretorius," said yet another officer, "though of course we don't know if we can trust him or indeed any Man, but at least he has what I shall call credentials." He stared at Circe. "What are yours?"

"Don't answer that!" snapped Michkag, and all eyes turned to him. "Once she has done her job, you will all know where her talents lay. In the meantime, I agree with Colonel Pretorius that we will keep our mission secret for the present except from those few officers who must participate in it."

Damn! thought Pretorius. *You're not bad at this!*

"All I can do now is tell the rest of you," continued Michkag, "that before two years have passed, each and every one of you will remember this night and be pleased that these two have come over to our side."

"But for fame and money, not principle?" said one of them dubiously.

"You are free to worry about motives," said Michkag with a touch of contempt and more than a little arrogance. "As for me, my position in the Coalition is such that I care only about results."

The officer began backtracking and apologizing.

"Enough!" snapped Michkag after another minute. He turned to Pretorius and Circe. "You two will go into the next room while I discuss this further with my officers. They must feel free to speak their minds."

They got up, walked into the bedroom, and waited for the door to slide shut behind them.

"Well?" asked Pretorius.

"Some of them doubt your motives," she said. "But none of them doubt Michkag's identity."

"That's all that counts," said Pretorius. "We're out of here in another day. He's here for the duration."

They sat in silence for another ten minutes. Then Circe tensed.

"What is it?"

"I don't know what he said," she replied, "but he's losing one of them."

"Can you tell which one?"

"Not without being in the room with him."

"Damn." He flicked his transmitter on with his tongue. "I don't know what you just said, but Circe tells me that they all believed you up to then, but you're losing one of them. If you can fix it, do so. If not, call us back in so we can at least identify him."

They spent another five minutes in the room. Circe shook her head at the end of it.

"You still haven't won him over," whispered Pretorius. "Bring us back, let Circe identify him, and let *him* take us to the tower. I'll have a reception committee waiting for him."

The door slid open after another minute, and Pretorius and Circe walked back into Zab 42.

"This meeting is now officially over. Pretorius and Circe, welcome to the Coalition."

"Third from the right," whispered Circe.

Pretorius whispered the information to Michkag.

"Zbagnorg," said Michkag, facing the Kabori in question. "Take our two new allies to the storage room high up in the East Tower. They will be shipping out incognito on a supply ship in the morning."

"Are you sure that's wise?" asked Zbagnorg.

"Tell him that he can come along to keep an eye on us," whispered Pretorius.

"I have a feeling that I have not quelled all your doubts about this mission," said Michkag. "Here is what I shall do. I relieve you forthwith of all other duties. From this day forward, you shall be their bodyguard, with the added duty of being their executioner if they behave in any manner that is not in keeping with their mission."

"I accept," said Zbagnorg, snapping a salute. "But of course, I do not know exactly what their mission is."

Michkag frowned. "You here are my most trusted officers, and I have no doubt as to your total loyalty. But should you fall into enemy hands, they have very efficient methods of extracting information, so I choose not to relate the details here." He paused thoughtfully. "I'll tell you what: you go up to the tower with them now, and wait there for me. I'll come up later, or at least before the supply ship leaves, and give you all the details. Does that meet your approval?"

"Yes, it does."

Michkag turned to Pretorius. "And you?"

"Who are we to dispute our commander's orders on our very first assignment?" answered Pretorius. "We will simply have to convince Zbagnorg through our ongoing efforts that we are exactly what we present ourselves to be."

"Then it is settled," said Michkag. "I want all six of you to accompany our new friends to the lift, to avoid any scenes with those who do not know they have become our allies. Only Zbagnorg need ascend to the tower with them, but your presence until then will avoid any awkwardness."

The door slid open, and Pretorius and Circe, escorted by six high-ranking Kabori officers, walked the length of the corridor, amid curious and hostile stares. Then, at the airlift, the other five waited until the two Men and Zbagnorg were slowly being lifted on a cushion of air, then went about their duties.

Pretorius coughed, covered his mouth, and whispered "Change of plans. Get Felix."

They rode the rest of the way in silence, stepped off at the proper level, and approached the door.

"I shall be watching you every second," said Zbagnorg to Pretorius. "I don't know how you fooled Michkag, but you are not fooling *me*. Sooner or later you will blunder, or *he* will blunder, and I will be there."

They reached the door, and as it slid open, Pretorius took a quick step backward and shoved Zbagnorg into Ortega's waiting prosthetic arms. The big man squeezed; they heard a loud *snap!* and four lesser ones as the door slid shut, and he let the Kabori fall to the floor.

"Dead?" asked Pretorius.

Ortega leaned over the body, then looked up. "He's still breathing," answered Ortega. "I wouldn't bet on his ever walking again, though."

Pretorius took out his screecher, turned it full force on Zbagnorg's head, and fired it.

"Well, he's dead *now*," said Ortega, "and that's for damned sure!"

"I suppose you want us to chop this one up too?" asked Snake with a grimace.

"Not necessary," replied Pretorius. "They know he'll be on the *Moonbeam*, so all we have to do is find some way to jettison him when we're a parsec or more away from here."

"So you really pulled it off?" said Djibmet.

"So far so good . . ."

"Then you're ready to go?"

"I've been thinking about it," said Pretorius. "And we're *all* ready to go. Including you."

"Me?" said Djibmet.

Pretorius nodded his head. "You."

"But . . . but he *needs* me!" protested the Kabori.

"He's had you since the day he was born," answered Pretorius, "and he's now in command not only of the fortress but of the whole damned Coalition. What does he need you for now?"

"There are little things, nuances and subtleties . . ."

"Djibmet, we've got the visual record here. There are between thirty and forty Kabori who saw you walking around here. You asked for the whereabouts of an officer who doesn't exist. Now, if you leave with us, that'll almost certainly all be forgotten, and if not, you were simply a spy who got away. But if you stay here under Michkag's protection, sooner or later someone will remember—and that could cast doubts on Michkag's judgment and maybe even his authenticity. Also, he's lived with these officers for years. They know you're not a fellow officer, they know you're not a close friend, they know he has no reason to offer you either a commission or his protection. Don't you think he's taking enough chances as it is?"

Djibmet was silent for a long moment, then looked up, his face a mark of pain and guilt. "I was being selfish and thoughtless," he said softly. "You are right, of course. I will leave with you."

"I'll let Michkag know," said Pretorius. "It'll give him one less thing to worry about."

There was another silence, broken by Proto. "Well, that's that!" he said.

"Yeah," said Pretorius. "Now we just have to get back through maybe a thousand enemy star systems without alerting any of them, and with no Michkag clone to intercede for us if push comes to shove."

"Damn," said Proto.

"What's the problem?"

"I don't even have a stomach—not the way Men and Kabori do—and suddenly you've made it start hurting."

32

Pretorius couldn't see any sense waiting in the tower, so he moved his crew and Michkag into the ship. Since it was all but empty, each of them took a large section for his or her own quarters. They designated one central area as a meeting room and promptly found themselves spending most of their time there. Pandora had no problem controlling and instructing the robots, and they made themselves reasonably comfortable for the next twenty hours, until the *Moonbeam* took off.

"Its itinerary seems simple enough," announced Pretorius. "It picks up a small amount of cargo on Althion II and Degma IV, and terminates on Vorrelb V."

"Speaking of cargo," said Circe, "what about our own?"

"I've got enough stuff to keep him sleeping for most of the trip, and tranquil for the rest of it," answered Pretorius. "We'll tube-feed him until he's awake enough to feed himself, which if things go as planned won't be until we're back in the Democracy on the final leg of our trip."

"Okay," said Ortega. "Getting back to the spaceports . . ."

"They're all within the Coalition's boundaries, of course," answered Pretorius, "so we're going to have hunt up a ship that can take us the rest of the way on one of those three worlds. Another cargo ship is out of the question. We might find one that goes over the border to No Man's Land, but we'll never get a Coalition ship that's going all the way to the Democracy."

"So we steal a ship?" said Snake with a smile. "I *like* it."

Pretorius merely stared at her.

"What?" she said at last.

"I know it's not to your taste," he said, "but I kind of thought we'd buy one with all that cash we got for the pelts on the way in."

"Damn!" she said. "I forgot all about that."

"Anyway, we don't want to do it at Vorrelb V, which figures to have the biggest spaceport."

"They'll have the most ships," said Ortega.

"Unquestionably," agreed Pretorius. "But they'll also have the most security, and along with Djibmet, who'd prefer not to have his face or voiceprint on any records, we'll be five Men and an alien I'll wager even their scanners have never seen before."

"I'm going to have to make the purchase," said Djibmet. "I'm the only Kabori here, and we're still in Coalition territory."

"Yeah, you're elected," answered Pretorius. "Anyway, we don't touch down on Althion II for three days, so just relax and try to catch up on your sleep." He walked over to where Pandora sat. "All except you. I need to see the layouts of the three spaceports."

"I anticipated as much," she said, bringing up a holograph of each in turn.

"Degma IV's so little I'm surprised it can accommodate the *Moonbeam*," he noted.

She smiled. "I knew you'd like it."

"Something that small can't just be hosting the occasional oversized supply ship."

"It's not," said Pandora. "It handles half the stellar traffic that comes to or leaves the planet."

"Just tell me we're going to be on the ground during the night."

"We land in the middle of the night and take off about two hours after sunrise."

"Perfect," said Pretorius.

"Good. Because you're not going to like the other two at all.

Althion II's in orbit between two stars, so it's never dark. And the Vorrelb V one is a major-league spaceport with major-league security."

"One's all we need," said Pretorius. He got up, walked back to his own private area, lay down, and was gently snoring a minute later. The landing and takeoff from Althion II was fast and efficient. Pretorius decided they were far enough from the fortress to jettison Zbagnorg's body and sent it spinning off into space.

Four days later they were cleared to land on Degma IV.

"Okay," said Pretorius, handing a stack of currency to Djibmet. "You don't want publicity, you might even be on the run from the law. It's strictly a cash-and-carry sale. You don't have to test it out, but you want to be sure it flew in on its own power, that it hasn't been sitting there for months waiting for some sucker to buy it. And make sure it's got room for five Men, you, Proto, and our sleeping passenger."

"And once the sale is made, what next?" asked the Kabori.

"Hopefully Pandora will have their surface scanner temporarily disabled by then. You have some friends, and you don't want the law to know they're with you. They might be smuggling something valuable in that box. Of course they're reluctant to even walk across the spaceport where they might be seen, so you want a transport vehicle, one with glass darkened and shades drawn, to pick us up and take us to the ship. And the only way the deal goes down is if you drive the vehicle yourself."

"They'll never go for it," protested Djibmet.

"Hey, Felix," said Pretorius, "what is one of those little spaceport transport vehicles worth?"

"Used? Maybe six thousand credits. I don't know how much that is in Coalition currency."

Pretorius peeled off more bills. "Your good-faith deposit," he said, handing them to Djibmet. "Think they'll still have a problem?"

"No," said the Kabori firmly. "No, they definitely won't."

"Okay, you know what size ship we need. Make the best deal you can."

"You can trust me," said Djibmet.

"If I didn't, what was left of you would be floating in space next to Zbagnorg's body."

The *Moonbeam* touched down, Djibmet left with the first load of cargo, and thirty minutes later a darkened vehicle approached the ship.

"He's back," announced Snake.

"Okay," said Pretorius. "Pandora, order the robots to move that huge crate next, and then the box with Michkag in it. We'll stand on the platform behind the crate as it lowers to the ground. Then we're just a few steps from the vehicle."

"I could have them move it once it's on the ground, so that it's still between us and the cameras, just in case they come back on."

"Couldn't hurt," agreed Pretorius. "How long has the system been down?"

"Since just before Djibmet left," she answered. "They ought to be bypassing what I did and getting back online any minute now."

"Okay, have the robots move the box the way you said."

And within ten minutes they had left the *Moonbeam*, driven across the spaceport to the ship Djibmet had purchased, boarded the ship, loaded Michkag onto it, and taken off.

"Done," said Circe with a sigh as they reached light speeds.

But of course, they weren't.

33

The voyage went smoothly for a week. Even after they passed out of Coalition territory Pretorius refused to send the news of their success to General Cooper. ("*We've* got a Pandora" was his explanation. "Who's to say *they* don't have one? We'll tell him when we see him.")

On the eighth day it became clear that they wouldn't have enough fuel to make it the rest of the way to the Deluros system, so they headed for an orbiting hangar and fueling station around Preston IV.

"Preston?" said Snake. "Isn't that a human name?"

"Yes," replied Pretorius.

"Then what the hell's it doing in No Man's Land?"

"He probably didn't know we weren't going to expand forever, back when he named it." Pretorius turned to the crew. "Since this *is* No Man's Land, there's no reason why Djibmet and the rest of us can't stretch our legs and get a look around while they're fueling us up." He turned to Proto. "Probably be best if you went as a Man."

Proto, who had appeared as a middle-aged man since leaving the fortress, nodded his agreement.

"I hate to ask, but how are we paying for this?" asked Pandora.

Pretorius pulled out the rest of the cash from the pelts and held it up. "It's Coalition money, but this is No Man's Land. They'll take it from them or the Democracy."

"But will they take Coalition cash from a Man?"

"Probably," answered Pretorius. "But just to be on the safe side, we'll let Djibmet pay for the fuel."

"There was *more?*" exclaimed Snake. "How the hell much were they worth? I think we're all in the wrong line of business."

"You held some back?" said Djibmet, frowning. "What if the person I bought this ship from had demanded more money?"

"Then he was a thief and you'd have found another seller," answered Pretorius.

They began approaching the station, and in another twenty minutes they had docked, Pretorius had ordered the fuel and paid for it, while Circe gave Michkag his daily intravenous meal. Then they went over to visit a restaurant that served all races, just to vary their diet after weeks in space.

While they were eating, a group of a dozen Torquals entered, each of them the usual nine to ten feet tall, each of them with the usual grim, unsmiling visage.

"*Men!*" growled one of them.

The others merely glared.

"And a Kabori," said another.

"We fight your wars, and you sit here and eat together."

They kept up the verbal harangue throughout the meal. Finally Pretorius and his group got up to leave.

"Where the hell's Security?" whispered Circe.

"Look at those little badges on their outfits," replied Pretorius. "These guys *are* Security."

"And liquored up or the equivalent," added Ortega.

"Why not?" said Pretorius. "Who's going to stop them?"

Snake stood up to leave. "I can't tell you how pleasant you've made this meal," she said.

"We didn't try to," said a Torqual.

"That's why I can't tell you."

Suddenly six of the Torquals were on their feet, and the others were starting to rise.

"I'll handle this," said Proto softly.

Pretorius looked at Proto in astonishment. "You?"

"Just be ready."

"We're not looking for trouble," said Pretorius. "Are you going to let us leave peaceably?"

The Torqual who seemed to be the leader pulled his burner and fired it just over Pretorius's head, then laughed. "Does that answer your question?"

"Absolutely not!" thundered Proto—and suddenly the Torquals were facing a thirty-foot-high nightmare creature that seemed to be all teeth and was roaring at them. They instantly turned their weapons on it, as Pretorius began shooting them down one by one with his own burner.

"Felix, get busy!" he snapped, and Ortega began blasting away with his built-in weaponry.

The image of the roaring, screaming face with the huge teeth moved to the right, then the left, then seemed to grow even larger. Finally one of the Torquals, realizing their fire was doing no good against the hideous beast, turned his fire on Pretorius, who instantly fell over, cursing a blue streak.

Then Ortega killed the last of them, instantly the image vanished, and Proto was briefly the misshapen lump that constituted his true appearance. He then became a middle-aged man again.

"God *damn* it!" muttered Pretorius from the floor.

"Are you badly hurt?" asked Circe.

"I'm not hurt at all," he growled. "But that's the third artificial foot I've had blown away. Can't any of these bastards ever hit anything else?"

"Just be grateful that they can't," said Ortega, lifting him up and supporting him.

"How's Proto?" asked Pretorius.

"I'm fine."

"I was starting to wonder," said Pretorius. "All those blasts . . ."

"They shot at the image," answered Proto with a smile. "If they'd aimed for its chin they might actually have killed me."

"We'll let that be our little secret," said Pretorius.

"You know," said Snake, "sooner or later they're going to summon another Security team—a sober one."

Pretorius nodded, then suddenly lurched forward and began losing his balance. "Get me back to the ship. I don't plan to spend the rest of the day leaning on Felix or having him carry me."

"Why not?" said Ortega. "After all, look how far *you've* carried *us*."

EPILOGUE

Pretorius looked over to the door as Cooper entered his hospital room.

"Got the foot again, I see," said the general with a smile. "At least we're not growing you any new organs this time. Evidently you're getting minimally better at your craft."

"Go to hell," said Pretorius.

"Just kidding, Nathan, my boy."

"Can you guess what I think of your sense of humor?"

Cooper chuckled. "Actually, it was a brilliant piece of work, and I've recommended medals for you and your whole team."

"I can't tell you how thrilled we are," replied Pretorius with a grimace.

"I mean it, Nathan," continued Cooper. "This is a truly remarkable team you've put together. It'd be a shame to split it up now."

Pretorius stared at him for a long moment. "Okay, let's have it," he said at last.

"This was a nice piece of work," said Cooper, shifting his weight uncomfortably, "but of course it was a pretty straightforward job."

"Right," said Pretorius. "Anyone could have done it."

"Oh, I wouldn't say that," replied Cooper, feeling more uneasy as he approached the point of his brief visit. "No, it really was a very competent job."

"I'm still waiting."

Cooper stared at him for a moment. "We've got a situation in the Antares sector that's a real stinker," he said at last. "We've lost three good teams trying to crack it."

"Shit!" muttered Pretorius. "Whenever you bastards reach a dead end, you come to me."

"To you and your team—your Dead Enders," agreed Cooper. He walked to the door. "Get well quick. I'd like to send you all out next month."

Pretorius was still glaring at the door minutes after Cooper had walked out.

APPENDIX 1

THE ORIGIN OF THE BIRTHRIGHT UNIVERSE

It happened in the 1970s. Carol and I were watching a truly awful movie at a local theater, and about halfway through it I muttered, "Why am I wasting my time here when I could be doing something really interesting, like, say, writing the entire history of the human race from now until its extinction?" And she whispered back, "So why don't you?" We got up immediately, walked out of the theater, and that night I outlined a novel called *Birthright: The Book of Man*, which would tell the story of the human race from its attainment of faster-than-light flight until its death eighteen thousand years from now.

It was a long book to write. I divided the future into five political eras—Republic, Democracy, Oligarchy, Monarchy, and Anarchy—and wrote twenty-six connected stories ("demonstrations," *Analog* called them, and rightly so), displaying every facet of the human race, both admirable and not so admirable. Since each is set a few centuries from the last, there are no continuing characters (unless you consider Man, with a capital M, the main character, in which case you could make an argument—or at least, *I* could—that it's really a character study).

I sold it to Signet, along with another novel titled *The Soul Eater*. My editor there, Sheila Gilbert, loved the "Birthright Universe" and asked me if I would be willing to make a few changes to *The Soul Eater* so that it was set in that future. I agreed, and the changes actually took less than a day. She made the same request—in advance, this time—for the four-book Tales of the Galactic Midway series, the four-book Tales of the Velvet Comet series, and *Walpurgis III*. Looking back, I see that only two of the thirteen novels I wrote for Signet were *not* set there.

When I moved to Tor Books, my editor there, Beth Meacham, had a fondness for the Birthright Universe, and most of my books for her—not all, but most—were set in it: *Santiago*, *Ivory*, *The Dark Lady*, *Paradise*, *Purgatory*, *Inferno*, *A Miracle of Rare Design*, *A Hunger in the Soul*, *The Outpost*, *The Return of Santiago*.

When Ace agreed to buy *Soothsayer*, *Oracle*, and *Prophet* from me, my editor, Ginjer Buchanan, assumed that of course those books would be set in the Birthright Universe—and of course they were, because as I learned a little more about my eighteen-thousand-year, two-million-world future, I felt a lot more comfortable writing about it.

In fact, I started setting short stories in the Birthright Universe. Two of my Hugo winners—"Seven Views of Olduvai Gorge" and "The 43 Antarean Dynasties"—are set there, and so are perhaps fifteen others.

When Bantam agreed to take the *Widowmaker* trilogy from me, it was a foregone conclusion that Janna Silverstein, who purchased the books (but moved to another company before they came out) would want them to take place in the Birthright Universe. She did indeed request it, and I did indeed agree.

A decade later I sold another *Widowmaker* book to Meisha Merlin, set—where else?—in the Birthright Universe.

And when it came time to suggest an initial series of books to

Lou Anders for the brand-new Pyr line of science fiction, I don't think I ever considered any ideas or stories that *weren't* set in the Birthright Universe. He bought the five Starship books, and after some fantasies and Weird Western excursions, he has now commissioned the Dead Enders series to be set there as well.

I've gotten so much of my career from the Birthright Universe that I wish I could remember the name of that turkey we walked out of all those years ago so I could write the producers and thank them.

APPENDIX 2

THE LAYOUT OF THE BIRTHRIGHT UNIVERSE

The most heavily populated (by both stars and inhabitants) section of the Birthright Universe is always referred to by its political identity, which evolves from Republic to Democracy to Oligarchy to Monarchy. It encompasses millions of inhabited and habitable worlds. Earth is too small and too far out of the mainstream of galactic commerce to remain Man's capital world, and within a couple of thousand years the capital has been moved, lock, stock, and barrel halfway across the galaxy to Deluros VIII, a huge world with about ten times Earth's surface and near-identical atmosphere and gravity. By the middle of the Democracy, perhaps four thousand years from now, the entire planet is covered by one huge sprawling city. By the time of the Oligarchy, even Deluros VIII isn't big enough for our billions of empire-running bureaucrats, and Deluros VI, another large world, is broken up into forty-eight planetoids, each housing a major department of the government (with four planetoids given over entirely to the military).

Earth itself is way out in the boonies, on the Spiral Arm. I don't believe I've set more than parts of a couple of novels on the Arm.

At the outer edge of the galaxy is the Rim, where worlds are spread out and underpopulated. There's so little of value or military interest on the Rim that one ship, such as the *Theodore Roosevelt* of the Starship series, can patrol a couple of hundred worlds by itself.

In later eras, the Rim will be dominated by feuding warlords, but it's so far away from the center of things that the governments, for the most part, just ignore it.

Then there are the Inner and Outer Frontiers. The Outer Frontier is that vast but sparsely populated area between the outer edge of the Republic/Democracy/Oligarchy/Monarchy and the Rim. The Inner Frontier is that somewhat smaller (but still huge) area between the inner reaches of the Republic/et cetera and the black hole at the core of the galaxy.

It's on the Inner Frontier that I've chosen to set more than half of my novels. In 1968's *Space Chantey*, the brilliant R. A. Lafferty wrote: "Will there be a mythology of the future, they used to ask, after all has become science? Will high deeds be told in epic, or only in computer code?" I decided that I'd like to spend at least a part of my career trying to create those myths of the future, and it seems to me that myths, with their bigger-than-life characters and colorful settings, work best on frontiers where there aren't too many people around to chronicle them accurately, or too many authority figures around to prevent them from playing out to their inevitable conclusions. So I arbitrarily decided that the Inner Frontier was where *my* myths would take place, and I populated it with people bearing names like Catastrophe Baker, the Widowmaker, the Cyborg de Milo, the ageless Forever Kid, and the like. It not only allows me to tell my heroic (and sometimes antiheroic) myths but also lets me tell more realistic stories occurring at the very same time a few thousand light-years away in the Republic or Democracy or whatever happens to exist at that moment.

Over the years I've fleshed out the galaxy. There are the star clusters—the Albion Cluster, the Quinellus Cluster, a few others.

There are the individual worlds, some important enough to appear as the title of a book, such as Walpurgis III, some reappearing throughout the time periods and stories, such as Deluros VIII, Antares III, Binder X, Keepsake, Spica II, some others, and hundreds (maybe thousands by now) of worlds (and races, now that I think about it) mentioned once and never again.

Then there are, if not the bad guys, then at least what I think of as the Disloyal Opposition. Some, like the Sett Empire, get into one war with humanity and that's the end of it. Some, like the Canphor Twins (Canphor VI and Canphor VII) have been a thorn in Man's side for the better part of ten millennia. Some, like Lodin XI, vary almost daily in their loyalties, depending on the political situation.

I've been building this universe, politically and geographically, for a third of a century now, and with each passing book and story it feels a little more real to me. Give me another thirty years, and I'll probably believe every word I've written about it.

APPENDIX 3

CHRONOLOGY OF THE UNIVERSE CREATED IN *BIRTHRIGHT: THE BOOK OF MAN*

YEAR	ERA	STORY OR NOVEL
1885 A.D.		“The Hunter” (IVORY)
1898 A.D.		“Himself” (IVORY)
1982 A.D.		SIDESHOW
1983 A.D.		THE THREE-LEGGED HOOTCH DANCER
1985 A.D.		THE WILD ALIEN TAMER
1987 A.D.		THE BEST ROOTIN’ TOOTIN’ SHOOTIN’ GUNSLINGER IN THE WHOLE DAMNED GALAXY
2057 A.D.		“The Politician” (IVORY)
2403 A.D.		“Shaka II”
2908 A.D.		1 G.E.
16 G.E.	Republic	“The Curator” (IVORY)
103 G.E.	Republic	“The Homecoming”
264 G.E.	Republic	“The Pioneers” (BIRTHRIGHT)
332 G.E.	Republic	“The Cartographers”

		(BIRTHRIGHT)
346 G.E.	Republic	WALPURGIS III
367 G.E.	Republic	EROS ASCENDING
396 G.E.	Republic	"The Miners" (BIRTHRIGHT)
401 G.E.	Republic	EROS AT ZENITH
442 G.E.	Republic	EROS DESCENDING
465 G.E.	Republic	EROS AT NADIR
522 G.E.	Republic	"All the Things You Are"
588 G.E.	Republic	"The Psychologists" (BIRTHRIGHT)
616 G.E.	Republic	A MIRACLE OF RARE DESIGN
882 G.E.	Republic	"The Potentate" (IVORY)
962 G.E.	Republic	"The Merchants" (BIRTHRIGHT)
1150 G.E.	Republic	"Cobbling Together a Solution"
1151 G.E.	Republic	"Nowhere in Particular"
1152 G.E.	Republic	"The God Biz"
1394 G.E.	Republic	"Keepsakes"
1701 G.E.	Republic	"The Artist" (IVORY)
1813 G.E.	Republic	"Dawn" (PARADISE)
1826 G.E.	Republic	PURGATORY
1859 G.E.	Republic	"Noon" (PARADISE)
1888 G.E.	Republic	"Midafternoon" (PARADISE)
1902 G.E.	Republic	"Dusk" (PARADISE)
1921 G.E.	Republic	INFERNO
1966 G.E.	Republic	STARSHIP: MUTINY
1967 G.E.	Republic	STARSHIP: PIRATE
1968 G.E.	Republic	STARSHIP: MERCENARY
1969 G.E.	Republic	STARSHIP: REBEL
1970 G.E.	Republic	STARSHIP: FLAGSHIP

2122 G.E.	Democracy	"The 43 Antarean Dynasties"
2154 G.E.	Democracy	"The Diplomats" (BIRTHRIGHT)
2239 G.E.	Democracy	"Monuments of Flesh and Stone"
2275 G.E.	Democracy	"The Olympians" (BIRTHRIGHT)
2469 G.E.	Democracy	"The Barristers" (BIRTHRIGHT)
2885 G.E.	Democracy	"Robots Don't Cry"
2911 G.E.	Democracy	"The Medics" (BIRTHRIGHT)
3004 G.E.	Democracy	"The Politicians" (BIRTHRIGHT)
3042 G.E.	Democracy	"The Gambler" (IVORY)
3286 G.E.	Democracy	SANTIAGO
3322 G.E.	Democracy	A HUNGER IN THE SOUL
3324 G.E.	Democracy	THE SOUL EATER
3324 G.E.	Democracy	"Nicobar Lane: The Soul Eater's Story"
3407 G.E.	Democracy	THE RETURN OF SANTIAGO
3427 G.E.	Democracy	SOOTHSAYER
3441 G.E.	Democracy	ORACLE
3447 G.E.	Democracy	PROPHET
3502 G.E.	Democracy	"Guardian Angel"
3504 G.E.	Democracy	"A Locked-Planet Mystery"
3504 G.E.	Democracy	"Honorable Enemies"
3505 G.E.	Democracy	"If the Frame Fits . . ."
3719 G.E.	Democracy	"Hunting the Snark"
4026 G.E.	Democracy	THE FORTRESS IN ORION
4375 G.E.	Democracy	"The Graverobber" (IVORY)
4822 G.E.	Oligarchy	"The Administrators" (BIRTHRIGHT)
4839 G.E.	Oligarchy	THE DARK LADY
5101 G.E.	Oligarchy	THE WIDOWMAKER

5103 G.E.	Oligarchy	THE WIDOWMAKER REBORN
5106 G.E.	Oligarchy	THE WIDOWMAKER UNLEASHED
5108 G.E.	Oligarchy	A GATHERING OF WIDOWMAKERS
5461 G.E.	Oligarchy	"The Media" (BIRTHRIGHT)
5492 G.E.	Oligarchy	"The Artists" (BIRTHRIGHT)
5521 G.E.	Oligarchy	"The Warlord" (IVORY)
5655 G.E.	Oligarchy	"The Biochemists" (BIRTHRIGHT)
5912 G.E.	Oligarchy	"The Warlords" (BIRTHRIGHT)
5993 G.E.	Oligarchy	"The Conspirators" (BIRTHRIGHT)
6304 G.E.	Monarchy	IVORY
6321 G.E.	Monarchy	"The Rulers" (BIRTHRIGHT)
6400 G.E.	Monarchy	"The Symbiotics" (BIRTHRIGHT)
6521 G.E.	Monarchy	"Catastrophe Baker and the Cold Equations"
6523 G.E.	Monarchy	THE OUTPOST
6524 G.E.	Monarchy	"Catastrophe Baker and a Canticle for Leibowitz"
6599 G.E.	Monarchy	"The Philosophers" (BIRTHRIGHT)
6746 G.E.	Monarchy	"The Architects" (BIRTHRIGHT)
6962 G.E.	Monarchy	"The Collectors" (BIRTHRIGHT)
7019 G.E.	Monarchy	"The Rebels" (BIRTHRIGHT)
16201 G.E.	Anarchy	"The Archaeologists" (BIRTHRIGHT)
16673 G.E.	Anarchy	"The Priests" (BIRTHRIGHT)
16888 G.E.	Anarchy	"The Pacifists" (BIRTHRIGHT)
17001 G.E.	Anarchy	"The Destroyers" (BIRTHRIGHT)
21703 G.E.		"Seven Views of Olduvai Gorge"

NOVELS NOT SET IN THIS FUTURE

ADVENTURES (1922–1926 A.D.)
EXPLOITS (1926–1931 A.D.)
ENCOUNTERS (1931–1934 A.D.)
HAZARDS (1934–1938 A.D.)
STALKING THE UNICORN ("Tonight")
STALKING THE VAMPIRE ("Tonight")
STALKING THE DRAGON ("Tonight")
STALKING THE ZOMBIE ("Tonight")
THE BRANCH (2047–2051 A.D.)
SECOND CONTACT (2065 A.D.)
BULLY! (1910–1912 A.D.)
KIRINYAGA (2123–2137 A.D.)
KILIMANJARO (2234–2241 A.D.)
LADY WITH AN ALIEN (1490 A.D.)
A CLUB IN MONTMARTRE (1890–1901 A.D.)
DRAGON AMERICA (1779–1780 A.D.)
THE WORLD BEHIND THE DOOR (1928 A.D.)
THE OTHER TEDDY ROOSEVELTS (1888–1919 A.D.)
THE BUNTLINE SPECIAL (1881 A.D.)
THE DOCTOR AND THE KID (1882 A.D.)
THE DOCTOR AND THE ROUGH RIDER (1884 A.D.)
THE DOCTOR AND THE DINOSAURS (1885 A.D.)

ABOUT THE AUTHOR

Photo by Hugette

Mike Resnick has won an impressive five Hugos and has been nominated for thirty-one more. The author of the Starship series, the John Justin Mallory series, the Eli Paxton Mysteries, and four Weird West Tales, he has sold sixty-nine science fiction novels and more than two hundred and fifty short stories and has edited forty anthologies. His Kirinyaga series, with sixty-seven major and minor awards and nominations to date, is the most honored series of stories in the history of science fiction. Visit him at his website, http://mikeresnick.com/, on Facebook, www.facebook.com/mike.resnick1, or on Twitter @ResnickMike.